Praise for V. L.

"One of my favorite authors, Val ~~McDermid is an important~~ writer—witty, never sentimental, taking us through mean streets with the dexterity of a Chandler." *Sara Paretsky*

"If you haven't discovered this award-winning trailblazer in lesbian detective fiction you're missing out on a good one."
Katherine V. Forrest

"There is no one in contemporary crime fiction who has managed to combined the visceral and the humane as well as Val McDermid.... She's the best we've got."
The New York Times Book Review

"Val McDermid is one of the bright lights of the mystery field."
The Washington Post

"McDermid's a skillful writer—comparisons with such American novelists as Sara Paretsky and Sue Grafton are appropriate."
Chicago Tribune

"Lindsay Gordon has got a heart of gold and a nose for trouble."
Randye Lordon

"Lindsay Gordon is smart, tenacious, daring, lusty, loyal, and class-conscious to the bone." *Barbra Neely*

Also by Val McDermid

The Distant Echo
Killing the Shadows
A Place of Execution

Lindsay Gordon novels
Report for Murder
Common Murder
Deadline for Murder
Conferences are Murder
Booked for Murder

Kate Brannigan novels
Star Struck
Blue Genes
Clean Break
Crack Down
Kick Back
Dead Beat

Tony Hill and Carol Jordon novels
The Mermaids Singing
The Wire in the Blood
The Last Temptation
The Torment of Others

Non-fiction
A Suitable Job for a Woman

HOSTAGE TO MURDER

BY
V.L. McDERMID

Bywater
BOOKS

Ann Arbor • New Orleans
2005

copyright © V. L. McDermid 2003

Bywater Books, Inc.
PO Box 3671
Ann Arbor MI 48106-3671

Printed in the United States of America on acid-free paper.

Bywater Books First Edition

Cover designer: Bonnie Liss (Phoenix Graphics)
Author photo by Alan Peebles

ISBN 1-932859-02-0

Acknowledgements

I had no plans to write another Lindsay Gordon novel until the British Council invited me to Russia. But I fell in love, and wanted to share my delight. Among those who contributed to the Russian end of this book are Kate Griffin, my minder, who showed me the ropes; Volodya Volovik, who shared his affection for his adopted city of St Petersburg; Seamus Murphy, whose enthusiasm took me places I'd never otherwise have seen; Irina Savelieva, who interpreted the dark and dangerous for me; Varya Gornestaeva, without whom none of it would ever have happened; Sasha Gavrilov for the encouragement and the good company; Marna Gowan, who exploited her contacts shamelessly; Maxim Shvedov, for all the St Petersburg sailing info; and Stephen Dewar who explained the intricacies of Russian customs and immigration. To all of you, thanks for being such generous companions.

Leslie Hills, who has forgotten more than I know about story structure, helped me hone the plot. Thanks for seeing me through the dark night of the soul and for always travelling off limits with me.

Thanks too to Brigid and Lisanne, who always believed in Lindsay.

In memory of Gina Weissand (1946-2001)
who was everything a friend should be.
You blessed us all, babe, and we miss you.

He that hath wife and children hath given hostages to fortune.

"Of Marriage and the Single Life"
Francis Bacon

PART ONE

Chapter 1

A murder of crows swore at each other in the trees that lined the banks of the River Kelvin. A freezing drizzle from a low sky bleached the landscape to grey. Nothing, Lindsay thought, could be further from California. The only thing in common with the home she'd left three months before was the rhythm of her feet as she ran her daily two miles.

On mornings like this, Lindsay found it hard to remember that she'd once loved this city. When she'd come back to Scotland after university and journalism training, she'd thought Glasgow was paradise. She had money in her pocket, she was young, free and single and the city had just begun the process of reinvigoration that had, by the millennium, made it one of the most exciting cities in Britain. Now, fifteen years later, there was no denying it was a good place to live. The cultural life was vibrant. The restaurants were cosmopolitan and covered the whole range from cheap and cheerful to glamorous and gourmet. There were plenty of beautiful places to live, and more green spaces than most cities could boast. Some of the finest countryside in the world was within an hour's drive.

And all she could think of was how much she wanted to be somewhere else. Seven happy and successful years in California had left her feeling that this long narrow land was no longer full of possibilities for her. Partly, it was the weather, she thought, wiping the cold mixture of sweat and rain from her face. Who wouldn't long for sunshine and the Pacific surf on a morning like this?

Partly, it was that she missed her dog. Mutton had always accompanied her on her runs, his black tail wagging eagerly whenever she walked downstairs in her jogging clothes. But she couldn't contemplate putting him in quarantine kennels for six months, so he'd been handed over to some friends in the Bay Area who guaranteed him a happy life. He'd probably forgotten her already.

But mostly, it was not having anything meaningful to do with her days. Lindsay would never have described herself as someone who was defined by her job, but now that she had none, she had come to realise how much of her identity had been bound up in what she did for a living. Without some sort of employment, she felt cast adrift. When people asked, "And what do you do?" she had no answer. There were few things she hated more than the sense of powerlessness that provoked in her.

In California, Lindsay had had a response, one she felt proud of, one she knew carried a degree of respect. She'd reluctantly abandoned her post lecturing in journalism at Santa Cruz to come back to Scotland because her lover Sophie had been offered the chair of obstetrics at Glasgow University. Lindsay had protested that she didn't have anything to go back for, but Sophie had managed to convince her she was mistaken. "You'll walk into a teaching job in Scotland," she'd said. "And if it takes a while, you can always go back to freelance journalism. You know you were one of the best."

And so she had stifled her doubts for Sophie's sake. After all, it wasn't her lover's fault that Lindsay had reached the age of thirty-nine without a clearly defined career plan. But now she was confronted by the cold reality of unemployment, she wished she'd done more to persuade Sophie to stay in California. She'd looked around for teaching work, but vocational journalism training wasn't nearly as widespread in Scotland as it was in the US. She'd managed to secure some part-time lecturing at Strathclyde University, filling in for someone on maternity leave, but it was dead-end work with no prospects. And the idea of going back to the overcrowded world of freelance journalism with a contacts book that was years out of date held no appeal.

So her days had shrunk to this. Pounding the walkway by the river. Reading the papers. Shopping for dinner. Arranging to meet old acquaintances for drinks and discovering how much distance there was between them. Waiting for Sophie to come home and bring her despatches from the world of work. Lindsay knew she couldn't go on like this indefinitely. It was poisoning her soul, and it wasn't doing her relationship with Sophie much good either.

She reached the point where she had to turn off the walkway and head up the steep hill to the Botanic Gardens, the halfway point on her circuit. Head down, she powered up the slope, too wrapped up in her thoughts to pay heed to her surroundings. As she rounded a blind bend, she realised she was about to cannon into someone walking down the hill. She swerved, but simultaneously, the other woman side-stepped in the same direction. They crashed into each other and Lindsay stumbled, smacking into a tree and falling to one knee, her ankle twisting under her. "Shit," she gasped.

"Oh God, I'm sorry," the other woman said.

"My own fault," Lindsay growled, pushing herself upright, then wincing as she tried to take her weight on the damaged ankle. "Jesus," she hissed, leaning forward to probe the joint with her fingers.

"You've not broken it or anything?" The woman frowned solicitously.

"Sprained, I think." She drew in her breath sharply when she touched the tender heart of the injury.

"Have you far to go? Only, I live just the other side of the river. My car's there. I could drive you?"

It was a tempting offer. Lindsay didn't fancy hiking a mile on a damaged ankle. She looked up, taking in her nemesis turned Good Samaritan. She saw a woman in her late twenties with an angular face and short blonde hair cut to fashionable effect. Her eyes were slate blue, her eyebrows a pair of dark circumflex accents above them. She was dressed out of Gap and carried a leather knapsack over one shoulder. She didn't look like an axe murderer. "OK," Lindsay said. "Thanks."

The response wasn't what she expected. Instead of the offer of an arm to help her down the hill and across the bridge, the woman looked taken aback, her eyes widening and her lips parting. "You're Lindsay Gordon," she said, bemused.

"Do I know you?" Lindsay leaned against the tree, wondering if she'd taken a blow to the head she hadn't registered at the time.

The blonde grinned. "We met about ten years ago. You came to the university GaySoc to talk about gays and the media. A bunch of us went out for a drink afterwards."

Lindsay strained at the locked gates of memory. "Edinburgh University?" she hazarded.

"That's right. You remember?"

"I remember doing the talk."

The blonde gave a rueful pout. "But you don't remember me. Well, that's hardly surprising. I was just a gawky wee fresher who was too overawed to open her mouth. But hey, this is terrible. Me standing here reminiscing while you're suffering like this." Now she extended her arm. "Lean on me. I'm Rory, by the way. Rory McLaren."

Lindsay took the proffered arm and began to limp gingerly down the slope. "I'm amazed you recognised me all these years later," she said. The least she could do was make conversation, even though she felt more like swearing with every step.

Rory chuckled. "Oh, you were pretty impressive. You're part of the reason I ended up doing what I do."

"Which is?"

"I'm a journo."

"Oh well, never mind," Lindsay said, attempting a levity she didn't feel. The last thing she needed right now was some bright and bouncy kid still jam-packed with idealism making her feel even more old and decrepit than she already did.

"No, I love it," Rory assured her.

"How do you manage that?" They had reached the bottom of the hill and were making their way across the bridge. Moving on the flat was easier, but Lindsay was glad she'd taken up Rory's offer, even if the conversation was depressing her.

"It's a long story."

Lindsay looked up at the climb that would take them back to street level. "It's a big hill."

"Right enough," Rory said. "Well, I started off on the local paper in Paisley, which wasn't exactly a barrel of laughs, but at least they trained me. I got a couple of lucky breaks with big stories that I sold on to the nationals, and I ended up with a staff job on the *Reporter*."

Lindsay snorted. "Working on the *Reporter* makes you happy? God, things must have changed since my day."

"No, no, I'm not there any more."

"So where are you now?" Even in her state of discomfort, Lindsay noticed that Rory seemed faintly embarrassed.

"Well, see, that's the long story bit."

"Take my mind off the pain and cut to the chase."

"I came up on the lottery."

"Jammy," Lindsay said.

"Aye. But not totally jammy. I didn't get the whole six numbers, just the five plus the bonus ball. But that was enough. I figured that if I invested the lot, it would earn enough in interest to just about keep a roof over my head. So I jacked the job in and now I'm freelance."

"And that's your idea of fun? Out there in the dog-eat-dog world?" Lindsay tried not to sound as sceptical as she felt. She'd been a freelance herself and knew only too well how tough it was to stay ahead of the pack.

"I figured what I needed was an angle. And I remembered something you said back at that talk at the GaySoc."

"This is surreal," Lindsay said. The word felt entirely inadequate to encompass the situation.

"I know. Wild, isn't it? I can't believe this is really you."

"Me neither. So what did I say that was so significant it came back to you all those years later?"

"You were talking about the ghetto mentality. How people think gays are completely different, completely separate from them. But we're not. We've got more in common with the straight universe than we have dividing us. And I thought, gays and lesbians don't just have gay and lesbian lives. They've got jobs.

They've got families. They've got stories to tell. But most folk in our world have no reason to trust journalists. So I thought, what if I set myself up as the journalist that the gay community *can* trust? What a great way to get stories to come to me." Rory's voice was passionate now, her excitement obvious.

"And that's what you did?"

"Right. I've been at it just over a year now, and I've had some fabulous exclusives. I mostly do investigative stuff, but I'll turn my hand to anything. And I'm making a good living."

They were almost out of the woods and on to the street. But although she desperately wanted to get the weight off her ankle, Lindsay didn't want this conversation to end. For the first time since she'd got back from California, she was hearing someone talk about her field with something other than apathy or cynicism. "So how did you get started?"

Rory pulled open the gate that led out from the river bank on to the quiet backwater of Botanic Crescent. "That's my flat, just on the corner there. I could fill you in over a coffee."

"Are you sure I'm not keeping you from anything?"

"God, no. Have you any idea how amazing it is for me to be talking to you like this? It'd have to be a bloody good story to make me miss a chance like this."

They crossed the road. Rory keyed a number into the security door of a red sandstone tenement and ushered Lindsay into a spotless tiled close. They made their way up one flight of worn stone stairs, then Rory unlocked the tall double doors that led into her first-floor flat. "Excuse the mess," she said, leading the way into the big dining kitchen at the back of the flat.

There was no false modesty behind Rory's words. It was, as she had said, a mess. A cat sprawled on a kitchen worktop by the window, while another lay curled on one of several piles of news-papers and magazines stacked on the floor. The tinfoil containers from the previous night's curry sat on another worktop alongside three empty bottles of Becks, while the sink was piled with dirty plates and mugs. Lindsay grinned. "Live alone, do you?"

"That obvious, is it?" Rory picked a dressing gown off one of the chairs. "Grab a seat. Do you want some ice for that ankle? I've got a gel pack in the freezer."

"That'd be good." Lindsay lowered herself into the chair. In front of her was that morning's *Herald*, the cryptic crossword already completed with only a couple of jottings in the margin.

Rory rummaged in a freezer that looked like the Arctic winter, but emerged triumphant with a virulent turquoise oblong. "There we go." She handed it to Lindsay and crossed to the kettle. "Coffee, right?"

"Is it instant?"

Rory turned, her eyebrows raised in a teasing question. "What if it is?"

"I'll have tea."

"I was only bothering you. It's proper coffee. I get it from an Italian café in town."

She busied herself with beans and grinder. When the noise subsided, Lindsay said, "You were going to tell me how you got started."

"So I was." Rory poured the just-boiled water on the grounds she'd spooned into a cafetiere. "I decided I needed to be visible. So I had a word with the guy who owns Café Virginia. You know Café Virginia? In the Merchant City, down by the Italian Quarter?"

Lindsay nodded. It hadn't been a gay venue when she'd lived in the city. It had been a bad pub that sold worse food, called something stupidly suggestive like Pussy Galore. But she was aware that it had been reincarnated as the city's premiere gay and lesbian café bar, although she hadn't paid it a visit yet. Sophie hadn't had much time for hitting the night life; she'd been too busy getting her feet under the operating table. Most of the socialising they'd done had been at dinner parties or in restaurants. Another sign of ageing, Lindsay had already decided. "I know where you mean," she said.

"I told him my idea, and we did a deal. Three month trial basis. He'd let me use one of the booths in the back bar as a kind of office. And I'd do bits and pieces of PR for him. So I wander down there most mornings and set up shop in the bar. Pick up the papers on the way, take my laptop and my mobile and get to work."

"And people actually bring you stories?"

Rory poured out the coffee and brought two mugs across to the table. She sat down opposite Lindsay and met her questioning gaze. "Amazingly enough, they do. It was a bit slow to start with. Just the odd gossipy wee bit that made a few pars in the tabloids. But then one of the lunchtime regulars who works in the City Chambers dropped me a juicy tale about some very dodgy dealing in the leisure department. I got a splash and spread in the *Herald*, and I was away. People soon realised I could be trusted to protect my sources, so everybody with an axe to grind came leaping out the woodwork. Absolute bonanza." She grinned. It was hard not to be seduced by her delight.

"I'm impressed," Lindsay said. "And it's not a bad cup of coffee, either."

"So what are you doing back in Glasgow? Last I heard about you was when you got involved in Union Jack's murder at the Journalists' Union conference. But the word was that you were living in California, that you'd given up the game for teaching. How come you're back in Glasgow?"

Lindsay stared into her coffee. "Good question."

"Has it got an answer?" There was a long silence, then Rory continued. "Sorry, I can't help myself. I'm a nosy wee shite."

"It's a good quality in a journalist."

"Aye, but it's not exactly an asset in the social skills department," Rory said ruefully. "Which would maybe be why, as you rightly pointed out, I live alone."

"I came back for love," Lindsay said. The kid had worked hard for an answer. It seemed a reasonable exchange for a decent cup of coffee and some pain relief.

Rory ran a hand through her hair. "God, what a dyke answer. Why do we ever do anything demented? Love."

"You think it's demented to come back to Glasgow?"

Rory pulled a rueful face. "Me and my big mouth. I mean, for all I know, California's not what it's cracked up to be. So, what are you doing with yourself now?"

Lindsay shook her head. "Not a lot. Mostly waiting for the love object to come home from the high-powered world of obstetrics and gynaecology."

"You don't fancy getting back into deadline city, then?"

Lindsay leaned back in her seat, trying to ease her teeshirt away from her shoulder blades now that the sweat had dried and stuck it to her skin. "I've no contacts. I've not written a news story in seven years. I don't even know the name of my local MSP, never mind who's running Celtic and Rangers. It'd be like starting all over again as a trainee reporter on the local weekly."

Rory gave her a speculative look. "Not necessarily," she said slowly.

"Meaning what?" Lindsay couldn't even be bothered to be intrigued.

"Meaning, you could always come and work with me."

Chapter 2

Morning rain on the Falls Road, grey sky only half a shade lighter than gunmetal; a comparison that still came too easy to too many people in Belfast. Ceasefires, peace deals, referendums and still it caught people by surprise that the disasters on the news were happening some other place.

A black taxi pulled up outside a betting shop on a street corner. By then, sometimes a black taxi was just a taxi. This one wasn't. This one was bringing Patrick Coughlan to work. To his official work. When he went about his unofficial work, the last thing he wanted to be seen in was IRA trademark wheels. In the days when he went about his unofficial work rather more frequently than of late, he had always gone under his own steam, in any one of a dozen nondescript vehicles. Of course the security services had almost certainly known Patrick Coughlan was a senior member of the IRA Army Council, but they'd never been able to catch him at it. He was a careful as well as a solid citizen.

The cab idled for a full minute by the kerb while Patrick scrutinised the street. If someone had asked what he was looking for, he'd have been hard pressed to answer. He only knew when it wasn't there. Satisfied, he stepped out of the cab and across the pavement. A man in his early fifties, obviously once very handsome, his features now blurred with slightly too much weight and high living, his walk betrayed a sense of purpose. His hair was a glossy chestnut, suspiciously so at the temples for a man who had lived his particular life. In spite of the laughter lines that surrounded them, his eyes were dark, shrewd and never still.

He pulled open the door on a gust of stale air and stepped inside. To the uninformed eye, just a busy Belfast betting shop, nothing to differentiate it from any other. Odds were chalked up on whiteboards, sporting papers pinned to the walls, tiled floor pocked with cigarette burns. The clientele looked like the unemployed, the unemployable and the retired. Every one of them was male. The staff were working hard behind metal grilles, but not so hard that they didn't all glance up at the opening of the door. The smoke of the day's cigarettes already hung heavy in the air, even though it was barely eleven.

Patrick crossed the room like the lord of the manor, nodding affably, waving a proprietary greeting to several regulars. They returned the greeting deferentially, one actually tugging the greasy brim of a tweed cap. It had never struck anyone as odd that so avowed a Republican should behave quite so much like an English patrician.

Patrick continued across the room towards a door set in the wall by the end of the counter. One of the counter staff automatically slid a hand beneath the counter and the sound of a buzzer followed. Without breaking stride, Patrick pushed through the door and into a dim corridor with stairs at the far end.

A door in the wall opened and a young woman with hair like a black version of Ronald McDonald and skin the blue white of skimmed milk stuck her head round it. "Sammy McGuire was on earlier. He said would you give him a call."

"I will, Theresa." Patrick continued down the corridor and up the stairs.

It would be hard to imagine how the office he walked into could have been more different from the seediness downstairs. The floor was parquet—the real thing, not those pre-glued packs from the DIY superstore—with a silver grey Bokhara occupying what space wasn't taken up by a Regency desk that looked almost too much for its slender legs. The chair behind it was padded leather, the filing cabinets that lined the wall old mahogany buffed to a soft sheen. Two paintings on the wall, both copies, one of a Degas and one of a Stubbs, both featuring horses. The only thing that let the room down was the view of the Falls Road.

He'd thought of having the window bricked up and replacing it with another Degas. But it didn't do to let people think you weren't keeping an eye on them. Information had always been a commodity in Belfast; and if you didn't yet have the information, it was almost as important to make it look as if there was no reason why you shouldn't. So the window stayed.

Patrick lowered himself gingerly into the chair, a martyr to his back as well as his country. Settled, he reached for the phone and pushed a single button on the speed dialler.

"Sammy?" Patrick said.

"Patrick. How're ye?"

"Well, Sammy. And yourself?"

"Ah well, no complaints, you know?"

"And the family?" The rituals had to be observed.

"They're all doing fine. Geraldine's got herself a nice wee job with the Housing Corporation."

"Good for her. She'll do well there, so she will. So, Sammy, what can I do for you?"

"Well, Patrick, it might be that I can do something for you."

Patrick opened the humidor on his desk and selected a King Edward half corona. "Is that so, Sammy?" he said, tucking the phone into his neck while he lit the cigar.

"Have you still an interest in Bernadette Dooley?"

Patrick clenched the phone in his fist. Only a lifetime of dissimulation allowed him to sound unruffled. "Now there's a name I've not heard these six years," he said genially. But his heart was jittering in his chest, the surge of memory flashing a slideshow of images across his mind's eye.

"Only, when she went missing, I seem to remember you were pretty keen to find out where she'd gone."

"I'm always concerned about my employees, Sammy. You know that."

"Oh aye," Sammy said hastily. "I know that, Patrick. But I didn't know if you were still interested?"

He couldn't maintain the pretence of disinterest any longer. "Where is she, Sammy?"

Patrick heard the sound of a cheap lighter clicking. "I was in Glasgow last weekend—a cousin of the wife's wedding. Anyway, I went into a supermarket to get some drinks in, and I saw Bernadette. Not to speak to, like, but it was definitely her, Patrick." Sammy spoke rapidly.

"Was she working there?"

"No, no, she was walking out with her shopping. I was at the check-out, in the middle of paying, there was nothing I could do..."

"What supermarket would that be, now?" Patrick said, as if it were a matter of supreme indifference.

"I'm not sure of the name of it, like, but it's right at the top of Byres Road. Behind the Grosvenor Hotel. That's where the wedding was, you see. I didn't know if you were still interested, but I thought, no harm in letting your man know."

"I appreciate that, Sammy. There's a twenty pound bet for you in the shop next time you're passing." It would cost him nothing. Sammy McGuire was one of life's losers. "Take care now."

Patrick terminated the connection. He leaned back in his chair and stared at the Degas, two frown lines between his eyebrows. Few people had ever touched his heart; Bernadette Dooley had been the only one of those who had ever dared to betray him. Even now, the thought of what he had lost when she had disappeared gave him physical pain. For seven years, he'd dreamed of finding her again, convinced that their paths would have to cross sooner or later. Not a day had passed without consciousness of what had gone when she had vanished from his life. At last, he had a chance to regain the peace of mind she had stolen from him. He flicked the intercom. "Theresa, Sammy McGuire's due a twenty on the house. He'll be by later on."

Then he hit the speed dialler again. The other end answered on the second ring, if silence could be called answering. "Michael?" Patrick said softly.

"No, it's Kevin."

Patrick stifled a sigh. The way it worked, you had to find a place

15

for the stupid ones because it was bad politics to turn them away. So you put one thick one on every team and hoped the others would keep him out of trouble. Funny, it always was a him that was the thicko. You could get away with it without too many problems usually, because one dummy in a cell of four or five wasn't too much of a liability. But in a team of two . . . it might be a different story. Patrick hoped not, for all sorts of reasons. "Put Michael on," he said wearily.

A long moment of silence, then Michael's hard voice cut through the ether. "Patrick," he said.

"Come in. I've got something for you." Patrick put the phone down. Only then did he realise his cigar had gone out.

The headlights turned into the drive. Lindsay checked that it was Sophie's car and reached for the phone. "Carry out, please," she said when it was answered. By the time the front door closed, she was listening to the invariable, "Twenty-five minutes, Mrs. Gordon." She twisted round on the window seat so she was half-facing the door. She heard Sophie's briefcase hit the floor, heard the snick of the cloakroom door shutting, then her partner's voice.

"I'm home," Sophie called. Her shoes clicked on the wooden flooring as she turned into the kitchen. "Lindsay?" She sounded puzzled.

"I'm through here."

Sophie appeared in the doorway, still elegant after a day's work in a tailored suit and plain silk shirt. She had the grace not to ask why Lindsay wasn't in the kitchen as usual, putting the finishing touches to dinner. "Hi, darling," she said, the smile reaching her tired eyes. Then she took in the bandaged ankle propped on a cushion and raised her eyebrows, concern on her face. "What on earth have you been doing to yourself?"

"It's just a sprain."

Sophie crossed the room and perched by Lindsay's foot, her hand drawn irresistibly to the neatly wrapped crepe bandage that swaddled the injured ankle. "Suddenly you're the doctor?"

"I'm the one with the sports injuries experience," Lindsay

16

grinned. "Trust me, it's a sprain."

"What happened?" Sophie tenderly stroked Lindsay's leg.

"I wasn't paying attention. I was running up the hill to the Botanics and I crashed into somebody."

Sophie shook her head, indulgent amusement on her face. "So how much havoc did you create?"

"None. She was absolutely fine. She ended up driving me home."

"Lucky for you her car was there."

Lindsay shrugged. "She lives just across the river. It was easier to give in and hobble there than to risk doing myself serious damage by walking all the way home."

"Still, it was nice of her to take the trouble." Sophie began gently massaging the relaxed curve of Lindsay's calf.

Lindsay leaned back against the folded wooden shutter. "Aye, it was. And then she propositioned me."

Sophie's hand froze and her eyes widened. "She what?"

Lindsay struggled to maintain a straight face. "She made me the kind of offer you're not supposed to be able to refuse, especially when it comes from a cute blonde baby dyke."

"I hope this is your idea of a joke," Sophie said, her voice a dark warning.

"No joke. She asked me if I wanted to come and work with her."

Sophie cocked her head to one side, not sure how much her lover was playing with her. "She offered you a job? On the basis of crashing into you and watching you sprain your ankle? She's looking for a bull in a china shop?"

"On the basis that I am still apparently a legend in my own lunchtime and she's got a very healthy freelance journalism business that could use another pair of hands." Lindsay let her face relax, her eyes sparkling with the delight of having wound Sophie up.

Sophie gave Lindsay's knee a gentle punch. "Bastard," she said. "You had me going for a minute there." She ran a hand through her silvered curls. "I don't believe you," she sighed. "Only you could manage to turn a jogging accident into a job opportunity. But how did she know you were a journalist? Is she someone you used to work with?"

"No. She was barely in the game by the time we left for California." Lindsay quickly ran through the details of the encounter with Rory that she'd been polishing into an anecdote all afternoon. "And so," she concluded, "I said I'd think about it."

"What's to think about?" Sophie said. "It doesn't have to be forever. If something else you really fancy comes up, you can always move on. Idleness makes you miserable, and it's not like you're snowed under with prospects."

Lindsay pulled a face. "Thanks for reminding me," she said frostily.

"I didn't mean it like that. I just meant that it sounds like what Rory's doing would be right up your street. Chasing the kind of stories that interest you. Working with a community you can feel part of."

Lindsay drew her leg away from Sophie and swung round to face the living room. "Never mind that I'd be working for somebody ten years younger than me. Never mind that she only offered it because she felt sorry for me. Never mind that it feels like backtracking to where I was fifteen years ago."

Sophie got to her feet and moved to turn on the lamps. "It doesn't sound like she felt sorry for you. It sounds like she was blown away by the chance of working with one of her heroes. Anyway, from what you've said, you wouldn't be working *for* Rory, you'd be working with her."

"And who do you think is going to get first dibs on the stories? They'd be coming from her contacts, not mine. Coming on the basis of her reputation, not mine. I'd end up with the scraps from the table. The stories that don't interest her. The down-page dross."

Sophie leaned on the mantelpiece, casting a speculative look at her lover. "It might start off like that. But it wouldn't be long before the word went out that Lindsay Gordon was back in town again. You'd soon be pulling in your own stories. Where's your fight gone, Lindsay? You've always had a good conceit of yourself. It's not like you to indulge in self-pity."

For a long moment, Lindsay said nothing. Finally, she took a deep breath. "Maybe I've been sitting in your shadow for too long."

Sophie's face registered shock. But before she could say anything, the doorbell rang.

"That'll be the takeaway," Lindsay said. "I hope you don't mind, but I didn't feel up to standing around cooking."

Sophie frowned. "Of course I don't mind. Why would I mind, for God's sake?"

"Because you'll be paying for it. You'd better go and answer the door. If we wait for me to stagger out there, it'll be cold by the time we get to eat it." She pushed herself upright and began to limp towards the kitchen, using whatever furniture was available as a prop.

By the time Sophie returned with a carrier bag full of Indian food, Lindsay had managed to put plates and cutlery on the kitchen table. Sophie dumped the takeaway on the table and headed for the fridge. "You want a beer?"

"Please." Lindsay busied herself with unpacking the foil containers and tossing the lids into the empty bag. When Sophie returned with a couple of bottles of Sam Adams Boston Lager, Lindsay looked up. "I'm sorry. That was out of order."

Sophie sat down and helped herself to pilau rice. "Is that how you feel? That you're living in my shadow?" Her voice betrayed the anxiety Lindsay's words had provoked.

Lindsay worried at a piece of naan bread. "It's not that. Not exactly. It's more that I feel like I've been drifting. No direction of my own. It's like the teaching job in Santa Cruz. I'd never have moved into teaching journalism if I'd stayed in the UK, but we went to the US for your career, and I had to find something to do."

"But I thought you enjoyed it?"

"I did. But that was just luck. It wasn't because I had a burning desire to teach. And if I'd hated it, I'd still have had to stick with it, because there was bugger all else I could do." Lindsay reached for the bottle and took a swig of beer. "And now, here we are, back in Scotland because of your career, and I'm still no nearer figuring out what I want to be when I grow up."

Sophie opened her mouth to say something but Lindsay

silenced her with a raised finger. "Don't get me wrong. I'm not saying that's your fault. Nobody is more pleased than me that everything's going so well for you. I know what it means to you. But it doesn't make it any easier for me. And you being so keen for me to hitch my wagon to Rory's star—that just feels like you being desperate for me to take up any kind of stop-gap that'll keep me from going out of my head with boredom and frustration. I don't want another stop-gap, Soph, I want to feel passionate about something. The way you do."

Sophie looked down at her plate and nodded. "I understand that," she said. "But you used to feel passionate about journalism. When I first knew you, ages before we got together, you really cared about what you were doing. You really believed you could make a difference."

Lindsay gave a bark of ironic laughter. "Yeah, well, we all thought we could change the world back then. I soon got that knocked out of me."

They ate for a few minutes in silence. Then Sophie reached out and covered Lindsay's hand with her own. "Why don't you give it a try? It sounds like Rory's way of working is light years away from the daily grind that turned you into a cynic. It can't hurt to put your toe in the water. Besides, when the gods drop such an amazing piece of serendipity in your lap, it seems to me it would be tempting fate to thumb your nose at it."

Lindsay tried to swallow her mouthful of bhuna lamb, but it seemed to have lodged in her throat. She'd never had any sufficient defence against Sophie's kindness. Her partner had never once complained about being the sole breadwinner since they'd returned from California, and Lindsay knew she genuinely harboured no resentment about it. All she wanted was for her partner to feel as happy and as fulfilled in whatever she chose to do as Sophie was herself. She hadn't applied any pressure, simply offered encouragement. The least Lindsay could do was kick her pride into touch and take a chance on Rory McLaren. "You're right," she said. "Heaven knows, I can't afford to fly in the face of serendipity. And besides, I've got nothing to lose, have I?"

Chapter 3

Lindsay squirmed around in bed, trying to get comfortable. The weight of the duvet made her ankle ache, distracting her from the Denise Mina novel she was trying to read. "Can you bring me a couple of ibuprofen when you come through?" she called to Sophie who seemed to be taking forever in the bathroom.

When she finally emerged and slipped into bed beside Lindsay, Sophie seemed unusually quiet. Lindsay swallowed the pills and put her book down. "Is something bothering you?" she said. "You've hardly said a word since dinner. Are you having second thoughts about me working with Rory?"

Sophie looked surprised. "No, not at all. Why should I?"

"No reason. But I couldn't think why else you'd gone so quiet."

Sophie sighed. "There's something we need to talk about. I was going to bring it up earlier, but we were talking about your future and it just didn't seem like the right moment."

Lindsay eased herself on to her side and put an arm around Sophie's waist. "That sounds ominous. I'll never sleep now, you know. You'd better tell me what's on your mind."

Sophie lay back and stared at the ceiling, one hand on Lindsay's encircling arm. "It's the baby thing."

Lindsay felt a pit opening in her stomach. Sophie's desire for a child had been an intermittent bone of contention between them for the past couple of years. Whenever Sophie had tried to discuss it, Lindsay had either stonewalled or blanked it. She might not have much of a life plan, but she knew for certain that parenthood wasn't part of it. So she'd worked on the principle that if she ignored it, Sophie would eventually get the message and it would all go away. And inevitably, the attrition of time would render it academic. But since they'd come back to Scotland, the subject had surfaced more regularly. Every few days, Sophie had raised the topic and Lindsay had tried to sidestep it. "You know how I feel about that," she said.

"Yes. I know how you feel about that. But I don't think you have the faintest idea of how I feel about it. Lindsay, it's all I think about," Sophie said, anguish unmistakable in her voice. "Everywhere I go, all I seem to see are pregnant women and women pushing babies in prams. I'm so envious it makes me feel violent. I can't even get away from it at work, because it's what I deal with all day, every day." Sophie blinked hard, and Lindsay couldn't avoid seeing the sparkle of tears in her eyes. "Lindsay, I'm desperate. I'm nearly forty. Time's running out for me. Already, the chances are that I'm not going to be able to conceive without some sort of clinical intervention. And there isn't a fertility clinic in the whole of Scotland that will treat lesbian couples. Not even privately. If I'm going to have any possibility of a baby, I need to start doing something about it now."

"Look, you're just broody. It'll pass. It always has before," Lindsay said wretchedly.

"No. You're wrong. It never passed. Sure, I stopped talking about it, but that was only because you were so negative about the whole thing, it felt like pushing a boulder uphill. Just because I stopped talking about it doesn't mean it wasn't always there, constantly nagging away at me. If I don't have a child, there's always going to be a hole in my life that nothing else will fill."

Lindsay drew her arm away and rolled on to her back. "You're saying I'm not enough for you. That what we have isn't good enough."

Sophie shuffled on to her side and reached for Lindsay's hand. "That's not what I'm saying. I love you like I've never loved anyone else. I want to spend the rest of my life with you. But this need in me—it's different. It's a kind of desperation. If you've never felt it, you can't know what it's like. If you could walk for five minutes inside my skin, you'd maybe comprehend how this is consuming me. I need to try, Lindsay. And I need to try now."

Lindsay squeezed her eyes shut. *Please, let this not be happening,* she thought. "I don't want a child." She spoke slowly and deliberately.

"You'd make a great parent."

"That's not the issue. The issue is that I don't want to."

"But I need to."

Lindsay jerked upright, oblivious to the stab of pain in her ankle. "So what are you saying? You're going to go ahead anyway? Regardless of how I feel?"

Sophie turned away. Her voice was shaky with tears. She feared she was driving Lindsay further from her with everything she said, but she couldn't keep the churn of emotions secret any longer. "Lindsay, if I have to lose you to have the chance of a child, then I'll do it. This is not about choice, it's about compulsion. This isn't some whim, some spur of the moment desire for a designer accessory. It feels like life and death to me."

Her words shook Lindsay like a physical blow. She pulled her knees up to her chest, gripping them tightly with her hands. She knew her lover well enough to realise that this was no empty ultimatum. Sophie didn't play games like that. And she was sufficiently resolute to carry out her stated intention.

This was the moment Lindsay had always dreaded, ever since the issue of motherhood had first raised its head between them. Her life had been bound to Sophie's for so long, she couldn't imagine what it would be without her. She didn't even want to try. But if she didn't give in, that would be exactly what she would have to face. "I can't believe you're making me choose between losing you or having a child with you," she choked out.

"I can't either," Sophie said. Her chest hurt, as if she was being physically rent in two. "Surely that alone tells you how powerless I feel? I'm in the grip of something I've got no control over, and it's killing me. But I've got to try, Lindsay. I've got to."

"I've got no choice either then, have I?" Lindsay said bitterly.

23

There was a long silence. Then Sophie said, "You have got a choice. You can stay with me and try to make a family with me and our child. Or you can choose to walk away."

Lindsay snorted. "Some choice. At least you've got a chance of getting something you want out of this. I don't. Either I lose you, which would break my heart, or I have to be a parent to a child I don't want. This is emotional blackmail, Sophie."

"You think I don't know that? You think I want to behave like this?" Sophie turned to face Lindsay, tracks of moisture glistening on her cheeks. "You think I like myself like this?"

Lindsay tried to stay resolute, to keep her eyes on the opposite wall. But it was more than she could manage. She slid down the bed and reached for Sophie. "You know I can't leave you," she mumbled into Sophie's hair.

"And you know I don't want you to. What would be the point in having a baby without you there to share it with?"

For a long time, they clung to each other, their tears salt against each other's skin. Then Lindsay leaned back. It was going to be a long night; time they made a start on what had to be said. "So. What's your next step?" she asked, resignation heavy in her voice.

Café Virginia was suffering its daily identity crisis in the hiatus between the after-work drinkers and the evening players. The music had shifted into more hardcore dance, making conversation more difficult, and there was a strange mixture of outfits on display, from business suits to teeshirts that clung to nipples and exposed midriffs.

The quietest place in the bar was the corner booth where Rory McLaren ran her business and held court. Nobody else ever sat in the booth, mostly because of the foot high scarlet neon sign that said, RESERVED. Rory had wanted it to say GONNAE FUCK OFF? but Mary the bar manager had vetoed it on the grounds that it would be too big for the table. Rory was hammering out the finishing touches to a memo on a story proposal for the Herald feature pages, occasionally pausing to sip at her bottle of Rolling Rock. She looked up, sensing company heading her way and saw a sharp-suited Asian woman with gleaming hair in a shoulder length bob weaving her way through the tables towards her.

Sandra Singh flopped on to the bench seat opposite Rory, dumping raincoat, handbag and briefcase beside her. "That jerk Murray," she spat.

"Thought as much," Rory said, giving Sandra the quick once over. "Love the earrings."

"A wee shop in Cambridge. I'm going to kill him, I swear to God. Three weeks hammering out the new format and then this morning it's, 'the network disnae like it.' I tell you, some days I wish I'd never left newspapers." She raked in her handbag and came out with a packet of Marlboro Red and a matchbook from last night's restaurant.

"You don't mean that." Rory leaned out of the booth and waved to the bar, holding up two fingers.

Sandra's grin was even sharper than her suit. "You're right, I don't." She sighed. "I just wish I did. So, any news?"

"You could say that. Looks like I might have got myself a partner."

Sandra snorted smoke. "As in, you got laid?"

Rory's attempt at dignity wouldn't have fooled a drunken child of two. "Sandra, there's more to life than sex."

Sandra's laugh attracted every woman in the place. "You didn't get laid, then."

"I'm talking business here, fool."

Sandra nodded acknowledgement to the barmaid who placed two sweating bottles in front of them. "You serious? I thought the whole point of this was being a one-man band?"

"I thought so, yeah. But this one's really special."

Sandra took a long swallow of her beer. "So you're planning on getting laid?"

Rory shook her head in affectionate exasperation. "No. Focus your mind above the waist for once, would you? I'm not looking for a shag, I'm looking to build a business. Listen, do you remember me telling you years back about Lindsay Gordon?"

Sandra frowned. "Lindsay . . . ? Oh, wait a minute. The great lesbian icon hack. The one that turned you on to the beautiful game. This would be that Lindsay Gordon?"

"One and the same. Well, you'll never guess what happened. You couldn't write this, people would just say, 'Yeah, right, and then the Pope said abortion was fine by him.' But this is the absolute, no messing, God's honest truth." Rory gave Sandra the full version of her meeting with Lindsay, punctuated by her friend's regular interruptions.

"That's wild," Sandra finally said. "So she said she'd think about it?"

"That was just for show. You could tell she's gagging to get back in harness."

"You wish." Sandra finished her cigarette and her beer. "Sorry, babe. I'm out of here. In fact, I never was in here. Got a date with a beautiful boy from Radio Clyde." She stood up, gathering her universe. She leaned across the table and kissed Rory on the cheek. "See you, darlin'."

On her way out, she passed a baby dyke, black leather waistcoat over white teeshirt, black jeans, dyed black cropped hair, bottle of Rolling Rock in her hand. "She's all yours," Sandra told her, patting her on the arm. The baby dyke flushed scarlet and edged towards the booth.

"I got you a drink, Rory," she said, a nervous smile twitching at the corners of her mouth.

"Thanks. You want to sit down?"

The kid squirmed into the seat Sandra had left. "You pay folk for stories, eh?" she scrambled out.

"Depends. What's your name?"

"I'm Kola. Wi' a K. Ma pal Ginger says you gien her a fifty for something she told you last year."

Rory nodded. Ginger had tipped her the wink about a candidate for the Scottish parliament with a sideline in cigarette smuggling. She'd got a splash in the *Herald* and follow-ups in all the dailies the next day. "I remember. How's Ginger doing? I've not seen her about the place for a while."

"She's went tae London. She got taken on by BHS. The clothes are shite, and so's the money, but she's having a ball. So will you pay me for a story?"

26

"Let me hear what you've got and I'll tell you what it's worth. OK?"

Kola thought about it. It was a bit more complicated than buying a drink or scoring some E so it took a minute or two. "How do I know you won't just write it anyway?"

"You don't. You have to trust me. But you know I didn't let Ginger down."

Kola nodded, her face clearing, relieved at having the decision made for her. "Right. OK. It's about Madonna."

Rory fought to keep her face straight. Whatever was coming, she didn't think it was going to keep the cats in Whiskas for life. "Madonna? We're talking the singer, not the one with the statues in the cathedral?"

It was beyond Kola, who frowned. "Aye, the singer. Her and that Guy Ritchie, they're gonnae buy a big house out in Drymen."

Stranger things have happened, Rory thought. *4, 6, 11, 24, 39 and the bonus ball is 47.* At least Drymen was the right sort of territory for someone like Madonna. Big houses, country estates, high walls and gamekeepers with shotguns. "In Drymen?" she echoed.

"You don't believe me, do you?" Kola accused her with the tired hurt of someone used to being taken for a liar.

"It's a bit... surprising," Rory said. "Gonnae tell me where you heard this?"

"It's right enough," Kola said defensively. "The folk that work for her have been on the phone to an estate agent out there."

"You're going to have to tell me how you know that, Kola," Rory said, suddenly wondering if the baby dyke might not be as daft as she looked.

Kola sighed in exasperation. "I'm shagging his wife."

Chapter 4

People would cross the road if they saw Michael Conroy walking towards them. Whether they knew him by sight or by repute or not at all, they instinctively knew better than to block this man's piece of the pavement. His eyes were the greenish amber of a bird of prey; his narrow face involuntarily called up memories of a wood-axe. He looked precisely what he was. Dangerous and mean. To Patrick Coughlan, this limited his usefulness. He'd never have dreamed of sending Michael undercover unless the aim was to scare the shit out of everybody he came into contact with.

Michael didn't mind. His idea of being a soldier wasn't pretending to be a librarian in North London or working on a building site in Derby while other people did the dirty work. He liked what he'd spent the past fifteen years doing. Ceasefire didn't suit him and he knew it.

He sat in the chair facing Patrick, his eyes calm and watchful. Dressed in an olive green combat jacket and blue jeans, he would have fitted in perfectly with any group of squaddies in a bar anywhere. Entirely self-contained, he cleaned his nails with the blade of a penknife, an absent-minded habit that he was unaware was marked down on the file MI5 had held on him for some years.

Kevin O'Donohue was the gopher. A thin, wiry greyhound, he fetched and carried without the wit to question what or why. Loyal to the point of stupidity, he was reliable only in the sense that he didn't have enough brains to act on his own initiative. He did what he was told, and mostly he did it well enough. Michael tolerated him for his sister's sake. Geraldine got Kevin's share of intelligence in the genetic share-out. It wasn't imbecility that had got her caught in the aftermath of the Docklands bomb. Just bad luck. Michael hadn't seen her for three years, but he'd kept his word and made sure Kevin was sorted. Kevin, of course, had no idea of this pact.

Kevin looked like a harmless rodent, which was appropriate enough. Coarse auburn hair badly cut so it emphasised the jut of his forehead, the sort of freckles that looked like a nasty rash and the fashion sense of Man at Millett's told any casual encounter all they needed to know. He fidgeted in his chair, nervous in the presence of Patrick, who always made him feel like he was about to make his first confession all over again.

"I've a wee job for you," Patrick said. "It's what you might call private enterprise. You'll need to keep your mouths shut, but you'll be well looked after."

Michael nodded. "Whatever you say, Patrick."

"It's a matter of finding somebody I have an interest in." Patrick pushed a photograph across the desk. Michael leaned forward and picked it up. He gave it the hard stare, then off-handed it to Kevin.

"She used to work downstairs," Michael said, his voice as uninterested as if he'd been asked the time.

"That's right. She did a disappearing act six, seven years ago with something that belongs to me. I've had the word out in a quiet sort of a way, and now I've got intelligence that she's in Glasgow."

"And you'd like us to find her for you." It wasn't a question.

"D'you have an address, then?" Kevin asked.

Patrick ignored him. "She was seen at the weekend in a supermarket at the top of Byers Road. Behind the Grosvenor Hotel. It's the only lead I've got. Obviously she's not going to be using her own name, so there's no point in looking in the phone book or the voter's roll."

Michael folded his knife shut. "We'll manage," he said.

Patrick opened his desk drawer and took out a brown envelope.

"I don't want you using any of our people over there. So you'll need a float. Theresa's got tickets downstairs for tonight's ferry."

"What about a car?" Michael asked.

Patrick raised one finger and smiled approvingly. "There's a British driving licence in the envelope. You can use it to hire a car if you need one."

Michael pocketed the envelope without looking at the contents. "Daily calls?"

"At least. You've got a clean mobile, haven't you?"

Michael's grin would have put Red Riding Hood's granny to shame. "Clean, not cloned," he said.

"Any questions?" Patrick asked, his voice a silky challenge.

"What are we supposed to do when we find her?" Kevin asked, oblivious.

"Whatever Patrick tells us," Michael sighed. He got to his feet. "I'll be in touch," he said.

Patrick inclined his head. "I can't wait." If they'd seen the look in his eyes, anyone with any sense would have already left town.

Lindsay stared out of the window of the cab, taking in nothing of the late morning bustle of Great Western Road. Normally, she'd have used the Clockwork Orange, Glasgow's underground system, to go into the city centre, but her ankle was stiff and swollen and today she cared more about comfort than being environmentally friendly.

It had been a long night. They'd talked for more than an hour after Sophie's bombshell, and it hadn't got any better from Lindsay's point of view. The revelation that had shocked her most of all was that Sophie had already identified a possible donor, had approached him and had secured his agreement. Fraser Tomlinson was a researcher in Sophie's department, a gay man in a steady relationship. He and his boyfriend Peter had been to the house for dinner, and Lindsay had found them pleasant company. According to Sophie, Fraser was HIV negative, his family medical history gave no grounds for serious concern and he had no desire to play any role in the life of any child that might result from the

30

donation of his sperm. It was so cut and dried, it had left Lindsay lost for words.

"And when were you thinking of starting?" she'd managed at last.

"I'm due to ovulate in a couple of days time," Sophie had said. "The best chance is to bracket the ovulation. I was planning to have the first go tomorrow night, then again two nights later."

Lindsay swallowed hard. "I can see why you wanted to bring it up now." Involuntarily, she moved so her body no longer touched Sophie's.

"I'm sorry to spring it on you like this. But we've talked and talked and got nowhere. I realised that we were never going to get anywhere unless I did something about it. Lindsay..." Sophie's voice was a plea. "Every time I bleed, it feels like a lost opportunity. I can't afford to wait. I've done the blood tests. So far, my hormone levels are OK. But every month that goes past takes me nearer the point where they're not going to be OK any longer. I've got a donor now, I'm not prepared to hang on until you come round to feeling positive about this."

"Fine. So we do it tomorrow night. What's the drill? Is there an etiquette here? Our place or theirs?"

"Fraser and Peter will come round here. What I hoped was that you would be here for me."

"You want *me* to do the thing with the turkey baster?"

"It won't be a turkey baster, for God's sake. It'll be a sterile syringe." Sophie reached for Lindsay's hand. "Please, Lindsay. I need you now more than I ever did."

Lindsay, who had always found it impossible to hold out against Sophie for any length of time, let her hand be held. "Fine. Whatever. Now, can I go to sleep?"

The end of the conversation had not led directly to sleep. Lindsay had lain awake long after Sophie's breathing became deep and regular. There was a hollow feeling in her stomach, a nameless grief that ached inside her. Something had shifted inside her tonight with the knowledge that she could never give Sophie enough to satisfy her. She had thought their life together was good, their relationship solid. Now, it felt as if her house was built on sand. Maybe it was true that she hadn't been hearing Sophie. But it was just as true that Sophie hadn't been hearing her.

She'd mooched around the house after Sophie had left for work, unable to settle to anything. She couldn't be bothered answering the morning's e-mails. She was impatient with the newspapers and their flood of irrelevancies. Finally, stir crazy, she'd decided to pay a visit to Café Virginia. Perhaps Rory McLaren had something to offer that would make her feel better about herself. But first, she had a couple of phone calls to make. Lindsay might have been out of the game for a long time, but she still knew one or two of the faces that counted. She wasn't going to hitch her wagon to Rory McLaren's star until she had confirmed that the world's estimate of the young freelance bore some relationship to the reality. In her early years as a national newspaper journalist, she'd wasted too much time chasing the fantasies of freelances keen to make an easy buck not to take any of the breed at their word.

On the other side of the city centre, Rory was swanning into the offices of the *Scottish Daily Standard*. The security men didn't care that she'd stopped working there six months before. They figured she'd had a better motive to blow the place up when she was on the staff than she ever could have as a freelance. She took the lift up to the editorial floor and walked into one of the side offices off the features area.

Giles Graham, lifestyle editor and secretly agony aunt of the *Standard* was stretched out on his sofa, reading the pained letters of his correspondents and eating very low fat cottage cheese and chives from the tub with a plastic spoon. Rory could never figure out how a man who managed such fastidious elegance in every other area of his life he could be taken for a gay man still managed such disgusting eating habits.

"That's disgusting," she said, crossing the room to sit in the swivel chair behind a worryingly tidy desk.

"I know. You'd think people would have the good sense not to go exploring their gay side with their brother-in-law, but they never learn," he said languidly in the English-accented speech of the privately educated Scot. He put his lunch down on the coffee table and carefully gathered the letters together before sitting up and brushing down his immaculate navy linen shirt for invisible crumbs. "How delightful to see you, Rory. Are we having social intercourse or is there a sordid financial motive behind your visit?"

"You want social intercourse? OK. How's Julia?"

Giles smiled fondly. His wife was the Member of the European Parliament for Central West Scotland. Julia's frequent absences, he maintained, were what rendered her capable of putting up with him. "She's on a jolly in Oslo."

"That's a contradiction in terms," Rory observed. "Give her my love next time you pass in the night." She leaned back in the chair and hitched her Gap-clad legs on to the desk. "I've got a very good tip for you, babe."

Giles groaned. "Why not copy? Why do I have to do all the work?"

"Because it's not my kind of story. I do investigative journalism, remember? Stories like this are the reason I quit working for the newsdesk."

"That and the thick end of a hundred and fifty grand," Giles said cynically.

"The lottery was the means, not the reason, as well you know. Now, do you want this story, or do you want me to toddle round to the *Sun*?"

Giles stretched his arms along the back of the sofa, languid as a trout stream on an August afternoon. "As if," he said. "So tell me what you know."

"Madonna's people are having hush-hush talks with estate agents about her buying a property on Loch Lomond. In the Drymen area."

Giles raised one eyebrow.

"Don't do that, you look like Roger Moore in a bad Bond movie," Rory complained. "It's straight up. I got it from the horse's mouth. Well, the groom's best mate's mouth. But I know for a fact that Struther Wilson have been approached, and if they've had the word, so have other people."

"If it's true, it's not a bad little tale," Giles said cautiously.

"It's me you're talking to, Giles. When you stand it up, it's a guaranteed splash and you know it."

His smile conceded. "How much are you looking for?"

"A generous tip fee. I've got to split it with my source. I'll leave the details to your sense of propriety."

Giles pushed his dark blond hair back from his forehead. "Very trusting."

"Hey, I know you're the only person under this roof who knows the meaning of the word." Rory dropped her feet to the floor and stood up. "I'll leave you to it. Some of us have got work to do."

He snorted. "Cappuccinos to drink, more like. By the way, Sandra tells me you think you're in with a chance with the woman across the landing."

Rory shook her head. "If you guys worked as hard at getting stories as you do at spreading gossip, I'd be out of a job. Let me know how you get on with Madonna."

Before he could reply, Rory was out the door. She had more than cappuccino on her mind, but that was none of Giles's business. She still couldn't quite believe in her encounter with Lindsay; it felt too good to be true. Her freelance business had begun to generate more business than she could handle alone, but she hadn't wanted to share with just anyone. She'd always been a loner, hiding her self-sufficiency behind a mask of easy charm, letting few people see the vulnerability and damage behind the façade. Sandra was one of a handful who had been allowed past the barrier of her public face, but Sandra was too much in love with the buzz of television to consider giving it up for the slog of freelancing. And there was nobody else that Rory had ever seriously considered working with.

But something had sparked between her and Lindsay Gordon, and it was something more than hero worship. They'd made an instant connection, and Rory still felt faintly baffled by the speed with which she'd offered Lindsay a share in her closely guarded world. She had no conviction that Lindsay would take up the invitation without more work on her part; her self-belief couldn't quite carry her that far. So somehow Rory was going to have to figure out how to entice her in.

Lindsay dipped another crispy chip into the bowl of relish and turned another page of the paper. She'd been waiting over an hour for Rory, but it hadn't been a problem. Somehow, the restlessness that had afflicted her earlier had dissipated in the congenial atmosphere of Café Virginia. And besides, she'd made good use of the time.

She'd limped in, her eyes roving round the bar area, taking in the décor that somehow managed to be stylish without being impersonal. Trance music played, not loud enough to make conversation uncomfortable. A handful of patrons sat on high stools at tables built on to the square pillars that supported the ceiling. A few glanced up as she walked in, but nobody gave her a second look as she made her way to the zinc-topped counter. Behind the bar, a woman with cropped black hair was stocking cold cabinets with bottled beers. As Lindsay approached, she turned and stood up. "What can I get you?" she asked.

"I'll take a cappuccino."

The barmaid nodded and moved to the gleaming coffee machine. While she fiddled purposefully with taps and spigots, Lindsay continued to scan the place. The bar area occupied the front of the café, but beyond she could see a bigger room. Wooden booths lined the back wall, but the rest of the space was occupied with round metal tables and Italian-style chairs with slender chrome legs. At two of the tables, lone women sat with coffee cups, cigarettes and newspapers.

Lindsay paid for her drink, then said, "I'm looking for Rory McLaren."

The barmaid smiled. "The Scarlet Pimpernel of the Merchant City." It came out with the smoothness of a familiar line. "She's no' been in yet."

"She's got a regular table, right?"

The barmaid leaned on the counter and pointed through to the back room. "Farthest booth at the end. She expecting you?"

Lindsay shrugged. "I suppose that depends on how confident she is of her pulling power."

The smile widened to a grin. "She'll be expecting you, then. Go away through. Mind you, there's no telling when she'll show up. If she's not in first thing, it could be quite a while."

"That's OK, I'm not in any hurry."

"Aye well, all good things come to those who wait."

"Will you have one with me while I'm waiting?"

The barmaid raised her eyebrows. "Aye, all right. I'll have a Diet Irn-Bru, if it's all right with you." She reached into the chill cabinet and pulled out a can, popping the top and taking a swig.

"Do you mind telling me your name? Only, I reckon there's a fair chance I'm going to be in here quite a bit, and, 'Hey, you,' isn't really my style."

"Oh God, not another smooth operator," the barmaid sighed, raising her eyes to the ceiling.

Lindsay grinned. "Truly, that wasn't a line. I might be doing a bit of work with Rory, and from what she's told me, this is where it all happens." She shrugged. "I prefer to be on friendly terms, that's all."

"What sort of work?"

"I used to be a journalist. And Rory seems to think I could be again." Lindsay's self-deprecating shrug was perfectly calculated.

"She can be very persuasive."

"So I've heard. But you need to be in this game. So humour me that I can still cut the mustard and tell me your name."

The barmaid grinned. She had a tiny diamond inlaid in her left canine. It added shock value to the smile. "I'm Annie," she said.

"And I'm Lindsay." She looked around. "Rory tells me she keeps pretty busy. Plenty stories coming in all the time."

Annie nodded. "Everybody knows her in here. You'd be amazed the things she picks up just hanging out. It was slow at the start, but these days she's always got something on the go. Mind you, I'm surprised she's thinking about working with somebody else."

"How so?"

"No disrespect, but Rory's no' exactly what you'd call a team

36

player. She likes her own company too much. Half the baby dykes in here are in love with her, but she never takes advantage. See Rory? She figures out what she wants and goes for it, and hell mend the hindmost. And people see that, and they trust her because of it."

"So you'd recommend working with her?"

"You could do a lot worse." Annie took a long swallow of her drink and put the can down behind the counter as another customer approached.

"I'll let you get on," Lindsay said, sliding off her bar stool and making her way through to Rory's booth. She smiled at the "Reserved" sign on the table, eased herself on to the padded bench seat and stared at the pile of morning papers neatly stacked against the wall. Her morning's research had been productive, and Annie's responses had confirmed her half-made decision.

The first journalist she'd spoken to had been a former colleague on the *Standard.* Gus was now news editor for BBC Radio Scotland and although their relationship had been closer to that of sparring partners than friends, he'd seemed pleased enough to hear from her.

Gus didn't like Rory. He thought she was a chancer who pushed the very limits with her stories and who didn't care whose toes she trampled on when she was on the chase. But then, Gus had never liked women, least of all dykes. If that was the worst he could find to say about Rory, Lindsay reckoned her potential workmate was probably almost as good as she'd said she was.

Lindsay's second call was to Mary Salmond. They'd both been active in the Journalists' Union at the same time, and Mary was now Women's Editor of the *Reporter.* She'd sounded positively delighted to hear Lindsay's voice and immediately insisted they have lunch together to catch up. Lindsay reluctantly agreed; she'd always found Mary far too Edinburgh earnest for her taste. But she wanted information, and she'd have to pay for it.

Mary had gushed at the mention of Rory's name. "She's done awfully well since she went freelance," she said. "Awfully well indeed. She's done the odd piece for me, always her own ideas, and her copy's a joy. She writes to length, she pitches it at the right level for my readers and she's got the knack of getting doors to open for her."

"What's she like personally?"

"I wouldn't say I knew her that well. She seems very private, never really gives much away. She's not one of those freelances who's always trying to freeload in the pub, you know the kind?"

Lindsay knew the kind. "But you like her?"

"Oh yes, I like her fine. She's very pally with Giles Graham, you know Giles? Such a sweetie. If Giles likes her, she must have something going for her, I've always thought he's an awfully good judge of character. I've seen her about with Sandra Singh as well. You won't know Sandra, she's a factual programmes producer at STV, after your time. Does that help?"

It had helped. Lindsay had instinctively liked Rory, but she was too shrewd an operator herself to trust her future to someone she knew nothing about. Now she knew enough to take a chance. She picked the top paper off the pile and began browsing. After an hour, she ordered a burger and fries. The burger turned out to be a very poor relation of what she was accustomed to in California, but the chips were glorious—fat chunks of real potato, golden brown and crunchy, the way she liked them and had seldom found them in America. *That would be how I stayed so slim over there,* she thought. She decided she'd give Rory till she'd finished her lunch, then she'd leave her a note and go. It really didn't do to seem too keen, after all.

A shadow crossed the page she was reading and Lindsay looked up to see Rory standing before her, laptop slung over one shoulder, a delighted grin on her face. "Couldn't stay away, huh?" Rory asked, sliding into the seat opposite Lindsay.

"Well, I could hardly go running, could I?"

Rory winced. "How is the ankle?"

"Sore. But not as swollen as it was. A week or so and it'll be back to normal."

"That's the official clinical view from the resident medic?"

Lindsay snorted. "Given Sophie's area of expertise, she'd take one look at a swollen ankle and probably tell me I was suffering from pre-eclampsia."

Annie arrived carrying a couple of cappuccinos. "There youse go. You want something to eat, Rory?"

"I'll take a plate of stovies, Annie."

The barmaid nodded and left them to it.

"Three cappuccinos in one day. I'll be jazzed till bedtime at this rate," Lindsay said.

"Would you rather have something else? Only, Annie said that's what you were on." Rory looked momentarily anxious.

She's trying to make an impression, Lindsay thought wryly. "No, that's fine. I suspect I'm going to have to have my wits about me to deal with you anyway."

"So, you've decided to take me up on my suggestion?" Rory kept her eyes on her coffee, but Lindsay could sense the eagerness underlying the question.

"I'm giving it serious consideration. But if it's going to stand any chance of working, we've got to be up front with each other." Rory's head came up as she registered the seriousness of Lindsay's tone. The banter was over, and it was time to get down to business.

"Point taken. So, what do you want to know?"

Lindsay sucked some foam off her cappuccino and wiped her top lip clean. "My big reservation is that initially, stories would only be coming my way on the basis of your reputation. Which obviously means you get first pick of whatever lands on the table. I have no idea what that means for me. If I'm just going to be running around doing the dross that doesn't interest you or that you think isn't worth your time and attention, then, frankly, I'm not interested."

Rory looked wounded. "No, that's not how I see it at all. See, the thing is, I already get more stuff coming to me than I can deal with. I end up selling stuff on as tips that I'd rather work myself, but if I'm in the middle of something big and I get a lead on a story that's time-sensitive, I have to let it go. The way I see it, when a story comes in, whichever one of us is free to take it runs with it. Anyway, the reputation you've got, you'll be pulling stories in yourself in no time."

Lindsay's eyebrows shot up. "The reputation I've got? Come on, Rory, I'm hardly a household name."

"I've just been in at the *Standard,* passing a tip on to Giles Graham. He remembers exactly who you are. And you didn't even work together. Your by-line will sell stories that I'd struggle to place. Lindsay, I'm not handing out charity here. You'd be doing me a favour by coming in with me."

Lindsay gave Rory a long, considering look. Sure, the kid was probably a bit starry-eyed about her, imagining a past crammed with glory days and twenty-two point by-lines. But surely that had to be better than trying single-handed to carve out a niche among the sceptical new faces that were running the newsdesks and magazine supplements these days?

It wasn't the hardest decision of her life. "OK. Let's give it a go. A month's trial, and at the end of it, either of us can walk away if it's not working out."

Rory punched the air. "Yes! That's brilliant, Lindsay. Hey, you won't regret this, you know."

I sincerely hope not, Lindsay thought. But she stifled her remaining reservations and extended a hand across the table. "Nor will you," she said.

"So. When do we start?"

Chapter 5

Kevin followed Michael out into the street and sniffed the air like a dog in a new wood. "So this is Glasgow," he said. "It's not that different, is it?" There was a note of disappointment in his voice.

Michael said nothing. He simply turned left and set off towards the bus stop he'd been told he'd find a couple of streets away. He carried his heavy holdall as lightly as if it held nothing more substantial than an evening newspaper. At the bus stop, he came to a halt, dropped his bag at his feet and lit a cigarette.

"Where is it we're going again?" Kevin asked.

"A bed and breakfast," Michael said. "Argyle Street."

"So what's the plan?"

"We'll take a wee look round the pubs near where she was spotted."

Kevin's face lit up at the prospect. "Sounds good to me, Michael."

A bus drew up and the two men boarded. It was almost empty and they had the rear area to themselves.

"We won't be drinking, Kevin. This is an operation, not a holiday," Michael said. His tone of voice would have signalled to anyone else that this wasn't a subject for debate.

Not to Kevin. He gave the cunning smile of the truly stupid. "But we'll need to fit in, Michael. We'll stick out like a sore thumb if we just go in and order a couple of cokes."

"That's why we won't be going in and ordering any cokes, Kevin," Michael snarled. "You'll be going up to the bar and asking for change for the cigarette machine. Or a box of matches. Meanwhile, I'll be taking a good look around. And if I see her, we'll be stopping for a glass of stout. And we'll be making it last."

Crestfallen, Kevin slumped in his seat, watching the unfamiliar city roll past the windows. He knew he was supposed to like Michael, for his sister's sake, but he was a moody bastard to work with and no mistake.

By closing time, Michael's mood had blackened to a pitch where even Kevin realised silence was the best option. They'd explored pubs ranging from raucous student bars with loud insistent music to more traditional pubs where old men nursed their pints with the tenderness of new mothers. Michael had cast an apparently negligent but actually sharp look over hundreds of women, none of them Bernadette Dooley.

They walked back through streets shared with drinkers heading home, the air aromatic with curry and fish suppers, to the scruffy B&B where they were inconspicuous among the transient workers and DSS claimants who made it their home. All the way back, a scowl deepened the crease between Michael's eyebrows. Kevin had lost count of the number of pubs they'd scouted out, but his pockets were bulging with boxes of matches and loose change. And not so much as a glass of stout had passed his lips.

Michael broke the silence as they turned on to Argyle Street. "We'll do a school in the morning."

"Eh?"

"Patrick says she has a child. A child has to go to school. We'll stake out the nearest primary to the supermarket."

"I don't remember anything being said about a child," Kevin complained.

"I checked in when we got here. You were in the toilet. Patrick said he'd forgotten to mention she has a child."

"I never knew that. From before, like. When she was working in the shop."

Michael made a kissing sound of exasperation. "She didn't have it then. Whoever it was who spotted her in the supermarket told Patrick she had a child with her."

"Maybe it's not old enough to be at the school," Kevin pointed out, proud of himself for coming up with the argument. "I mean, it's only six years since she left."

Michael flashed a look of surprise at Kevin. It was always a shock when he said something that wouldn't be self-evident to a three-year-old. "Maybe not. But apart from hanging around the supermarket, we've got nothing else to go at. She'll not be on the voter's roll or in the phone book, not if she's got any sense. So we'll check out the primary schools on the map and we'll be there first thing."

Kevin saw the prospect of a decent night's sleep rapidly receding. "Right you are," he sighed. "The school it is."

Kevin wasn't the only one who reckoned sleep might be elusive. Lindsay had had one of the worst evenings in living memory, and the turmoil of emotions raging through her didn't feel as if they were going to subside any time soon. Part of her wished she'd taken Rory up on her suggestion of a celebratory meal out to cement their new partnership and to hell with the consequences. But she knew that, being who she was, that would always have been impossible. She couldn't be sure whether it was cowardice, love, good manners or fear that meant she had to go home and participate in the insemination she dreaded; all she knew was that she couldn't bring herself to do otherwise.

She'd returned via the greengrocer in Hyndland who seemed somehow always to have the freshest vegetables in town. Sprue asparagus, a selection of wild mushrooms, fresh strawberries, peaches and raspberries. She'd remembered Fraser's boyfriend was vegetarian, and while deep down she longed to serve them all congealed Kentucky Fried Chicken, her need to see the world well fed wouldn't allow it. It was a mark of pride to Lindsay that when people ate in her kitchen, they ate memorably and well. So she'd take the time and trouble to produce grilled asparagus, wild mushroom risotto garnished with parmesan and rocket, and a fresh fruit salad. If she'd liked them better, she'd have made a meringue shell for a pavlova, but her soul wasn't feeling that generous.

She'd thought that Sophie would be home early for once, but her lover only just made it through the door ahead of their guests. "Trying to avoid talking about it?" Lindsay had said sourly when Sophie finally walked into the kitchen and came up behind her to kiss her on the neck.

"No," Sophie replied evenly, refusing to be drawn. "I was called in on an emergency consult at the Western. You'll be pleased to hear we saved the baby and the mother, though it was touch and go with the mum."

Guilt tripped, Lindsay said nothing, taking out her spleen on the parmesan, producing a pile of extravagant curls.

The rest of the evening hadn't gone any better. Fraser and Peter had clearly already been to the pub before they arrived, drowning their apprehensions in whisky, to judge by the smell on their breath as they leaned forward in turn to plant air kisses on Lindsay's cheeks. "So, what's the drill?" Fraser had demanded with an air of forced gaiety. "Is there some ceremony to the Goddess, or do we just run away through to the spare room and have a wank?"

Lindsay closed her eyes momentarily, biting down hard to keep her mouth firmly shut. "Don't be daft," Sophie said, her voice more affectionate than Lindsay could ever have managed in the circumstances. "We'll eat first. Lindsay's cooked us a lovely meal. And then..."

"He can provide his specimen, eh?" Peter chipped in, his ferret smile disturbingly predatory. Lindsay was glad Sophie had asked Fraser to be their donor; at least he looked like a human being, not an escapee from a vivisection lab. Sophie's chosen donor would be a good match for her, Lindsay thought dispassionately as she poured wine for everyone. Like her lover, Fraser was above average height, especially for a Scot, and he had the same trim build. His hair and eye colour were close to Sophie's and like her, he had good facial bone structure.

Lindsay supposed it made sense to have a donor who resembled Sophie so closely. It increased the chances of any baby that resulted resembling its mother. But she couldn't help feeling an irrational pang of exclusion that Sophie had never even bothered to ask if she'd like them to find a donor who was a match for her, so that there would be at least a chance that any child would look like an amalgam of both of them, rather than be so clearly Sophie's child.

The dinner conversation had been gruesome. When the two men had eaten with them previously, it had been an easy and comfortable evening. But what lay ahead sat like a ponderous elephant in the middle of the dinner table, impossible to ignore yet equally unfit for discussion according to any rules of decorum.

Fed up of the dismal attempts at small talk that kept running aground, Lindsay finally said, "You don't want to be a parent, then, Fraser?"

Fraser looked startled. "Well, not in the sense of day-to-day involvement, no. Though I like the idea that my genetic material will continue after I've gone."

Selfish bastard, Lindsay thought. She wondered why he thought his genes were so special they deserved to be preserved, but realised this wasn't a line of conversation that would endear her to Sophie. "So you're not going to be popping round to take the wean to the football? Or the Scottish country dancing," she added as an afterthought, remembering that Peter had revealed that he and Fraser had first met at a gay and lesbian ceilidh. The sort of event she would have slit her throat rather than attend. Lindsay had grown up in the Highlands and knew what ceilidhs were supposed to be like. She thought Peter and Fraser would last about ten minutes tops at any village dance she'd ever attended.

Fraser smiled uncertainly, unsure if he was really hearing hostility. "I'm happy to let you and Sophie bring up the child without any interference from me," he said cautiously. "I don't mind it knowing I'm the other half of its genetic make-up when it's older, but I'm not planning on being a father in any active way."

Lindsay smiled. Out of the corner of her eye, she could see Sophie suddenly look apprehensive. "Let's just hope he doesn't decide when he's thirteen that he'd rather live with the other half of his genetic make-up, then," she said.

"Lindsay, do stop trying to frighten Fraser," Sophie said. Her voice was light, but the look she gave Lindsay would have melted the snows of Kilimanjaro. "Now, would anyone like any more fruit salad?"

Fraser and Peter exchanged a swift glance "Maybe we should just cut to the chase, Sophie," Fraser said.

"I'll show you to the spare room," Sophie said, ushering them out of the dining room and throwing a warning look over her shoulder at Lindsay. When she returned a few minutes later, she found Lindsay clattering the dirty plates into the dishwasher.

"Are you deliberately trying to fuck this up for me? Or are you just behaving inappropriately because you're nervous?" Sophie demanded.

"Neither. I was just trying to make sure we all knew what the ground rules were." Lindsay closed the machine forcefully.

"But I told you all that last night. You knew I'd already been through all that with Fraser."

Lindsay tipped the remains of the fruit salad into a plastic container and headed for the fridge. "I wanted to hear it from the horse's mouth." She leaned against the worktop, her arms folded across her chest. "I'm sorry, Sophie, but it's hard for me to take your word for things when I know how desperately you want this. You'd tell me black was white if you thought it would prevent me standing in the way of you chasing this particular dream. So I don't think it was out of order for me to ask Fraser what I did."

Sophie's grey eyes blazed anger. "I don't suppose you stopped to think that it made us look like anything but the close and confiding couple?"

Lindsay shrugged. "Maybe Fraser will just figure that I'm cautious. Which is a sensible thing to be."

Sophie ran her hands through her silvered curls. "Jesus. I'm supposed to be in a relaxed and receptive state for insemination and look at me. Wound up like a fucking spring thanks to you."

Her partner's anguish worked on Lindsay as no rational argument could have done. She put her arms round Sophie and murmured, "Oh, Christ, I'm sorry. Come on, let's get you sorted."

Sophie led the way through to their bedroom. Somehow, she'd

found the time to lay out a sterile plastic syringe by the side of the bed. "What's the drill?" Lindsay asked grimly.

"Peter will bring the sperm through in a glass. It starts to thicken once it leaves the man's body, so we have to keep it at blood heat for about ten to fifteen minutes so it'll liquefy again."

"Too much information," Lindsay muttered.

"The best way to do that is to put the glass between your breasts."

"*My* breasts? What's wrong with yours?" Lindsay demanded.

"I'll be lying on my back with a pillow under my hips, Lindsay," Sophie said impatiently as she began to undress.

"Great," Lindsay muttered. "Then what?"

"You take it up into the syringe and inject it as far up my vagina as you can get."

"And that's it?"

Sophie, by now stripped down to her underwear, had the grace to look embarrassed. "Not quite. There's strong anecdotal evidence that an orgasm around the time the sperm is introduced increases the chances of success."

Lindsay looked appalled. "You're not suggesting we . . . ?" Then she suddenly saw the funny side and burst out laughing. The release of the tension that had them both clenched in its grip brought them together again like a stretched elastic band snapping back into shape. "I really don't think I can do it," Lindsay spluttered.

Sophie finished undressing, slipping quickly beneath the duvet. "I don't think I could keep a straight face now. Probably better if I do it myself."

Lindsay closed her eyes and rubbed her eyelids with thumb and forefinger. "I think that might be best," she said, shaking her head incredulously, a final snigger escaping her lips.

Before she could say more, there was a tentative tap at the door. "All ready, girls," Peter sang out from the hall.

Lindsay opened up and stared down in disbelief at the glass being proffered to her. A large gob of off-white mucus clung to the bottom of the Edinburgh crystal, as viscous and slimy as phlegm. Wordlessly, she took it and closed the door. "You gave him one of my whisky tumblers," she said plaintively. "How can I ever drink out of them again?"

Sophie snorted with laughter. "That bloody dishwasher's about as hot as an autoclave. Trust me, you're not going to catch anything."

"It's not a matter of hygiene, it's a matter of taste. And I'm not talking flavour," Lindsay growled, thrusting the glass down the front of her shirt to nestle in her bra between still firm breasts. "Oh God, the smell," she moaned as the sharp tang of the sperm invaded her nostrils. "It's like municipal swimming pools. Jesus, I really thought being a dyke meant I'd never have to deal with this gunge again. This is so disgusting, Sophie."

"You think I don't know that? Listen, you're not the one facing the prospect of having it inside you."

Lindsay gave a savage grin. "It's not too late to change your mind."

"Very funny. Come and give me a cuddle, please?"

Gingerly, careful of her cargo, Lindsay edged alongside Sophie. With her free hand, she stroked Sophie's hair, letting her lips brush against the top of her head. "I don't think I've ever felt less sexual," Sophie said, her voice wavering on the edge of tears as she struggled for arousal.

You and me both, Lindsay thought grimly. But she kept her thoughts to herself and dropped her head to Sophie's breast, gently nuzzling her nipple. She licked it harder, sucking it into her mouth and tonguing it firmly. She was rewarded, as she knew she would be, with a soft moan and the arching of Sophie's spine.

Then suddenly it was all action. Lindsay had to pull away to draw the sperm into the syringe. Placing her hand over Sophie's, she slid the barrel into her lover's vagina as far as it would go, then depressed the plunger. There was a desperation in Sophie's cries as she came almost simultaneously. When Lindsay dared look up, she saw tears tracking down Sophie's cheeks. She knew her own eyes were pricking almost to overflowing.

Their reasons, she knew, were dangerously different.

Lindsay leaned against Sophie's bent legs, her cheek against Sophie's knee. As soon as was decently possible, she pulled away.

"I'm going to see if the guys need a drink," she said. Anything to get out of there and find a moment to get her face in order.

Now, two hours later, Lindsay was staring out of the living room window to the moonlit playing fields across the road and the tawdry glitter of the city lights beyond. She had shared a large malt with Fraser and Peter then seen them out. She'd made a cup of herbal tea for Sophie, whose body had overnight become a temple worshipping very different gods from before. She'd climbed into bed as she suspected she was expected to do and had faked sleep. Once she'd been certain that Sophie's deep and regular breathing wasn't feigned, she'd slipped out of bed, poured herself another Caol Ila and sat on the window seat wondering how much of her future lay within these walls, and how much within the walls of the Café Virginia.

Chapter 6

A few miles away, Rory McLaren was also pondering Lindsay's future, though not in quite the same terms as the subject of her plotting. She swigged greedily from a bottle of water and let herself slide down the wall she was leaning against until she was hunkered down level with Sandra. Sweat streaked their faces and bodies as they grinned inanely at each other in the chilling out space in the basement of Escape, their favourite dance club which occupied a former warehouse where Garnethill merged into Cowcaddens.

They'd split a tab of ecstasy earlier in the evening, they'd danced like dervishes and now they were both starting the gradual descent to the point where sleep might be possible at some point in the not too distant future. But for now, they were content to let the gentle throb of the ambient track ease them down gently.

"What're you thinking?" Sandra said after a few minutes.

"How useful Lindsay's going to be."

"That would be in a work context?"

Rory giggled softly. "I was thinking about work. But you never know..."

Sandra groaned. "Stick to the work. Useful how?"

"Well, take Keillor. I've got the tip, I've hardened it up pretty well, but I need some solid evidence. But Keillor knows me so I've got no chance of scamming him. But he's never seen Lindsay. Maybe between us we can figure out how to have him over and she can do the sharp end."

Sandra's mouth curled up in a feline smile. "Oh yes, I like it. Nail the wee slug to the floor."

"I'll talk to her about it in the morning."

"It's already the morning."

"Only technically." Rory hugged herself and scrunched her face up in an expression of amused cunning. "A couple of real buzzes like creepy Keillor and she'll be so hooked. Which will be nice."

Sandra chugged on her own bottle of mineral water. "Uh oh."

"I mean it'll be nice to have somebody around to work with. I never thought I'd miss the newsroom, and I don't, not really. But it does get lonely sometimes. Everybody in the bar is a potential source, so I can't afford to let them be my friends. So I spend most days not really talking to anybody unless you or Giles stops by. Lindsay . . . now, there's somebody I can talk to. Nice woman. Very nice woman."

"She's also a happily married woman, Rory. Tell me you're not going to crash through her life like an express train on speed," she sighed.

Rory shook her head vigorously, droplets of moisture scattering from her sweat-darkened hair. "Hey, she's a grown up. She can make her own choices. I don't force myself on anyone."

Sandra snorted. "Little miss butter wouldn't melt. Rory, just for once, leave it alone. You know you don't do relationships. You're the emotional equivalent of a hit and run driver. You never get hurt yourself, you just leave a trail of wreckage in your rear view mirror."

Rory pulled a face. "Yeah, well. When the only relationship you've ever seen close up was as fucked as my mum and dad's was, you'd be mental to think it was as easy as falling in love. Dive in, dive deep and then climb back out and dry off before you catch a cold, that's what works for me. And if it makes you any happier, I promise not to make a move on Lindsay. OK?"

Sandra put an arm round her friend and hugged her close. "It's not about making me happy. It's about you making yourself happy."

"Which I do, with lots of girlies." Rory's smile was wry. "Only, never for very long."

"Just remember that if Lindsay starts looking like Mount Everest."

"Eh?"

"You don't have to climb it just because it's there. You'll have more fun in the long run working with her."

"Sandra, are you sure you're not Jewish?"

Sandra gave her an affectionate punch in the ribs. "Fuck off, Rory. C'mon, let's go and have a last dance and see if I can pick myself up some wee boy who wants to be initiated into the secret world of the older woman."

Rory chuckled as she got to her feet. "And you've got the nerve to talk about me."

Sandra rumpled Rory's damp hair. "Difference is, I can do the serious thing just as well as I do the playing." She pushed past and made for the stairs leading to the main dance floor, entirely missing the momentary flash of sadness and longing that crossed Rory's face.

The raw cold ate into Kevin's bones. Michael seemed oblivious to the weather, as affected by the penetrating damp as were the concrete and glass of the primary school they were watching. The school was near the Botanic Gardens, in a quiet side street lined with tall sandstone tenements, which posed something of a problem for them. There was no convenient bus shelter or phone box to use as a surveillance point. Nor was there a handy café with windows overlooking the school entrance. And in these days of paedophile paranoia, nothing would provoke a call to the police faster than two men standing on a street corner scrutinising the children arriving at a primary school.

If it had been up to Kevin, they would have gone back to bed after their preliminary reconnaissance at half past seven had demonstrated how apparently impossible was the task facing them. But this was the school nearest the supermarket where Bernadette Dooley had been spotted, so they had to start here, Michael decreed. And besides, he had spent long enough on the front line to have honed his improvisational skills. As they had walked up Byres Road towards the school, he'd noticed two youths by the Underground entrance handing out copies of a free newspaper to the commuters hurrying into the station. When he realised how exposed the school was from a surveillance point of view, he'd remembered the newspaper distributors.

He'd marched Kevin back down to the station and gone into a huddle with the youths. A threatening look from his amber eyes would probably have been enough to achieve his goal, but Michael didn't want to be fixed in anyone's memory as a bad lad. Not just yet, anyway. So a couple of tenners were swapped for two bundles of freesheets and they walked back to the school, where they took up position at either side of the gates, handing out the paper to teachers and parents as they arrived.

Nobody gave them a second look.

"Won't she recognise you?" Kevin had asked as they'd walked back.

In reply, Michael had taken a pair of glasses from his inside pocket. They had thick black frames and lenses tinted blue. He put them on and simultaneously let his shoulders slump. In that instant, the threat disappeared like the sun behind a cloud.

"No, right, I see what you mean," Kevin muttered.

Now, he watched how Michael scrutinised every face that approached. When the electric bell finally sounded on the dot of nine o'clock, he was satisfied that Bernadette Dooley was not among the parents who had delivered their offspring to Botanics Primary.

"So what do we do now?" Kevin asked forlornly, clutching the leftover newspapers to his chest.

"We go and see if that supermarket's got a café," Michael said. "And if it hasn't, we find someplace to watch it from. And this afternoon, we find another primary school at chucking out time." He was already striding down the street.

Two hours and forty-three minutes later, Kevin shifted in his plastic chair. "She's giving us funny looks, that woman on the till," he muttered.

Michael scowled. "You're too fucking obvious, that's why." He glanced at his watch. Three teas each and a couple of bacon butties. The worst part was not being able to smoke. *No*, Michael corrected himself. The worst part was having to work with a fucking eejit like Kevin who could no more blend into the background than a naked woman at High Mass.

"I'm not doing anything," Kevin whined.

Michael bit back a vicious response. He sipped his lukewarm tea. "Away and get me a fresh cup of tea. And when you've done that, you can go into the supermarket and buy me some bananas."

"Bananas?" Kevin frowned in puzzlement.

"They're a good source of potassium. Just do it, Kevin."

Kevin pushed himself up from the table. He strolled over to the counter, his attempt at nonchalance setting all the till operator's antennae jangling. She couldn't figure out his game at all, but she was mentally rehearsing his description. When he returned with the tea, Michael said, "Fine. Now the bananas, there's a good lad. And take your time about it. Have a browse. See if there's any new flavours of Pot Noodle to get you excited." The sarcasm was wasted on Kevin, who shrugged and walked off to join the milling shoppers.

Left to himself, Michael pulled out his mobile and called Patrick. "It's me," he said as soon as they were connected. "So far, no joy."

"I didn't expect anything so soon." Patrick's voice was flat, unreadable. "Stay on it. Call me tomorrow."

The line went dead. Whatever Bernadette had taken from Patrick, it had clearly pissed the man off more than Michael would have risked lightly. He put the phone back in his pocket and continued his scrutiny of the entrance to the store. Barely taking his eyes off the harassed mothers and the slow-moving pensioners who made up most of the clientele at that time of the morning, he sugared his tea and began to drink it. This was probably a total waste of time, but they had nothing else to chase. As long as Patrick was willing to spend his money, Michael was content to watch and wait.

Time ticked inexorably past and still Kevin didn't return. He was probably memorising the Pot Noodle flavours, Michael reckoned. Then suddenly, all thoughts of Kevin disappeared. He went immobile as a lizard that knows it's been spotted and still hopes its camouflage will keep it safe.

It was her. Pushing past an elderly couple, dark hair swinging round her head in a long bob, heavy coat wrapped round her, disguising a figure that Michael remembered had always been worth noticing. Bernadette Dooley was hurrying into the supermarket, making straight for the counter that sold cigarettes, confectionery and lottery tickets.

If he leaned over in his seat, he could see her back view. She was scrabbling in her bag for her purse, pulling it out, opening it, taking out a couple of notes. She handed over the money and received a carton of 100 Silk Cut in return. Then she was turning away, pushing the cigarettes into her bag, head down, making for the door again.

Michael was on his feet. By the time she made it to the street, he was a handful of steps behind her. He glanced quickly over his shoulder. Where the fuck was Kevin? Ah, the hell with it. Bernadette was the important one. Kevin would doubtless sit in the supermarket till it closed. Either that or he'd have the sense to make his way back to where they were staying. Wouldn't he?

Bernadette turned right out of the store and headed down Byres Road. The pavements were busy enough to give him cover. With the total focus of the hunter whose oblivious prey is well upwind and living on borrowed time, Michael began stalking Bernadette Dooley.

Rory was already settled into her booth at Café Virginia when Lindsay arrived. "Hey," she greeted her, "You look worse than I do, and I was clubbing till gone three."

Lindsay squeezed out a vague smile. "I was up half the night. And not in a good way."

"Must have been something you ate, eh?"

"Must have been. So, what's doing?"

Rory pushed a manila folder across the table as Lindsay's cappuccino arrived. "Take a look at that."

Curious, Lindsay studied the contents. The first page was a memo to herself from Rory:

> Tip re Keillor/Kilwinning. CCD, the multinational phar-
> maceutical and agrichemical company have a small plant
> on the outskirts of Kilwinning. Just over a year ago,
> local farmer sells biggish chunk of land to a suit from
> down south, who says he wants to retire and do rare
> breed sheep. Few months later, planning application
> goes in for change of use from agricultural to light
> industrial. Turns out land now belongs to CCD, they
> want to expand in unspecified ways to extend their
> research. Locals convinced they're going to be poisoned
> with chemicals or overrun with cloned sheep. Think the
> local plan will keep them safe. But Chief Planning
> Officer David Keillor leans heavy on councillors and the
> change of use goes through. Source tells me that Keillor
> is running round in a brand new BMW 4x4, costs about
> a year's salary new, and his wife has a neat wee Porsche
> Boxster. Source also tells me that vehicles were originally
> registered to CCD.

The other documents were reports of the planning committee meetings and transcriptions of Rory's interviews with the farmer who sold the land and various locals with an axe to grind. Lindsay digested the material then looked up and said, "And?"

"Well, obviously, we need to get a look at the vehicle registra-tion document for Keillor's Beamer."

Lindsay nodded. "Obviously. So what's been keeping you?"

The sarcasm was gentle enough for Rory to grin. "Keillor knows me. We had a wee bit of a head to head a few years ago when he was working for the city planning department. Something to do with selling off school playing fields. So there's no way I can get close enough. I thought maybe you'd have an idea how we could pull it off?"

Lindsay scooped the froth off her coffee and slowly licked it off the spoon. "How bent do you want to get?" she asked thoughtfully.

Rory scratched an eyebrow. "Run it past me."

"Do you happen to know if Strathclyde Police have changed their warrant cards in the past two years?"

Before Rory could answer, Sandra breezed up to their table. "Hiya, girls." She inclined her head towards Lindsay. "You must be Splash Gordon." She thrust a hand out. "I'm Sandra Singh. I'm supposed to be this one's best pal." Lindsay took the offered handshake with a nod.

Rory gave an exasperated little smile. "Lindsay, meet Sandra. Sandra is a factual programmes producer/director up the road at STV. She hates her boss, she likes boys that are barely old enough to shave and she thinks that since my mammy's dead, she should poke her nose into my business all the time."

Lindsay moved up the bench to make room for Sandra. "Good to meet you. It's nice to know there's somewhere I can go to get the dirt if I need an edge."

Sandra shook her head at the available seat. "I'm not stopping. I was passing and I thought I'd just say hello. You girls plotting?"

Lindsay said, "Yes," at the precise moment Rory said, "No."

"I'll take that as a yes, and leave you to it. Catch you later." With a wave of her slender fingers, she was off.

Rory raised her eyes heavenwards. "Something else."

"Clearly. So, do you have an answer?"

Rory looked momentarily bewildered. "An answer?"

"Warrant cards."

"Right. Eh, not as far as I know. Why?"

"I think this comes into the category of what you don't know can't hurt you. Have you got an address for Keillor? There isn't one in the file."

Rory dug around in her backpack and produced a battered filofax. She rummaged around inside and finally unearthed a torn scrap of paper. She tore a sheet out of the notebook on the table and scribbled down an address in Milngavie. "You sure you don't want to talk it through?" she said almost wistfully as she handed it over.

"I'm sure. If it all goes horribly wrong, at least you'll be able to

57

put your hand on your heart and say it was nothing to do with you."

"Well, damn," Rory said. "Haven't you figured out yet that I like trouble?"

"All the more reason not to tell you what I've got in mind," Lindsay said dryly. "I can get into enough trouble for both of us, all by myself."

Rory grinned. "Oh good. You know, I think we're going to be pure dead brilliant together."

Lindsay's smile didn't make it to her eyes. It wasn't so long ago that she would have said the same thing about her and Sophie. Now, she really wasn't sure any more.

Chapter 7

Bernie Gourlay took the washing out of the tumble drier and began to fold it. She noticed that one of Jack's school sweatshirts had begun to split at the shoulder seam and put it to one side to sew up later. She often heard mothers complaining about the things they had to do for their kids. But she'd never once felt like that. She knew what a miracle he was, and she counted it a privilege to be able to take care of the details of his life. She'd been conscious ever since he'd been placed in her arms that his dependency on her would wane consistently as he grew older, and she'd determined then that she would enjoy every moment, every phase of his development, but that she'd let go when she had to.

She was, she thought, the luckiest person she knew. She'd escaped from a life that was difficult and anxious, and although the journey hadn't been without its ups and downs, now she'd achieved something she'd never have believed possible. Happiness. Jack was growing strong and healthy, a cheerful child whose face never seemed crossed with shadows. And she had Tam. Big, daft, lovely Tam who had swept her off her feet and never minded that Jack was another man's son, nor that she was incapable of having more children by him. Tam, who had bought this beautiful big garden flat for them to live in, who saw to it that none of them ever went without, who worked hard to take care of them all but who never let his business interfere with enjoying his family to the full.

Bernie glanced at the clock. Ten minutes before she had to leave and pick up Jack from school. Tam dropped him off in the mornings, but she always made sure she was there in plenty of time to pick him up. She couldn't bear the thought of him standing at the school gates, worry at her lateness puckering his face and darkening his china blue eyes. Soon enough, he'd be begging her to let him walk home with his pals, but for now, he was still pleased to see her when the bell went.

The electronic chirrup of the phone disturbed her cheerful thoughts. *Probably Tam,* she thought, reaching for the handset. It was seldom that a day went by without him calling just to say hello. Four years married, and he was still a big soft romantic at heart.

But the voice that insinuated its way into her brain wasn't Tam's. It was a voice she'd often prayed she would never hear again. It was a voice whose very tone was a masquerade, disguising the viciousness behind it with a beguiling softness. Bernie wasn't beguiled. She was terrified. She felt as if a block of ice was dissolving in her stomach, sending cold trickles through her whole body. She clung to the phone, mesmerised, unable to put it down even after the line went dead.

Staggering slightly, she collapsed into a kitchen chair. Tears pricked her eyes and her dry lips trembled. Eventually, she got to her feet, still shaky. Although she had prayed she'd never have to put it into action, she had a contingency plan in place. She took a well-worn leather address book from a kitchen drawer and looked up an unfamiliar number. She keyed it into the phone and waited for the international connection. When the phone was answered, she gave the name of the person she desperately needed to talk to. Another pause. Then Bernie closed her eyes with relief. "It's Bernadette," she said. *Please God, let this work.*

Late the following afternoon, Lindsay drove out through the south side of the city towards the prosperous suburb of Milngavie. She never failed to be struck by the contrasts in Glasgow, even

60

between areas that superficially seemed to have much in common. The average income in Milngavie was probably only marginally above that in the smart part of the West End where she and Sophie lived. But culturally, it felt like a different world. The West End had always been traditionally more genteel, drawing its residents from the academics at the university and the medical staff at the city's hospitals. Now, it had added media, IT professionals and the arts to the mix, making it a place where Lindsay felt as at home as she was ever going to be.

But Milngavie had always felt more culturally barren. The money here came from retail empires, from accountants, from people who preferred Andrew Lloyd Webber to Mozart or the Manic Street Preachers. The difference was obvious to her even in the architecture. This was the land of bungalows and detached houses, where to inhabit a semi was somehow to have failed. There was nothing here to compare with the grandeur of the red sandstone tenements of Hyndland or the imposing houses of Kelvinside. Lindsay knew she was indulging her prejudices with such facile thoughts, but she didn't care. From everything she'd read about David Keillor, she'd have been astonished to find him living anywhere else.

She turned into the quiet side street where Keillor lived and cruised slowly down till she spotted his house. It was a two-storey detached property in a decent sized garden, a double garaged tacked on to one side. The brilliant white harling that covered the house looked as if it had recently been repainted, and the double glazing was the expensive sort that mimicked traditional sash windows. It didn't look as if Keillor was strapped for cash. She parked just past the entrance to his drive and settled back to wait.

She'd borrowed Sophie's car for the afternoon, knowing that the anonymous saloon her lover drove was more appropriate for what she had in mind than the classic MGB roadster she'd bought on her return to the UK. Sophie had teased her about having a mid-life crisis, but Lindsay had pointed out that she had always driven classic cars and because she'd previously owned an MGB, she knew enough to carry out her own maintenance. Since she couldn't hope to do that with a modern car crammed with electronics, she was effectively choosing the budget option, she'd argued. Sophie had just laughed and kissed her.

If she has a baby, I'll have to ditch the MGB, Lindsay thought sourly. She knew Sophie well enough to realise that no child of hers would be allowed on the narrow bench seat in the rear of the 1974 sports car lest it fly into the air and disappear from the rear view mirror, bouncing down the motorway. Her life would have to change in far more profound ways, she knew that. But today, what rankled was the potential loss of her car. She knew she was being childish, but she was the only person who knew that, so it didn't count.

Lindsay forced herself to stop thinking about the baby and concentrate instead on what she had to do. She dug into her jacket pocket and took out the small black leather wallet with the Strathclyde Police crest on it. A couple of years before, she'd been instrumental in saving an American friend, Meredith Miller, from facing a murder charge. A few weeks later, the fake warrant card had arrived in the post, along with a brief note. "You're better than the real thing. I though this might amuse you. Thanks. Meredith." She'd never imagined using it, but then she'd never imagined being a journalist again, particularly not in Scotland.

She adjusted her rear view mirror so she could see approaching traffic and settled down for a wait. She didn't expect it to be too long. Officials like David Keillor left the office on time. It was only their minions who had to stay late to deal with their workloads. With luck, he'd be home very soon. She wanted to hit him as soon as he got out of the car, catch him on the back foot before he could settle in to his normal evening routine.

Lindsay had guessed right. A mere twenty minutes after she'd arrived, a black 4x4 BMW rolled into sight. As the electronically operated gates opened to allow the car to enter, she was on the pavement, walking briskly on to the herring-bone brick of Keillor's driveway. His face swung towards her, a look of suspicious surprise narrowing his eyes.

Lindsay smiled disarmingly and walked right up to the driver's door. The window sank down a few inches. "What are you doing? This is private property," Keillor snapped. He had the well-groomed appearance of a man who knows the importance of first impressions. His dark hair was cut short, the shape sharp and well-defined. His skin was lightly bronzed, his eyebrows neatly trimmed. He smelled of mint.

Lindsay produced the warrant card and held it open long enough for him to see her photograph but not much else. "DC Lindsay, Strathclyde Police. You're Mr. Keillor? Mr. David Keillor?"

His frown deepened. "Of course I am. Who else would be driving my car into my drive? What's this about?" He began to open the door, forcing Lindsay to step backwards.

"I wanted to ask you a few questions regarding an inquiry we're conducting."

Keillor tutted as he climbed out of the car. He was surprisingly short, making his exit from the high vehicle comically awkward. "You'd better come in, then."

Lindsay followed him round to the front door and into the hall-way. "In here," he said, ushering her into the dining room. A gleaming oval table was surrounded by six matching chairs. An antique sideboard stood against one wall, crystal glassware and silver sparkling in the late afternoon light from the bay window. Keillor gestured to a chair but remained standing as Lindsay sat down. "So what's this all about?" he demanded again.

Lindsay found his arrogance surprising. Most people, confronted by a police officer, were at the very least apprehensive, in her experience. Everybody felt a twinge of guilt about something; either that or a twinge of fear that something terrible had hap-pened to someone they loved. But Keillor's self-confidence seemed impossible to dent. This was a man who was very sure he was untouchable. It would be a pleasure to rock that self-satisfaction to its foundations.

"We're investigating a serious incident that happened late last night in Giffnock. A hit and run. The elderly gentleman who was knocked down is quite poorly in hospital. We have a witness who saw the vehicle. The description he gave us corresponds to your car, as do a couple of the letters of the registration. So, I've come along to ask you one or two questions and have a wee look at your vehicle. If you don't mind."

Keillor shook his head. "Look all you like. But this is a waste of time. I was at home yesterday evening. We had friends round for dinner. They left around half past eleven then my wife and I went to bed. The car wasn't out of the garage all night. So whoever your witness saw, it wasn't me. Or my car."

Lindsay nodded, taking her notebook out of her bag. "So you won't mind giving me the names of you dinner guests?"

Keillor sighed impatiently. "For Christ's sake."

"We do have to take these things seriously, sir. If it had been you or your wife who'd been run over, you'd want us to do our job. The names?"

"Charles Wayne and his wife Sarah."

"And where might I contact Mr. and Mrs. Wayne?"

"He's the managing director of CCD Scotland," Keillor said, as if this were a fact any child should have known.

Lindsay couldn't believe her luck. Things couldn't have worked out better if she'd planned it. Whatever happened now, she could place the MD of the pharmaceutical company in David Keillor's dining room. Now she wished she'd bothered to tape the conversation. Time away from the sharp end had definitely laid a layer of rust over her skills. "So I could get him at his work?"

"I imagine so. Now, is that everything?"

"Just for the record, could I check your vehicle documents? Your insurance and your log book? And I'll need to take a look at the car."

"Why? This is nothing to do with me."

Lindsay shrugged. "It's procedure, sir. If you wouldn't mind getting the documents, I can be checking your vehicle. Save time that way." She got to her feet and smiled.

"Oh, all right." Keillor showed her out and returned indoors.

Lindsay made a pretence of studying the front nearside wing of the big BMW, crouching down to peer at the bumper. She was straightening up when Keillor re-emerged with a plastic folder in his hand. "Looks all clear to me, sir," she said.

"Of course it does," he said impatiently. "How many times do I have to tell you? Whoever knocked down your old man in

Giffnock, it wasn't me and it wasn't my car." He thrust the folder at her. "There you are."

Lindsay opened the folder. She glanced at the insurance certificate then looked at the vehicle registration. She forced herself not to smile in triumph. There was all the evidence she needed. The previous owner of the BMW was there in black and white. CCD (Scotland). *Gotcha*, she thought. "That all seems to be in order." She handed the paperwork back to Keillor. "I'm sorry to have troubled you. I'll have to speak to Mr. Wayne. Just a formality, obviously. But we have to go through the motions."

At last, Keillor smiled. "I appreciate that, officer. But I'm a very busy man. I haven't got time to waste."

"In that case, I won't occupy you any longer." Lindsay nodded a farewell and headed back down the drive. She found it hard to keep a spring out of her step. Somehow, she'd managed to forget the galvanising buzz that hit at the moment when a difficult story suddenly cracked open. If Rory McLaren had done nothing else, she had reminded Lindsay of the sheer delight of using her skills to bring down someone else's nasty little castles in the air.

First thing in the morning, she'd make the innocuous call to Charles Wayne. And this time, she'd tape it. OK, it wasn't strictly speaking her story. And they'd have to put it out under Rory's by-line to protect Lindsay from any comeback on her strictly illegal scam. Probably best to leave it a week or so, just to be on the safe side.

But she'd done it. She'd copper-bottomed the story. Splash Gordon was back. And it felt so good.

The high lasted as far as the Western Infirmary, where she'd arranged to pick up Sophie. Her lover stood by the outpatients entrance, deep in conversation with Fraser. Lindsay closed her eyes momentarily. *How could I have forgotten it's the second attempt tonight?* she wondered bitterly. *How could I have imagined I was going to be allowed to have a life?*

A couple of miles away, Bernie Gourlay let herself into the house. She'd walked Jack round to a friend's house for a birthday party, and she had a couple of hours to herself before Tam would pick him up on the way home. Normally, she'd indulge herself in a long bath heavily scented with essential oils, a gin and tonic and a glossy magazine. But relaxation was beyond her just now. Fear gnawed at her, its sharp teeth cutting into her peace of mind and ripping it to shreds.

With a deep sigh, she dropped her handbag on the hall table and walked through to the kitchen. She knew at once that something was wrong, chill damp air hitting her where warmth should have been. Her eyes darted round the room and terror gripped her chest in a physical constriction. The window by the back door was shattered, the glass crunched into fragments on the tiled floor. And on the kitchen table, clear when she had left, was a sheet of paper.

On automatic pilot, Bernie crossed the room. She gazed down and read, in thick black capitals, **NO HIDING PLACE, BERNIE**. She gave a faint whimper of anguish and crumpled into the nearest chair. Dear God, he could put his hand on her any time he chose. Her breathing was fast and shallow as dread coursed through her. What was she going to do?

"Get a grip," she admonished herself, trying to draw herself upright. Somehow, she had to keep this from Jack and Tam. She had to protect them from what she knew. Numb, Bernie pushed herself to her feet. Things to do. There were things to do. She found the Yellow Pages and looked for emergency glaziers. It didn't matter if the man was still here when Tam got back. She could make up some story about slipping on the floor and losing her grip on a tin which had smashed the glass. First, find a glazier. Then clear up the broken glass. Burn the note. Make everything normal again.

It was, she knew, a losing battle. Nothing was ever going to be normal again. But she had to try.

Chapter 8

The school playground was deserted. By the gates, a man leaned against the wall. If it hadn't been for his air of relaxed noncha-lance, the sense of entitlement that seemed to emanate from him, he'd have looked worryingly out of place in his stylish Italian suit and glossily polished loafers. His dark hair was cut short, apart from a heavy, side-swept fringe that fell just above his eyebrows. Without his beak of a nose, he'd have been handsome in a heavy-lidded Southern European way. He carried a smart briefcase and a plastic bag with the logo of a computer shop on the side. His eyes scanned the street constantly, but without disturbing his appear-ance of self-containment.

The shrilling of the interval bell rang out from the school building and a stream of chattering, liberated children began to emerge. The man calmly pushed himself off from the wall and walked through the gates, his attitude suddenly intent. His eyes lit on a dark-haired six year old, careering round in a game of tig with half a dozen others. The man headed straight for him.

As he approached, the boy caught sight of him and stopped dead, his face uncertain. The man walked up to him and dropped into a crouch, meeting him eye to eye. "Ciao, Giaco," he said, his eyes crinkling in a smile.

Jack Gourlay said nothing. He broke eye contact and looked at the ground.

"Didn't your mamma tell you I was coming today?"

Jack shook his head. The man held the bag open and showed it to Jack. While he peered into it, the man looked swiftly around, to check if he'd been spotted. Seeing nothing to worry him, he said, "Look, Giaco. It's for you. A Nintendo. For taking on holiday. You're coming on holiday with me. Today."

The boy shook his head. "I can't."

"You can't? Who says you can't come on holiday with your papa?"

"I've not got my jammies or anything."

"We'll buy anything you need. Come on, Giaco, it's an adventure. I thought you liked adventures? It's been so long since we had fun together. I really missed you." He dropped bag and briefcase and put his hands on the boy's shoulders. "You miss me too?" he asked softly.

"Yeah, I suppose," Jack said, still not meeting his eyes.

"So now we make up for lost time, OK?"

"I better tell Jimmy."

It was, the man recognised, capitulation. "Who's Jimmy?"

"Jimmy Doran. He's my pal. The one over there with the ginger hair. He'll wonder what's happened to me if I don't tell him."

"OK. Tell him you've had to go off with your dad. But be quick. We've got a plane to catch."

Jack's face lit up. The prospect of a plane journey clearly dispelled any lingering doubts he had about entrusting himself to Bruno Cavadino.

It had been a toss-up whether Lindsay would call Charles Wayne from home or wait till she arrived at the Café Virginia. If she did it from home, she could present Rory with a *fait accompli*, all the loose ends tied up in a neat wee parcel, Charles Wayne on tape admitting he'd had dinner with David Keillor as the glittery silver bow on top. But if she did it from the flat, she'd have to contend with Sophie, who was working from home that morning with her feet up on the window seat, presumably to minimise any sudden

68

movements that might dislodge any potential embryo. Sophie certainly wouldn't approve of the co-parent of her potential offspring committing an arrestable offence under the family roof. On the other hand, Lindsay didn't really want Rory eavesdropping on her impersonation of a police officer either.

In the end, she compromised. On her way to the Hillhead underground station, she took a detour down Ashton Lane and slipped into Bean Scene. Armed with a large cappuccino, she huddled into the farthest corner, jacked the mobile into her mini-disk recorder and called the main CCD switchboard. After a little preliminary jockeying with a secretary then a personal assistant, she was finally put through to the great man himself. His voice was a light tenor, its strangulated vowels testifying to its owner's origins somewhere around the Thames Estuary.

"Mr. Wayne? This is DC Lindsay, Strathclyde Police. I'm sorry to bother you. I wondered if you could help me with a wee inquiry."

"Of course, of course." Wayne sounded both enthusiastic and unctuous. "Anything to assist the police. We like to foster good relations here at CCD."

I bet you do, she thought. "I've got a witness statement from Mr. David Keillor that says you spent the evening before last dining at his house. Would that be correct?"

"Spot on, Detective. A lovely evening it was too. But why are you interested in my social engagements?" Now there was a note of caution.

"I'm trying to eliminate Mr. Keillor from an inquiry into a road traffic accident. Could you tell me what time it was when you and your lady wife left the Keillors?"

"Let me see . . . I paid off the babysitter just before midnight, so we must have left there somewhere between half past eleven and twenty to twelve."

"And Mr. Keillor was with you all evening?"

Wayne chuckled. "Naturally. David's always a very good host."

"Thank you very much, Mr. Wayne. I'm sorry to have taken up your time."

"No problem. Glad to be of help."

Lindsay pressed the stop button on the recorder as she hung

up. She plugged in the headphones and listened with satisfaction. It couldn't have been better. A little judicious editing of the conversation to eliminate any reference to her subterfuge and she was home and dry. Not only did she have Wayne's admission that he had dined with David Keillor, she had the implication in his last statement that this was far from the first time the men had met socially. It would be fun watching Keillor try to wriggle his way out of this one. A pity it would be Rory doing the showdown. But she was going to have to get used to this way of working, alien as it was to her natural instincts. She'd spent years guarding her exclusives against her rivals; it wasn't going to be easy to trade that for sharing.

Rory was already online in her booth when Lindsay arrived at Café Virginia. Rory raised one finger to indicate she was in the middle of something so Lindsay booted up her own laptop and started writing up the notes of her conversations with Keillor and Wayne. Before she could finish, Rory folded her screen down and raised her eyebrows. "Well?" she said. "How did it go?"

For one crazy moment, Lindsay thought she was referring to the previous evening's insemination. She was about to open her mouth and say, "Gruesome," when she realised the topic under discussion was the story. She outlined her progress to Rory, whose grin spread wider as she grasped the full implications of what Lindsay had established.

"You are fucking outrageous," she spluttered. "They didn't call you Splash Gordon for nothing, did they?"

"I think you'll find it was more ironic than admiring," Lindsay said, remembering the less than supportive atmosphere of the newsroom. "And I wasn't exactly on the ball. I didn't tape my little chat with Keillor."

Rory shrugged. "Irrelevant. You got Wayne on tape, which is even more damning. We're going to have to wait a couple of weeks before I hit Keillor, though. If we're really, really lucky, he won't make the connection with your thespian activities."

"We'll keep my name off the finished piece, all the same," Lindsay said firmly.

"Aye. There's time enough for glory."

"I sincerely hope so."

Bernie stood outside the school gates, chatting idly to a couple of the other waiting mothers whose children were in Jack's class. The bell sounded, the doors opened and children of all shapes, sizes and colours began to pour out of the building. After a few minutes, the stream had slowed to a trickle. The other mothers were gone, one with a chattering daughter, the other with a son interested only in the collection of football cards he'd pulled out of his pocket as soon as he'd cleared the school entrance. But still there was no sign of Jack.

She felt a strange fluttering in her stomach, a physical manifestation of an undefined fear. Now, no more children emerged. It was time to panic, she realised. Bernie walked through the gates then, as she neared the school doors, she broke into a trot.

Unnoticed by her, the man leaning against the bus stop twenty yards down the street suddenly shifted. Michael hastily put away the knife he'd been using to clean his nails and began to stroll up the street towards the school. Whatever was going on with Bernadette Dooley, it wasn't in the script. Not as he understood it, anyway. Where was the boy? What was going on?

What he couldn't see was Bernie running down the school corridor to the classroom where Mrs. Anderson taught Year Two. She grabbed the lintel and swung herself into the room, her breath catching in her throat. "Where's Jack?" she demanded, her voice shrill.

Mrs. Anderson, a comfortably plump woman in her mid-forties, looked puzzled. "It's Mrs. Gourlay, isn't it?"

"Where's Jack?" Bernie was shouting now, not caring what the teacher thought of her. "He didn't come out when the bell went. Where is he?"

Mrs. Anderson's face sagged. "I don't understand. Mr. Gourlay came and fetched him at morning interval. Didn't you know?"

"Tam?" Bernie looked thunderstruck. "Tam came to the school and took Jack away?" She shook her head incredulously.

"That's what Jimmy Doran told me. When the children came back after break, Jimmy came up to my table and said Jack Gourlay had told him to tell me that he'd had to go away with his dad."

"And you thought he meant Tam," Bernie's voice had dropped to a whisper. Staggering, she collapsed into a child's chair, leaned her head on the desk and sobbed in wild, uncontrolled gasps that made her whole body shudder.

"Oh, my goodness," Mrs. Anderson said, suddenly understanding that there might be valid reasons for such distress. "I'd better get the head teacher."

At that precise moment, Jack Gourlay—né Cavadino—was thirty-five thousand feet above Germany. He looked up from his Nintendo, an anxious frown on his face. "Mum won't be angry with me, will she?"

Bruno Cavadino gave his son a hug. "Why would she be angry with you? I told you, she said we could go away together."

"She's never let us go away together before," Jack said suspiciously.

"She thought you were too little to be away without her. She thought you would cry because you missed her. But I told her, he's old enough now to understand that a holiday is a holiday, not forever. You won't cry, will you?"

Jack gave a tight, apprehensive smile. "No, papa. Can we phone her when we land?"

Bruno shook his head. "You don't want her to think you're a big baby, do you? She'll call us in a couple of days. Don't worry."

The siren call of Nintendo dragged Jack back from the conversation to his screen. Bruno looked down at him with a surge of affection that surprised him. He was a good kid. Bernie had made a decent job of bringing him up. But she'd had her chance. Now it was up to him to do his best for the boy. It wouldn't be easy, but he had plans for Jack.

Bernie was sobbing into a handkerchief while a woman police constable patted her awkwardly on the shoulder. Mrs. Anderson sat at her table, fingers twisting round each other as Sergeant Meldrum took her through the events of the morning.

"I thought nothing of it, you see. I mean, obviously you don't.

The boy, Jimmy Doran, he said that Jack had told him he had to go off with his dad. Naturally, I assumed he meant Mr. Gourlay."

Sergeant Meldrum nodded, scribbling something in his notebook. "So, the last you saw of the boy would be when, exactly?"

"When the bell went for the morning interval. Five to eleven."

The classroom door burst open and Tam Gourlay burst in. He was a bear. Six feet and six inches of brawn, topped with a thick head of dark auburn hair and a full, neatly trimmed beard one shade lighter, he stormed into the classroom like a force of nature. Without pause, he rushed to Bernie, pushing the policewoman to one side. "Has that bastard Bruno taken him?" he demanded.

"Tam, oh Tam, I'm so sorry," Bernie sobbed.

"Sorry? It's not your fault you married a bastard first time round." He glared belligerently at Sergeant Meldrum. "So what the hell are youse doing to stop him? Christ knows where he'll take the boy."

"We've already circulated a description to the ports and airports, sir. We're doing everything we can," the policeman said, his tone placatory.

It didn't work. "Is that all you can say? Have you not got weans? Jesus, man, can you not see the state she's in? You've got to find the boy."

"Was Mr. Cavadino ever violent during the marriage?"

"What's that got to do with anything?" Tam demanded.

"No, he wasn't," Bernie cut in.

"And has he had access to Jack since the marriage broke down?" Meldrum continued.

"He's taken him out him half a dozen times when he's been in the country," Bernie said, sounding calmer now her husband was present.

"Mrs. Gourlay, do you think he'd offer any kind of physical threat to Jack?"

She shook her head. "Bruno wouldn't hurt a hair on his head."

"You see my problem, sir?" Meldrum asked, his tone that of sweet reason. "The child doesn't seem to be at risk. OK, Mr. Cavadino didn't have permission for this custody visit, but he has

73

previously returned Jack safely. We've no reason to think a crime has been committed."

"I don't believe I'm hearing this," Tam roared. "Our boy gets kidnapped and you think that's OK?"

"With respect, sir, that's not what I said."

Tam looked at the sergeant as if he wanted to hit someone and he was the best candidate. "Listen, pal," he growled. "Get your finger out and get our boy back. Or else you'll wish you'd never joined the polis. And that, my friend, is a promise."

Lindsay poured two glasses of pinot grigio and took them through to the living room, where Sophie was sprawled on the sofa, a book on preparing for pregnancy open on her lap. "There you go," Lindsay said, offering Sophie a drink. "I've just put the potatoes in the oven. Dinner'll be about three quarters of an hour."

Sophie shook her head. "No wine for me, love." She patted her flat stomach. "Better safe than sorry."

Lindsay put both glasses on the end table and slid on to the sofa, lifting Sophie's feet into her lap. "Sorry, force of habit. I forgot your body's a temple now. How are you feeling?"

Sophie snorted with laughter. "Exactly the same as usual. I don't think you get symptoms within twenty-four hours of insemination. What about you? How's the ankle? You should be the one with your feet up."

"Ach, it's not too bad. It's more stiff than sore now. Do you mind if I put the local news on?" she added, reaching for the TV remote control.

"News junkie," Sophie teased her. "Of course I don't mind."

The screen came alive on a police press conference. A uniformed chief superintendent sat behind a table. Next to him, a woman with red swollen eyes looked as if she was holding herself together by sheer force of will. Her hand was held by a giant of a man with a neatly barbered mane of hair and a heavy beard. What could be seen of his face looked sullen. The sound faded up on the police officer's voice. "... during the morning interval. We have reason to believe that the boy has been snatched by his natural father. We're obviously concerned that Mr. Cavadino will try to

74

take Jack out of this jurisdiction, even though he has no legal right to do that. If anyone has seen the boy or his father, they should contact Strathclyde Police."

Two photographs appeared side by side on the screen. The boy grinned cheerfully at the camera with the gap-toothed smile of childhood. His resemblance to the woman was obvious. The man whose photograph appeared next to him looked unmistakably Italian, his easy smile making his face more attractive than it would have been in repose. After a moment, the camera returned to the press conference.

"Mrs. Gourlay, have you a message for your former husband?" the policeman asked.

The woman took a visible breath and looked straight down the barrel of the camera. "Bruno, if you're watching this . . . I know you mean well, but Jack's safety is the most important thing in the world to me." Her voice cracked and broke and tears welled from her eyes.

The picture changed to a reporter standing outside police headquarters. "Photographs of Jack Gourlay and his father Bruno Cavadino have been circulated to ports and airports. But tonight, fears were growing that they have already left the country."

"That poor woman," Sophie said, reaching for Lindsay's hand. "She must be going through hell. I can't imagine what that must be like. Not to know where your child is or what's happening to him."

"It's despicable," Lindsay said.

"What? Putting that woman on the telly?" Sophie sounded offended.

"No, of course not. I meant that thing that couples get into when they split up, using their kids as weapons against each other. It's so bloody selfish."

"That's not going to happen to us, you know," Sophie reassured her.

"What? Breaking up or fighting over the kid?"

"Neither one. It's going to be OK, Lindsay. No, it's going to be better than OK. It's going to be wonderful."

Lindsay grunted. "If it happens."

"It's going to happen. I'm sure of it. If it doesn't work this time, we'll just try again."

"And when do you stop trying?" Lindsay couldn't help herself. "How long are you giving this?"

"As long as it takes. I thought we'd try the insemination for six months, and if that doesn't work, we can look at assisted conception."

"You mean IVF?"

Sophie nodded. "I don't want to go there, but if that's what it takes, yes."

"I thought you said lesbians couldn't get IVF treatment in Scotland," Lindsay said mutinously.

Sophie squeezed her hand. "Lindsay, I'm professor of obstetrics at Glasgow University. Trust me, I've got the contacts."

Lindsay's heart sank. She saw her future contract to a pinprick focus on the business of conception. It wasn't a pretty picture.

Chapter 9

Afternoons in the Café Virginia were subdued affairs. Solo coffee drinkers flicked through newspapers, bar staff cleared lunchtime debris and cleaned tables, Horse sang "Breathe Me" and Rory wrote copy. Lindsay was online, browsing the newspaper archives, trying to get up to speed with her native land in the third millennium. There was, she thought, something very soothing about it all. She could hardly believe how quickly her general sense of malaise at being back in Scotland had fled. If nothing else, it told her how much she needed work to give her a sense of purpose. Now, if only Sophie would give up this madness, she would be entirely content.

The calm was shattered by a new arrival. His voice carried from the front bar right through to the back booth. "I'm looking for Rory McLaren," the thunder said. Lindsay looked up to see the husband from the previous evening's police press conference waving a twenty-pound note under Annie's nose.

"Through the back, corner booth," she said, trousering the twenty without missing a beat in her stocking of the fridge.

The man mountain looked around suspiciously as he wove a path through the tables towards their corner. Why, Lindsay wondered, did straight people always think they were about to be propositioned as soon as they entered a gay establishment? Had they even looked in a mirror lately?

He stopped at the table, his eyes swivelling from one to the other. "Rory McLaren?" he asked, almost hesitant.

Rory finally looked up and said wearily, "Tam Gourlay. As in," she slipped into mimicry of a semi-hysterical radio advert, "'Gourlay's Garage, your first choice for previously owned vehicles.'"

"Very funny," Gourlay growled.

"The exposé I did on the tricks of the second hand car trade, right?"

"Hey, nobody was happier than me to see you closing down the toerags and the cowboys," he protested.

"So what do you want with me, Mr. Gourlay? Come to shop some more of your dodgy colleagues?" Rory looked back at her screen, giving off boredom like musk.

"There's somebody I want you to meet."

Rory flicked him a glance, amused and questioning.

"I've got a taxi waiting outside."

She snorted. "And that's the pitch, is it? Go off in a taxi with a strange man who associates with a bunch of people I've put out of business. Very tempting."

"I thought youse investigative reporters were supposed to be fearless?"

"Fearless isn't the same as stupid."

"Rory?" Lindsay thought she'd better intervene before Gourlay burst a blood vessel. Rory raised her eyebrows. "I don't think Mr. Gourlay is here because of cowboy car dealers. I think the person he wants you to meet is his wife. Her wee boy got snatched by his natural father yesterday. Tug of love kidnap."

"Right," Rory said, instantly grasping the tabloid shorthand. She looked up at Gourlay, her smile apologetic. "I'm sorry for your trouble. But I don't do stories like that. I think it's a private eye you need."

Gourlay shook his big head. "Christ. I don't just want the boy found, I want the world to know about this cover-up. It's a scandal, that's what it is. But you? You're as bad as the fucking polis.

78

Just because Bruno Cavadino's a diplomat, nobody wants to know."

"A diplomat?" Lindsay interrupted, her interest pricked.

"Aye. So all we're getting is, 'there's bugger all we can do, dinnae rock the boat, be a good boy.' And all the time, my wife's going off her head with worry. Who knows where the fuck the boy is now? And apart from us, it seems like nobody cares either." His frustration was obvious.

"Rory, let's go and have a wee chat with Mrs. Gourlay. This diplomatic angle, it's interesting. Could be a good piece in it," Lindsay said, sounding more casual than she felt.

Rory sighed. "Oh, all right. It's not like we're snowed under with work."

Lindsay smiled up at Gourlay. "Give us a minute to get sorted here, we'll meet you outside." She extended a hand which was enveloped in a meaty paw. "I'm Lindsay Gordon, by the way. Rory and I work together."

"Thanks," he said gruffly, then turned and walked out.

"I can't believe you think this is worth pursuing," Rory grumbled as she closed her computer down. "Tug of love, ten a penny, Hague Convention doesn't work, so what's new?"

Packing up her laptop, Lindsay said, "Abuse of diplomatic immunity. You can always get a good head of moral indignation going on that one. And this is a wee bit tastier than cultural attachés not paying their parking tickets. Look, if you don't want to come, I'll handle it."

"No, you're all right. I've done more or less all I was going to do this afternoon anyway. I might as well come along for the ride."

She doesn't quite trust me yet, Lindsay thought ruefully as she followed Rory out into the street. Tam Gourlay was leaning against a black cab, waiting for them. As they headed west past George Square, Gourlay leaned forward and frowned at Rory.

"So how come you ended up with a man's name?"

"My mother's sentimental. I was conceived in a field just north of Aberdeen."

Both Gourlay and Lindsay smiled. "Aurora Borealis. Helluva

79

mouthful for a wee lassie," he said, reaching for his cigarettes and lighting up.

"Hey," the cab driver protested. "Can you no' read? It says no smoking."

"I've got to smoke," Gourlay said. "I've got a doctor's line. See if I don't smoke, I lose the place and rip the heads off taxi drivers. OK, pal?"

"It's true," Lindsay confirmed. "I've seen him. We've had him on tablets, patches, the lot. It's only the fags that keep him stable."

The taxi driver shook his head in mock disgust. "See Glasgow and die, right enough."

The living room of Tam and Bernie Gourlay's flat spoke of an unpretentious comfort. It felt lived in, with a child's toys piled into a couple of boxes in one corner, shelves that contained a mixture of popular women's fiction and sports videos, Monet's *Water Lilies* on the walls. When they arrived, Bernie was sitting by the bay window in the late afternoon dusk. Gourlay switched the light on as he entered, but Bernie didn't react. She continued to stare out of the window, smoking with an air of desperation.

"Bernie?" he said. "Bernie, this is Lindsay and Rory. They're going to help us find Jack. They're journalists."

At the word "journalist," Bernie's head jerked sharply towards them. "I'm sorry," she said coldly, her flat Belfast accent as strong as the day she'd left. "He's been wasting your time. Everybody's written the story already."

Rory shrugged and looked at Lindsay, who kept her expression blank. "This is our best chance," Gourlay protested. "The polis willnae help, they wankers at the Foreign Office willnae help. We need somebody in our corner that knows what they're doing. Somebody that'll no' let them get away wi' it."

"No, Tam. I said no, and I meant it. A few stories in the papers won't bother Bruno. You don't know what you're getting into here." Her red-rimmed eyes stared unblinking at him, but her hands were trembling.

"This is Glasgow, no' bloody Sicily. Christ, Bernie. I don't understand you. Do you not want the boy back, or what?"

"Of course I do." For a moment, her façade wavered and Lindsay could see naked fear in Bernie's eyes. "But what can they do to help? We've already held a bloody press conference, for all the good that did us."

"Listen, this pair, they investigate things. They expose scandals. It's what they do. And this diplomatic immunity bullshit, that's a scandal if ever there was one."

Seeing Rory edging towards the door, Bernie said triumphantly, "See for yourself. She knows it's a waste of time. Go on, darlin', away back to the pub."

Rory shrugged. "I already told your husband what you needed was a private eye. But he insisted."

This time, there was no mistaking the look of panic in Bernie's eyes. "A private eye?" she gasped.

"They're good at finding missing persons," Rory said gently. "They've got a lot of experience. I could give you a couple of names if you like?"

Bernie's eyes widened and her mouth opened. But no words came. Lindsay watched Bernie, assessing her. Something was off-key. Bernie Gourlay just wasn't behaving like a desperate mother who'd move heaven and earth to get her child back. Intrigued, Lindsay said, "Of course, a private eye will want to keep everything under wraps. Personally, I think publicity's your best chance of finding out where your son is. And that's the first step to getting him back."

Bernie snatched at the chance. "You know, I think you might be right," she gabbled. "All right. I'll talk to you. But don't you ever forget, Tam Gourlay. It was you that set this ball rolling."

Gourlay looked baffled but clearly wasn't about to question her surrender. "I'll make a pot of tea," he said, backing out of the room. Rory had the good sense to settle herself in an armchair and try to blend into the background.

"So, Bernie, what exactly does Bruno do for the Italian Foreign Office?" Lindsay asked.

"He's a commercial attaché."

"And where's he stationed now?"

"The last I heard, he was in Belgrade."

"Not exactly a place you'd want your six year old son to be, I imagine."

Bernie said nothing. But Lindsay wasn't giving in so easily. "How would Bruno get him out of the country?"

"Jack has two passports. I've got his British one and Bruno's got his Italian one."

"Convenient for Bruno. So, how did you two meet?"

"I'd just come over from Ireland. I was working as a waitress in a hotel in town. Bruno used to come in a few times a week. He asked me out, and we just clicked. We were married two months later." Bernie lit another cigarette.

"So what went wrong?"

"Italian men don't want wives. They want servants. Just because I was a waitress when I met him, it doesn't mean I wanted to wait on him hand, foot and finger for the rest of my days. Besides, I don't think I was smart enough to make the right sort of embassy wife." There was no mistaking the bitterness now. "So I left him. Jack was only a year old."

"That must have been tough," Lindsay sympathised.

"What would you know about tough?" Bernie demanded contemptuously. "Yes, it was tough. I hooked up with one of the women I used to work with at the hotel. I minded her kids in the evenings when she was working, and she looked after Jack during the day so I could get a job. And that's when my luck turned. Tam advertised for a receptionist, and I answered the ad. I thought I'd finally fallen on my feet. It should have occurred to me that Bruno would hate the idea of another man bringing up his son."

"So Bruno tried to get custody of Jack?" Lindsay asked.

"He tried, and he failed. I thought he'd given up the idea, but clearly I was wrong." Bernie bit her lip. Now her distress was clearer than at any time since they'd arrived. Taking advantage of it, Lindsay continued to probe for more background details on Bruno, managing to extract from Bernie that he had originally come from the Val d'Elsa area of Tuscany. But whenever she tried to get Bernie to talk about Jack, she clammed up. After half an hour, Lindsay had to concede defeat. She wasn't going to get any further with Bernie Gourlay. She promised to do everything in her power to track down Jack's whereabouts, then she and Rory made their escape.

"That was seriously weird," Rory said as they walked down the street, the red sandstone tenements stained the colour of dried blood by the early evening gloom. "You'd think she'd be desperate for help. But it was like she couldn't get us out of there fast enough."

"Yeah, I know. There's something not kosher there. Maybe our Bruno is something a wee bit more dodgy than a commercial attaché. Maybe he's a spook. Or maybe he has connections." Lindsay glanced at her watch.

"What? You mean, as in, 'Respect the family'?" Rory said in a terrible impersonation of Marlon Brando.

Lindsay winced. "I know, I know, you can be Italian without being a Mafioso. But I'm curious, just the same."

"Maybe there's another reason why she's ambivalent about Jack coming home," Rory said slowly.

"How do you mean?"

"Maybe it's not all happy families in Kinghorn Drive. Maybe Tam's abusing the boy?"

Lindsay turned the idea over in her mind and dismissed it. "He's not the type," she said decisively.

"Suddenly there's a type?" Rory demanded.

"Of course not, I'm not that naïve. But Tam Gourlay is possibly the least sleazy guy I've met in years. Besides, abusers don't do *anything* to draw attention to their relationship to their victims, and Tam's hardly trying to hush things up."

Rory shrugged. "It would explain what we've just seen."

"I don't buy it. My gut says no." They walked on in silence for a few yards, approaching the corner where their routes home would naturally separate.

"Hey, you know what?" Rory said suddenly, bright as fresh paint.

"What?"

"This is your very first proper story. We should go out and celebrate. A bottle of champagne, a nice dinner. What do you say?" If she'd had a tail, she'd have been wagging it in supplication.

83

It was tempting. An evening with Rory would have seemed like an attractive option at the best of times. And whatever this was, it wasn't the best of times. Almost anything would have sounded more fun than another evening discussing conception. But giving in to temptation wasn't the most sensible way to fixing things between her and Sophie. "I'd love to, Rory, but I need to get back."

They'd reached the corner. "Fine," Rory said, her nonchalance obviously forced. "Another time, maybe. When you've cleared it with Sophie."

Before Lindsay could protest that she didn't need to clear her social engagements with her girlfriend, Rory had swung off down the street. Oh well, Lindsay thought as she trudged up the hill towards home. At least she had a story of her own to get her teeth into.

Michael Conroy waited for the cover of darkness before he made his latest reconnaissance of the street where Bernadette Dooley lived with her husband. Jesus, Joseph and Mary, but the husband was a big fucker. Michael feared no man, but he liked the odds to be weighted in his favour, preferably with serious hardware. Whatever it was that Bernadette had taken from Patrick, he'd be happy if it could be recovered without a direct confrontation with the big man.

Patrick had gone very quiet when he'd reported back about Bernadette getting her name all over the papers. Michael knew his boss well enough to read the silence, to realise that Patrick was seriously unhappy, not least because Michael's direct warning had proved unproductive. He figured Patrick had maybe been planning to use threats against the boy as further leverage, so his disappearance would be a helluva spoke in your man's wheel.

All the same, it was some coincidence, the lad getting snatched just when Patrick took an interest in the mother. But coincidences happened. Michael knew that. A couple of his best friends had done long stretches inside because of coincidence. It didn't worry him.

At least, it didn't worry him nearly as much as Patrick's instructions to keep Bernadette under close surveillance. Kinghorn Drive, where she lived with the big fucker, was a quiet residential street. The kind of place where, even if there wasn't an official Neighbourhood Watch, there was bound to be some nosy old bitch twitching the nets day in, day out. If they tried keeping watch from a car, one of the local busybodies would be on to the police within the hour.

Where the hell else could they watch from? There wasn't a single vantage point anywhere in the street that would avoid suspicion.

The answer came on his third pass along the street. A couple of doors down from the Gourlays' flat, on the opposite side of the street, a second-floor flat had a poster in the window announcing it was for sale. Peering up through the dark, Michael could make out the absence of curtains, a sure sign of vacant possession. He'd pulled a stunt like this once before with an empty flat.

Tomorrow morning, he'd present himself at the estate agent's, clean and shaved. A film maker looking for a location. Willing to pay top dollar for the use of an empty flat for a couple of weeks. An empty flat like that one he'd noticed on Kinghorn Drive. Surely the owner would be happy to make a few bob at no inconvenience to himself? It wasn't as if there would be any obstacle to potential viewing. At an hour's notice from the agent, the film crew could be up and away, as if they'd never been there.

Michael walked briskly back to the pub where he'd left Kevin supping Guinness. With a bit of luck, he'd be able to satisfy Patrick without taking any risks. In Michael's book, that made it a very good day indeed.

Chapter 10

Even if you wanted to hide from someone on Hillhead under-ground station in the middle of the morning, it was too quiet for that to be a serious possibility. Not that Lindsay had any desire to hide from Rory, exactly. She just felt it would be easier to handle their relationship if they kept it within professional parameters. Sharing the same journey into work somehow felt a little outside the boundaries. But she could hardly ignore the familiar figure slouched against one of the pillars, waiting for the train. She walked up and tapped Rory on the shoulder.

Her head snapped round, eyes wide, eyebrows arching in surprise. "Oh, hiya," she said, her face lighting up when she realised she wasn't being assailed by the loony on the train or importuned by a beggar. She gave Lindsay a one-armed hug and a peck on the cheek. "How're you doing, Splash?"

"Good. You?"

Rory groaned. "Sandra turned up with a bottle of vodka and the burning desire to whinge about her boss. So I'm feeling a wee bit frayed round the edges."

"I should have come out with you after all. Saved you from yourself," Lindsay said.

Rory's reply was drowned by the arrival of the bright orange train. With its carriages smaller than most public transport systems, it always made Lindsay feel she was travelling in Toytown.

She half-expected Noddy and Big Ears to board at Kelvinbridge, hotly pursued by the golliwogs.

Once they were sitting down, Rory repeated herself. "I said, are you always so uxorious?"

"Is that how you see me?" Lindsay stalled.

"Well, I've only known you a few days, but you always seem to be in a hurry to get home at the end of the day. Which is not a criticism," she added hastily. "It's just...well, it's just unusual, when you've been together as long as you two."

"Yeah, well, that would be because unusual is where we are right now." Lindsay tried to keep her voice light. She failed.

"Hey, I'm sorry if I said the wrong thing," Rory said anxiously.

Lindsay shook her head. "It's OK." She stared at the floor between her feet. "Look, if we're going to work together, I guess I should tell you what's going on in my life. At least then you'll know if I'm being moody, chances are it's nothing to do with you."

"Listen, you don't have to tell me anything you don't want to." Impulsively, Rory reached across and squeezed Lindsay's hand. She was entirely unprepared for the charge she felt when Lindsay returned the pressure.

"It's entirely selfish, believe me. I need to talk to someone about it before I go mad. And all the friends I would normally offload it on are either in California or London. So you got the short straw."

"Hey, that's cool. I mean, I want us to be friends, you know?"

"I know. But let's wait till we're sitting comfortably, eh? Preferably with a coffee in front of us."

Twenty minutes later, they were ensconced in the back booth. Now the moment was upon her, Lindsay felt a strange reluctance, as if talking about what ailed her was somehow a betrayal of Sophie. But it was too late for that. Rory was staring at her with the patient anticipation of a child who knows it will get the biscuit if it just sits still for long enough. It was time to cut to the chase. "Sophie wants a baby," she said flatly.

"Ah," Rory said.

"She's been talking about it for a while. But I kept blanking it. I thought if I just ignored it, she'd get the message and it would go away." A tired smile. "I couldn't have been more wrong."

"Would I be right in thinking you're not exactly enthusiastic about the idea of parenthood?"

Lindsay stirred the froth on her cappuccino. "That would be an understatement. I like my life. And I've never wanted a kid."

"Hard to argue with the biological imperative, though."

"That's the trump card, isn't it? But it's hard to understand when it's not something you've ever experienced. See, I've never been possessed by anything the way this has got Sophie in her grip. It's obviously not just some whim. It consumes her. She's obsessed. It's like I'm not even there in her heart, in her head. There's no room for me any more, just this overwhelming need." Lindsay sighed.

"So you're at an impasse?"

Lindsay shook her head. "No. It's gone past that. A few days ago, she announced that she'd found a donor. She's been inseminating this week."

Rory looked appalled. "You mean, she's gone ahead without your agreement?"

"Well, it's more that she backed me into a corner. The only choices I had were to stay and support her in something that I hate the idea of, or else to walk away. And I love her, Rory. I couldn't leave her. That was the gamble she took. And she won."

"That's a helluva gamble."

Lindsay shook her head. "Not really. Deep down, she knows how committed I am to her, to this relationship. At some level, she knew I'd have to give in to the emotional blackmail."

"I'm sorry, I know you love her, and I don't know the woman, but I think that's a terrible thing to do. It's really selfish, really calculating." Rory's face revealed disgust and contempt in equal measure.

"The thing is, Rory, Sophie isn't selfish. And she isn't some hard, calculating bitch out for number one. She's actually the most generous and kind person I know. She's a lot nicer than me, trust me on that. It's a measure of how much this need has hold of her that she's behaving like this, and I don't think she's proud of it. In a funny kind of way, I suspect she feels as trapped by this as I do."

Rory looked bemused. "You're being a lot more generous than I would be in your shoes. I mean, the bottom line is, she's going for the thing she wants regardless of what it means to you, to your relationship."

Lindsay took a sip of her coffee and met Rory's eye with a rueful smile. "Looks like it."

"You deserve better than that," Rory said fiercely.

Lindsay laughed. "You really don't know me very well, do you? Mostly, I feel like I don't deserve someone as honest, as loyal or as supportive as Sophie. So," she continued, her tone becoming businesslike. "Now you know what it is that's doing my head in. So if I lose the plot, it's probably because I'm panicking about parenthood. OK?"

"Thanks for telling me." Rory reached across the table and laid her fingers on Lindsay's wrist. This time, she wasn't the only one who felt the electricity. "Any time you want to dump, feel free."

Looking startled, Lindsay dipped her head in acknowledgement. "Duly noted. But for now, I need to crack on with the tug of love kid." She switched on her laptop, connected to the internet and a few minutes later, jotted down the number of the Italian Embassy in Belgrade.

Rory, who was flicking through the morning papers, looked up in surprise as Lindsay launched into fluent Italian. She waited till the call was over, then said, "How come you speak Italian so well?" she asked.

"I lived in Italy for six months a few years back."

"You were a journalist in Italy?"

Lindsay grinned. "No. I was the winter caretaker on a campsite."

Rory looked puzzled. "How come?"

"It's a long story. Some other time. The main thing is, Bruno Cavadino isn't at work and he's not due back for another three days. I'm going to have to see if I can track down any family he's got in Italy." She frowned, trying to come up with a solution to her problem. "What are you up to today?" she asked absently.

"I'm taking a contact out to lunch. He thinks he's got a story about at the submarine base at Faslane. Probably the usual load of

89

rumour and gossip, but you never know." She looked at her watch. "In fact, I better make tracks if I'm going to get to Helensburgh in time."

Lindsay nodded. "See you when I see you, then." She waited till Rory had left, then dug her electronic organiser out of her bag and checked a number. Although she hadn't worked as a reporter in Italy, her boss had a cousin who worked for one of the dailies there. They'd met at a New Year party and bonded via their common experience at the sharp end. *"Buongiorno,"* she said when she was connected. *"Vorrei parlare con Giulia Garrafo, per piacere...Si, va bene...Giulia? C'e* Lindsay Gordon...Yes, I know, it's been far too long. But I'm back living in Glasgow now, so coming to Italy isn't going to be such a big deal in future." The two women caught up with each other then, the demands of friendship satisfied, Lindsay said, "Listen, I need your help with a story I'm working on."

She outlined the background to Jack Gourlay's disappearance. "Cavadino isn't back in the office in Belgrade for another three days, so I reckon he's probably getting the boy settled in with his family. But all I know is that he grew up in the Val d'Elsa area. Any chance you can find out if he still has family there?"

"It's a long shot. But I know a good stringer near there, and I have a couple of contacts in the Foreign Ministry," Giulia said. "If I have to use the stringer, you'll pay freelance rates, yes?"

Lindsay thought for a moment. Unlike private eyes, who go paid for their work regardless of results, freelances like her and Rory only earned once they'd achieved success. Paying an Italian journalist to make inquiries on her behalf could leave them out of pocket if she couldn't make a story stand up. But she also understood the need at this point in her career of speculating to accumulate. "Yes, of course," she said, hoping it wouldn't be a long job.

"Great. Give me your number, I'll get back to you."

Lindsay ended the call feeling slightly hopeful. It was good to know she hadn't completely lost her touch. Time, she thought, for another wee chat with Tam Gourlay.

♦ ♦ ♦ ♦ ♦

Gourlay's Garage occupied a corner site on Maryhill Road. The cars were a typical mix of sales reps' saloons and dinky hatchbacks for school and supermarket runs. "Tam's Temptation of the Week" was a three-year-old Ford Mondeo with sports wheels and a wood veneer dashboard. Lindsay wasn't tempted.

The office was a Portakabin that managed to exude an air of homely comfort. No girlie calendars or car advertising posters here, just a series of dramatic photographic prints of Highland scenery and the smell of lavender pot pourri. Lindsay suspected the ambience had more to do with the woman answering the phone than Tam. The woman, a motherly fifty-something, smiled as Lindsay entered and held up a finger, indicating she was almost finished. She put down the phone with a cheery farewell and swivelled in her chair to face Lindsay. "Good afternoon, and welcome to Gourlay's Garage. How can I help you?"

"Is Tam in?"

"Mr. Gourlay? Yes, he's here. Who shall I say is calling?"

The door behind her opened and Tam's head appeared in the gap. "Oh, it's you," he said, sounding faintly disconcerted. "I thought we had a customer. Come away through." He stood back and held the door open for her.

The inner office was a tidy, businesslike domain that reeked of cigarette smoke. Tam dropped into a leather executive chair and waved Lindsay to one of the less comfortable client seats on the opposite side of a cheap metal desk. "Any news? Made any progress?" he asked.

"I've got some inquiries on the go. But I wanted to have a chat with you, clear up some details. To be honest, your wife wasn't exactly one hundred per cent cooperative last night."

Tam looked embarrassed. "Aye. I'm sorry about that. She's just kind of close to the edge the now, know what I mean?"

"She bound to be upset. But when I've done stories like this in the past, I've always found the parents were desperate to grasp at any straw that might help to get their kid back."

Tam reached for an open packet of cigarettes and took one out. "Sure. But take it from me, Bernie's desperate, right enough.

91

Having said that, she's scared of what Bruno might do if the pressure goes on."

"Like what?"

"She says he might just do a runner with the boy. Walk away from his job, disappear into the wide blue yonder."

Lindsay looked sceptical. "It's not very likely, is it? What would he do for money?"

"Bernie seems to think his family would see him right. And she's the one that knows the guy, right?"

If Bernie genuinely believed that too much publicity might drive her ex-husband underground, it went a long way towards explaining her hostility the previous evening, Lindsay thought. Writing a story with an unwilling interviewee wasn't a recipe for success. And it certainly didn't make for a good follow-up if it turned out to have a happy ending. Maybe she should think about a more proactive approach to the problem of Jack Gourlay's kidnapping. "Tell me something, Tam. Supposing I find out where Jack is, what were you thinking of doing about it?"

Through the haze of smoke, she thought she detected a moment's shiftiness. "Well, obviously, we'd have to go through the legal channels in whatever country he's got him in."

"So you weren't thinking about snatching him back?"

There was a long silence that Lindsay was determined not to break. "What if I was?" Tam said eventually.

"Well, it would be a bloody sight more interesting as a story than some long drawn out court battle," Lindsay said casually.

Tam looked at her shrewdly. "Are you saying you'd help?"

Lindsay held her hands up, palms facing him. "I never said that. But obviously you'd need help. And obviously, if you asked for help from somebody who also had something to gain from a successful operation...well, that would be a way of making it more secure, wouldn't it?"

"I hear what you're saying," he said slowly.

"If he's abroad, it might be difficult. And expensive."

Tam shrugged. "To hell with the expense. I'm not exactly on the breadline. I'll spend whatever it takes to get Jack back."

"That's good to know. But first, we've got to find out where he is." Lindsay got to her feet. "I'll be in touch as soon as I hear anything."

She walked out of the Portakabin, shaking her head in wonder. What had she just signed up to? Why did she always have to jump in at the deep end? Some people couldn't live without the edge of risk in their lives. Was that what the possibility of parenthood was turning her into? Or was it that she was starting to feel that she might as well be reckless since she didn't have much left to lose? Pushing the uncomfortable thought away, she headed back to her car.

Lindsay polished off the last mouthful of her baked potato with chilli and pushed the plate to one side. Working from the Café Virginia had definite advantages, she reckoned, thinking back without nostalgia to her previous life as a journalist, to canteen meals drenched in saturated fats and sandwiches gobbled on the run. She'd just opened that day's *Scotsman* when an immaculately dressed and perfectly groomed man slid into the seat opposite her. He wore an expectant expression, and although he looked familiar, Lindsay couldn't place him at once.

Seeing her confusion, he held out his hand with an accompanying smile. "Giles Graham. Lifestyle editor of the *Standard*. Our paths crossed briefly in a past life."

"Of course," Lindsay exclaimed. "I'm sorry, it was seeing you out of context, I couldn't make the connections." She shook his hand. "Are you looking for Rory?"

"I am indeed. I was passing, and I thought I'd buy her a coffee. A small thank you for a tip she gave me that seems to be panning out rather nicely. But since she's not here, perhaps you'd let me buy you one instead?"

Lindsay shook her head. "I'm awash with the stuff. But don't let me stop you."

Giles leaned round the corner of the booth and managed to catch Annie's eye. He was, she thought, the kind of man who was accustomed to catching women's eyes, regardless of their sexual

93

orientation. "I hear you and Rory are going to be working together," he said. "About time she had someone with a bit of sense to temper her wilder excursions."

"And you think I'm that person?" She could only think that Giles had somehow managed to avoid some of her more legendary exploits.

"Absolutely. You've been there, done that, sold the tee-shirt at a charity auction. Nobody knows better than Splash Gordon the kind of trouble a journalist can get into before she loses her idealism. So it seems to me that there's no better brake on Rory's excesses than someone who understands the dangers they can lead to."

It was, she thought, charmingly put. But before she could respond, her phone rang. "Excuse me," she said, picking it up. "Lindsay Gordon."

"*Ciao, bella*. It's Giulia."

"Wow, that was quick. I take it that means you have an answer for me?"

"*Vero*. I don't think it's the one you want to hear, however. The freelance I contacted managed to track down Cavadino's mother. The family owns a café on the road from Colle Val d'Elsa to Grosseto. He got the mother into conversation, and the kid's definitely not there. The old lady was complaining about never seeing her grandchildren, especially the one in England."

"Scotland," Lindsay corrected automatically. She sighed. "Never mind. You did your best."

"I'm not finished," Giulia protested. "My boyfriend's sister-in-law, Lucia, works in the personnel department of the Foreign Ministry. I didn't want to say anything before in case she couldn't help, but now I can boast about it." She gave her trademark giggle, a breathy sound that always reminded Lindsay uncomfortably of Jennifer Tilly in *Bound*. "Cavadino has a sister. She is married to another diplomat, a former colleague of her brother's. Apparently, sister and brother are very close."

"And where is the sister based?" Lindsay asked eagerly.

"According to Lucia, Maria Padovani is with her husband. He's the commercial attaché at the St Petersburg consulate."

94

"St Petersburg? As in Russia?"

"*Vero.*"

"Why there? Isn't the embassy in Moscow?"

"Sure. But everybody has a consulate in St Petersburg. All that shipping, you know? They have to maintain a presence to look after their commercial interests. Not to mention all those sailors who get into trouble ashore."

"Of course, I wasn't thinking. So, what's the score with Maria Padovani? Is the boy there?"

"Lucia said she was checking visa status for dependants. And according to the person she spoke to in the consulate, the Padovanis applied for a multi-entry diplomatic visa for their nephew soon after they arrived in Russia. They were claiming him as a dependant. Apparently the line was that his father wasn't able to look after him and he had asked them to take charge of the boy. But they don't live in the residence, so nobody really knew if the boy was there or not. Sounds like Cavadino has been planning this for a while, no?"

"He certainly set it all up well in advance," Lindsay said. "I'll have to see what I can find out about the St Petersburg end of things. Thanks a million, Giulia. I owe you."

"You can pay me in *frascati* in Rome."

"It's a deal." Lindsay hung up and gave Giles an apologetic look "Sorry about that. A story I'm working on."

"With a St Petersburg connection?" he asked. "I'm not fishing, just interested," he added hastily, seeing Lindsay's look of suspicion. "I went there last year with Julia, my wife. She's an MEP, had to go there on some fact-finding mission about Russian education and I managed to ride her coat-tails. Marvellous city."

"I've never been."

"You should go, before the Russians get the hang of mass tourism and it gets ruined."

I could end up there sooner than you imagine, she thought wryly. "I don't suppose you've got any contacts there?" she asked without much hope that serendipity would weigh in on her side.

He shook his head. "Not journalists, no. I got quite pally with a chap from the British Council. He does a lot of liaison work with the local schools and colleges, which is why we ended up spending quite a bit of time with him."

A faint glimmer of an idea flickered at the edge of Lindsay's brain. "Do you think he might be up for a bit of intrigue?"

Giles laughed. "Probably. British Council bureaucracy doesn't exactly make for an interesting life. I expect he'd be terribly grateful for a bit of excitement. Do you want me to call him?"

In reply, Lindsay handed him her phone.

"You don't mess about, do you?" he said, amused. He looked up a number on his electronic organiser then dialled it. "Hello? Is that Gareth? Gareth, it's Giles Graham here. Julia's husband. How are things with you?" He listened politely for a minute. "Oh, we're both fine," he continued. "Listen, Gareth, a colleague of mine has a need for a little clandestine information gathering in your fair city. And I wondered if you'd be willing to help her? ... I'm not entirely sure, but I suspect it's not the sort of thing she could put through official channels ... You would? Hang on, I'll pass you over to her."

He handed the phone to Lindsay with a wink. "I think you'll be OK there."

"Hello? Gareth, my name's Lindsay Gordon. I really appreciate you talking to me."

"No problem," he said, his Geordie accent immediately obvious. "A change is as good as a holiday round here. If I can do anything to help, I will."

"Great. This is all a bit delicate, and I don't want to drop you in it professionally, so it's probably better if I don't go into the reasons why I need this information. Are you OK with that?" Lindsay's voice was warm and persuasive, honed over years of persuading the reluctant to talk.

"I suppose so," he said dubiously. "It's not anything illegal, is it?"

"No, of course not. I just don't want to put you in an embarrassing position."

"So what is it you want to know?"

"I'm trying to track down a six-year-old boy. I think he might be in St Petersburg, and if he is, I'm sure he'll be going to school. He's a native English speaker, which I guess would narrow the options down quite a bit. I wondered if you could maybe let me have a list of places he could possibly be enrolled?"

"That's it? That's all you want to know? No problem. Just let me make a couple of calls. Can you ring me back tomorrow on this number? Make it around the same time, if you can."

Lindsay punched the air and gave Giles the thumbs-up. "That's great, Gareth. I really appreciate this."

"Like I said, no problem. You tell Giles, next time he comes, he owes me a bottle of Bowmore."

Lindsay ended the call, her eyes sparkling with satisfaction. "Giles, you are a prince among men. That espresso is on me."

Chapter 11

People were so gullible, Michael mused. No, on second thoughts, people were so greedy. The estate agent had been a pushover as soon as the words, "I'd pay cash, of course. No need to bother the taxman, is there?" had left his mouth. You'd think with the damage Republican bombs had done over the years that any Brit with half a brain would think twice before they rented out an empty flat to a man with an accent like his. But the magic of money worked the trick every time.

It was perfect. The view from the bay window of the living room couldn't be bettered. They could see the Gourlays' front door and they could catch glimpses of Bernadette as she moved across the living room. The only thing Michael had to worry about was whether Kevin had the attention span to keep a proper watch when it was his turn.

So far, there hadn't been much to see. The big fucker had gone off in his shiny maroon Jag at twenty to nine. Bernadette had emerged just before ten and Michael had followed at a discreet distance. She'd walked down to the supermarket and bought a chicken, a bag of spuds, a cabbage, a bottle of Scotch and 200 cigarettes. She'd moved like a zombie, he'd thought. If he'd jumped up in front of her and shouted, "Boo!" he didn't think she'd have broken stride.

On the way back, he'd caught himself wondering what the point of this was. Patrick knew where she was living. He'd given her one scare already with the note he's had Michael leave on the kitchen table. Presumably, he was also leaning on her via the phone to get her to give up whatever it was she'd walked off with. But surely he must have realised by now that the softly-softly approach wasn't getting him anywhere? Michael couldn't understand why he hadn't been instructed to try a more direct method of persuasion.

However, the habit of obeying orders was ingrained in Michael. If Patrick was holding back, there had to be a reason. It was possible he wanted to front her up himself. Christ Almighty, Michael thought, if I'd robbed Patrick Coughlan and he showed up on my doorstep, I'd sign away everything I owned in the world to see the back of him. If that was the game plan, it was possible that the delay was because Patrick hadn't been able to get away. He wasn't simply a busy man; he was important too. Just because there was a ceasefire, that didn't mean Patrick could disappear on his own private business whenever it suited him.

All in good time, Michael had told himself as he watched Bernadette let herself into the home she probably still saw as a sanctuary. For now, he was content to wait.

Sophie had woken up feeling sick. When she passed the news on, Lindsay felt sick too. "Does that mean it's worked?" she'd asked.

"I'm not getting my hopes up," Sophie had said. "It could be psychosomatic, it could be that I ate too much of your wonderful tomato and artichoke risotto last night."

"And it could be that you're pregnant." Lindsay rolled over and sat on the edge of the bed, wondering for how much longer it would just be the two of them.

"What are you so scared of, Lindsay? Are you worried I won't love you any more when the baby comes?" Sophie squirmed across the bed and put an arm round her lover's naked back.

"I suppose that's part of it. The baby will come first with you, it's the way the biology works. But mostly, it's just that I like my life the way it is. I like the choices we have. Where to live, where to go on holiday, when to go to the pictures, when to go out for dinner. We've worked hard for the right to those choices and it feels like madness to throw all that away." She got to her feet and padded across the room to get her dressing gown.

"We'll have different choices," Sophie said, her voice tinged with sadness. "We'll have a lovely life, Lindsay, I promise you."

"Yeah, but on balance, I prefer the devil I know."

Her words came back to her as she sat in Café Virginia browsing the morning papers. She hadn't seen Rory since the previous morning, and had no idea what her business partner was up to. Presumably pursuing the Faslane story, whatever it had turned out to be. She wondered if they needed to set up an agreed system for communicating what they were up to, or whether that would feel too much like keeping tabs on each other. She was fairly sure Rory would hate to feel checked up on almost as much as she would.

So, what was she doing with her much-vaunted choices today? Not a lot, came the answer. She'd spent half an hour checking out St Petersburg on the internet, formulating ideas and discarding them as fast as she thought of them. Eventually, she'd come up with the bare bones of a plan. But she needed to know she wasn't setting herself an impossible task. Three hours till she could phone Gareth in St Petersburg, and damn all to fill them with. Lindsay needed to dig up some stories for herself, but she wasn't going to do that sitting on her backside in the café. She was about to go off in search of a newsagent that sold out-of-town weekly papers when her phone rang. She grabbed it eagerly and said, "Hello? Lindsay Gordon."

"Lindsay? It's Gareth here. I got your number off Giles, I hope you don't mind?"

"Not at all, no."

"Only, I've got that information for you, but I've got to go to a meeting this afternoon, so I thought I'd better get back to you before then."

"That's great,' Lindsay said, elation swelling inside her. "What's the score?"

"There's three schools that could take an English-speaking six-year-old. I can email you the details, it would be easier than trying to spell them out to you."

Lindsay's heart sank. "Three?"

"Yes. They're all fairly central, and they're all much of a muchness when it comes to the quality of teaching, as far as I can gather."

"Is there any one in particular that caters to the diplomatic community?" Lindsay asked, desperate to narrow down the search.

"I don't know about catering to the diplomatic community specifically, but there are a couple of people here with kids who send them to the international school on Konstantinogradskaya Ulitsa. I've heard that quite a few of the kids there have parents who are EU diplomats."

"That's brilliant, Gareth." She gave him her email address. "I really appreciate you going to this much trouble."

"It was no trouble. I'll email those details to you right away."

Lindsay hung up. She dialled a new number and waited.

"Gourlay's Garage, your first choice for previously-owned vehicles, how may I help you?" She recognised the voice of Tam's receptionist.

"Can I speak to Tam, please? It's Lindsay Gordon."

The line went hollow as she was put on hold. Then Tam Gourlay's voice boomed in her ear. "Have you got some news for me?"

"I've got a pretty good idea where Jack is."

The roar of delight nearly blew the electronics in Lindsay's phone. "That's fantastic! Amazing! So where is he?"

"I think the chances are strong that he's in St Petersburg."

A moment of stunned silence followed by, "You mean, in Russia?"

"That's right."

"What the fuck's he doing in Russia?" Tam sounded genuinely bewildered.

"Bruno's sister is married to another Italian diplomat. They've had it set up officially for ages for Jack to go and live with them. I can't see any reason for that unless they were planning to look after him once Bruno had snatched him. Even if it's only for a short time, until the fuss dies down."

"Fuck. What do we do now? I mean, Russia. I don't even know how you get there. Or how long it takes."

"Well, funnily enough, I've got one or two ideas about that. It's going to be risky, and it's going to cost a lot of money."

"I told you," Tam interrupted. "Money is not an issue here. All I want is to see Bernie happy again."

"OK. So, this is what I'm thinking." Lindsay leaned back in the booth and outlined her plan.

Two hours later, the MGB was powering up the long rise of the Rest and be Thankful. Blessedly, there hadn't been much traffic on the Loch Lomond road and she'd made good time. With luck and a continued absence of caravans and motor homes, she'd be at her parents' house in an hour and a half. The heather was turning purple on the hills, and the familiar grandeur of the landscape made Lindsay feel at home as the city never would. She recognised her membership of the national trait of sentimentality for her native land, but she didn't care. The sense of ownership she felt driving through Argyll to the Kintyre peninsula was something that could never be taken from her.

Sophie hadn't been best pleased when she'd called to tell her she was going up to Invercross overnight. It wasn't that she minded Lindsay being away; she minded not coming with her. "We don't see enough of your parents," she'd said plaintively. "Tell them to come down and visit soon."

Aye, right, Lindsay thought, knowing how little time her fisherman father was ever prepared to spend away from the sea. Her mother enjoyed the opportunity for shopping in the big city, but watching her father fret always spoiled Lindsay's joy in her mother's pleasure. "We'll go up for a weekend soon," she promised Sophie.

"A shame it couldn't wait till the weekend this time," Sophie said.

"You know how stories don't wait." Well, it was almost the truth

"I know. It's good to see you enjoying yourself again, Lindsay. I'm really glad you're working with Rory." They'd left it at that, neither mentioning what was uppermost in both their minds.

Lindsay was changing down to negotiate a series of bends when the phone rang. She pulled over into a viewpoint and picked up the phone. "Hello? Lindsay Gordon."

"Hey, partner, where are you?" Rory sounded cheerful. "I just got this bizarre message from Giles saying I better catch you before you went chasing off to Russia. What's going on?"

"I'm on the A83, west of Arrochar, heading down towards Loch Fyne. Which, as far as I'm aware, is not the way to Russia."

"What are you doing there?"

"I'm on my way to Invercross, to visit my parents."

"Invercross? Where the hell is that?"

"Half way down the Mull of Kintyre, on the west side. Where I grew up. Possibly one of the most beautiful places on the planet."

Rory snorted. "Compared to Castlemilk, almost anywhere qualifies for that description. So what's all this about Russia?"

"I think I've tracked down Jack Gourlay. It's looking likely that he's in St Petersburg."

"Wow! Bizarre. So, is Bernie going to court to get him back?"

Lindsay took a deep breath. "Not exactly."

Rory picked up on the hesitation. "Oh no. Don't tell me. Big Tam wants to play at *Where Eagles Dare*."

"Something like that. So, do you fancy a trip to Russia?"

PART TWO

Chapter 12

The first thing Lindsay noticed about Pulkovo Airport was the cigarette smoke. Accustomed to American airports where no tobacco had burned for years, she was taken aback to see people smoking everywhere. It reinforced what had already struck her on the approach to the runway—that she was heading somewhere very foreign indeed. This wasn't a landscape she'd seen anywhere else in Europe. From the plane window, it looked like Legoland: the buildings neat, square blocks, anywhere from six to twelve storeys high, laid out in grids. Sticking up apparently at random were factory chimneys, red and white striped, also like something from a child's construction kit, plumes of smoke coming out of them at right angles in the stiff wind. There seemed to be nothing organic about this landscape; it was as regimented as humans could make it.

Then, as the plane dipped down, Rory pointed out a landing strip exclusively for helicopters. There were dozens of them, in various liveries. "It's a flock of petrol budgies," she exclaimed.

As the plane approached the runway, silver birch trees took over. As far as the eye could see, ghostly white trunks stood in the dimming afternoon light, topped by naked branches like a very bad perm, the chimney stacks sticking out of them, still red and white, still spewing out ribbons of white smoke across a sky the blue of robin's eggs.

When the wheels touched down on the tarmac, the Russians on board applauded loudly. "Tells you all you need to know about Aeroflot," Lindsay commented.

"Where do we go?" Rory asked anxiously as they emerged into the terminal building. She'd admitted to being less than intrepid when it came to abroad, and being confronted with signs in Cyrillic everywhere clearly wasn't helping her confidence.

"Follow the crowd," Lindsay said. "We've all got to jump through the same hoops." They descended a flight of stairs and found themselves in a high-ceilinged immigration hall, queues snaking the length of the room. Lindsay headed for what looked like the shortest line, and resigned herself to a long wait. In the week since she'd discovered Jack Gourlay's whereabouts, she'd set herself a crash course in figuring out Russia, and she knew getting through immigration could take a while.

She'd thought the whole process would be nightmarish and complicated, but the travel agent had made it all look desperately simple. Arranging visas had taken no more than a couple of days once they'd filled in the forms and supplied passport photographs. The hotel booking was confirmed and the flights arranged. But a lot of what happened now they were here would be up to her. She'd learned the alphabet, the words for "please" and "thank you" and the invaluable sentence, "I don't speak Russian." She'd studied a street map of the city, got her head round the metro system and read the *Rough Guide*.

All that had been easy compared to explaining to Sophie why she had to go off on such a risky venture at all. Her partner had seemed emotionally vulnerable, a state Lindsay wasn't accustomed to dealing with. Sophie was the rock in their relationship, the one who was always calm in a crisis. Lindsay was the volatile one, impetuous and prey to insecurities. She didn't know how to respond when Sophie accused her of abandoning her at a crucial time. She knew she was supposed to be supportive, she just didn't seem to be able to find the necessary vocabulary. Instead, she retreated into mutinous self-justification, which only made things worse. She wasn't sure why she was behaving so badly, and she was too scared of the answers to examine her motives too closely. When she'd left that morning, she'd found herself wondering if she could ever manage to be the person Sophie appeared to need her to be. Or if she even wanted to be.

But she couldn't think about that now. She was the pivot around whom a meticulously constructed plan had to move like clockwork. That was going to take all her concentration. She was glad Rory was there to share the load, although persuading Rory to come had been almost as hard as overcoming Sophie's objections.

"You're mad," Rory had objected when Lindsay had first run the outline of her plan past her.

"Why?"

"For one, you don't even know for sure that Jack is in St Petersburg at all."

"Cavadino wouldn't leave him with strangers, and he's due back at work any minute now. Besides, Maria and her husband have had Jack down on their list of dependants since they first arrived in Russia. Where else is he going to be?"

"That could be a red herring. He could be anywhere on the planet."

"But on balance, he's more likely to be in St Pete's," Lindsay said reasonably. "And if he's not, Tam Gourlay will be the poorer, not us. Tam's prepared to fund it, so what have we got to lose?"

"Life, liberty and the pursuit of happiness?" Rory hazarded. "Lindsay, it's like a jungle on the streets of Russia. Do you really think Jack will be running around without protection? These guys shoot anybody that gets in their road. And if the Mafia don't get us, the cops probably will. I don't want to end up in a fucking gulag for kidnapping a wee boy."

"Well, please yourself. It's a risk I'm prepared to take. If you won't come with me, I'll just have to manage without you."

Now real concern crept into Rory's voice. "Lindsay, what are you trying to prove here? What's with the recklessness? You know yourself this is an act of total lunacy. And yet you're going at it like a bull at a gate. What's going on?"

"Nothing's going on," Lindsay said gruffly, denying the questioning voices inside her own head yet again. "When I say I'll do something, I do it. And I said I'd do my best to get Jack Gourlay back. So I'm going to Russia. All right? It's my life. I can take risks with it if I want. Christ, why is it all the women in my life think it's their job to tell me what I should and shouldn't do?"

Two days of frosty silence later, Rory had plonked herself down in the booth, held her hands up in capitulation and said, "OK. Count me in. All for one and one for all, right?"

"What changed your mind?"

"Sandra reminded me that you had been a better reporter than I will ever be and if you thought it was worth going for it, you were more likely to be right than a big jessie like me."

Lindsay grinned. "Thank you, Sandra." She remembered the moment now as the line shuffled forward at reasonable speed. Ever since she'd agreed to come, Rory had been reminding Lindsay on a more or less hourly basis of the dangers that lay ahead. But in spite of her apprehension, she was still here, at Lindsay's side.

After a twenty-minute wait, Lindsay finally handed her passport over to an unsmiling immigration official who seemed to spend forever scrutinising her seven-day visa and entering details into his computer. At last, he stamped passport and visa and she was released into the baggage hall, where a couple of carousels grunted and wheezed under their burden of luggage. The screens that should have indicated which belt carried the bags from their flight were resolutely blank. "You stay by this one and I'll go over to the other one," Lindsay said to Rory.

Eventually, their holdalls appeared on Rory's carousel and they made their way through the green channel into a morass of people peering through the doors in an attempt to glimpse their loved ones. Lindsay pushed forward, craning her neck, trying to find their driver.

They were almost at the doors leading to the car park outside when she spotted a burly old man with a shock of silver hair resembling Boris Yeltsin's. But there the resemblance ended. This man was clear-eyed, erect and handsome, his skin the weathered tan of an outdoorsman. He spread his arms wide and shouted in a deep voice, "Lindsay! You grow more lovely with every passing

109

year." He pulled her into a bear hug, smacking kisses on both cheeks.

Lindsay freed herself and stepped back to include Rory in the group. "Honestly, Sasha, age hasn't slowed you down, has it? Rory, meet Sasha Kuznetsov. Sasha, this is my colleague, Rory McLaren."

Sasha enveloped Rory's hands in both of his. When Lindsay had told her she had enlisted the help of one of her father's friends, she hadn't known what to expect. She'd imagined the former skipper of a Russian factory ship to be as dark and forbidding as the waters he fished, but this man was as warm and sturdy as a sun-bathed rock. Something about Sasha's solidity gave her more confidence than anything she'd seen or heard since Lindsay had dragged them into this folly. "Pleased to meet you," she said, meaning it.

"The pleasure is always mine when beautiful women are concerned." He winked to emphasise the lack of threat behind his gallantry, then reached for their bags. "Welcome to Russia. Now, follow me."

He led them outside to an elderly but gleaming Peugeot. It was as warm and sticky outside as it had been inside the terminal. "Is it usually this hot at the beginning of September?" Lindsay asked as they climbed into the car.

"Not always. This year, we have a lot of sunshine. More than normal. Maybe it will be cooler in a day or two."

"Please God. I don't know if I can think straight in heat like this," Lindsay said.

"Let's hope none of us has too much thinking to do. Now, best if you relax and gather your strength. We have plans, and in the morning, we work. But for tonight, I will leave you in peace to recover from plane."

"Sounds good to me," Lindsay said.

As they reached the outskirts of the city, Sasha began to point out sites of interest. "This is the Moscow Prospekt, this triumph arch was once the largest cast-iron structure in the world. Dostoevsky lived here. And here also. He lived a lot of places, I think they paid him to live in their buildings so they could put up a sign saying, 'Dostoevsky lived here' and put the rents up." He guffawed at his own joke. "Senate Square, with the bronze horseman, Peter the Great. The gold dome, that's the Cathedral of St Isaac. The Admiralty. Palace Square and the Hermitage."

The names flowed over Lindsay as she drank in the sights. She'd seldom seen anywhere so imposing. Even the apartment blocks were built on a scale to command admiration. The late afternoon sun seemed to pull all the colours out of the buildings, emphasising the ochres, yellows, blues, pinks, sage greens and browns of the flaking and faded stucco. The years of Soviet neglect had left St Petersburg looking raddled and decayed. But it was clear that a massive programme of restoration was under way. There was scarcely a street without signs of building work.

Rory was unusually quiet, clearly struck by her surroundings. "I can't get over the churches," she said eventually. "Every time we turn a corner, there's another one. All those gilded domes and glamorous colours, all those gold crosses. I thought the Communists pulled all the churches down."

Sasha chuckled. "They never wasted a building. They just used them for other things. Builders' yards, carpentry workshops, that's what they turned them into. One of the finest churches in the city, they made it the Museum of Atheism. Now, the church makes them good again."

"All they need to do now is fix the roads," Lindsay said dryly as Sasha swerved wildly to avoid yet another pothole. "I thought at first all the drivers must be drunk, then I realised they were avoiding the ruts and the holes in the road."

"It's getting better," he said as they left the grand façade of the Hermitage behind and swept across the steel grey River Neva. "Vasilievsky Ostrov," he added. "Vassily's Island, where your hotel is. Also, where I live. When Peter the Great built the city, he wanted the island to be another Venice. All the streets in the main part are in a grid. They were supposed to be canals, but it never happened. There are three big parallel avenues, and the streets that cross them are numbers. You are on the Seventh Line. Near McDonalds."

"McDonalds?" Rory echoed faintly.

He turned off the wide boulevard into a broad street. "We are here." He helped them out with their bags and walked them into the hotel. "OK. I go. You need me, you have my number. I am near, on the Tenth Line. But I will be here in the morning at seven. There is good restaurant up the street, Georgian restaurant." He gave Lindsay a hug and shook Rory's hand again. "We will do well. Enjoy your evening." With a wave of his big square hand, he was gone.

Checking in proved painless, since the reception staff spoke English. Within minutes, they were walking into their third-floor suite. Lindsay didn't know what she'd been expecting, but it wasn't this. The two rooms were airy and spacious, freshly decorated and furnished in contemporary style. "Amazing," Rory said, wandering through the rooms. "Hey, we've got two bathrooms. I thought it would be like some bed and breakfast in Rothesay, all 1950s furniture and no mod cons. But this is lush."

There was, Lindsay noted, a single divan in the living room of the suite. Just as well, since the bedroom contained only a double. She'd asked for twin beds, but the message had clearly got lost in translation somewhere. "Yeah, it looks like we landed on our feet with this place." She unzipped her holdall and started unpacking.

"Sasha's terrific," Rory said.

"I've known him since I was a kid. Luckily my dad and him stayed in touch after he gave up the fishing. When my dad called him and said I needed his help, he jumped at the chance to pay back a wee bit of the hospitality he's had from his Scottish friends over the years. I'd trust him with my life."

Rory snorted. "Isn't that exactly what we're doing?"

"I think it's more that we're putting him on the line. He's the one that gets left behind to face the music if it all goes sour on us. Which, by the way, it's not going to do, OK?"

Rory pulled a face and began browsing the Guests' Guide to the hotel. "Hey, there's a leaflet here about a Russian banya. It sounds a bit like a sauna. Do you fancy doing that tonight?"

"Is it not hot enough for you already?"

"I wasn't thinking about the heat, I was thinking about the

experience. We're not going to have much time to do anything touristy, we should at least get a flavour of Russia." She waved the flyer under Lindsay's nose. "Look, it's not a communal thing. We could hire it for an hour. Four hundred roubles, that's only a tenner, isn't it? It would give us a chance to talk in private about what we've got to do."

Lindsay relented in the face of Rory's enthusiasm. Besides, she could use some relaxation. "OK. Let me unpack, then I'll go downstairs and ask them to book it."

An hour later, they were standing outside an archway, exchanging anxious looks. "It doesn't look very promising," Rory said dubiously.

"It's the address the receptionist gave me," Lindsay replied, sounding more confident than she felt. She walked through the archway into a courtyard and found herself in what looked disturbingly like a scrap yard. There was an assortment of vehicles in various stages of dismemberment, a fork-lift and a pick-up truck, and a row of lock-up garages. There was nothing that looked remotely like a bath-house. A man emerged from one of the lock-ups and said something incomprehensible. Lindsay took a deep breath and said, "Banya?"

The man pointed to a rickety wooden staircase that resembled a fire escape on the point of being condemned. Somewhat apprehensively, they mounted the stairs and arrived at a door with a handwritten sign next to a doorbell. "In for a penny," Lindsay muttered and pressed the bell.

The door was opened by a young man dressed in a clinical white uniform. Lindsay uttered her one Russian sentence and he nodded. "Angliski, da? Is OK, I do English. I am Dimitri." He ushered them in and handed them a pair of rubber flip-flops each, then escorted them to what looked like a 1950s family living room, minus the TV. Fake wooden cladding covered the bottom half of the wall, complete with highly visible nails. The top half of the wall rejoiced in imitation stone wallpaper. There was a black leatherette sofa with a couple of tears patched with packing tape, a few hard chairs and a table holding a samovar, some teacups, teabags and sugar. This, it emerged, was the changing room. Dimitri gave them a couple of white sheets each, then disappeared.

"This is a bit wild," Rory said.

"At least you're having your post-war chic experience," Lindsay said, stripping off with her back to her business partner and wrapping herself in a sheet.

When they emerged, Dimitri was waiting. He led them down a corridor and opened a door leading into the business end of the banya. He showed them two wooden cabins—one, a Swedish-style dry sauna, the other a traditional Russian banya. There was also a plunge pool, inexplicably empty. But he pointed out a row of shower cabinets that would provide the necessary freezing cold shock to the system.

He led them into the Russian banya, pointed to a low wooden bench and said, "You sit here." It looked like a sauna, Lindsay thought, taking in the brazier filled with stones, and the bucket of water with a ladle. Then Dimitri revealed the difference. He poured what seemed like an absurd amount of water on the coals to activate them. The heat rose dramatically, along with the humidity. But bizarrely, there was no accompanying cloud of steam.

Dimitri left them to it, and inside a minute, the heat hit 80 degrees and the humidity 95 per cent. Within seconds, their bodies were slick with a mixture of sweat and steam. "My God," said Lindsay. "What a sensation." Her skin tingled, her face prickled and she could feel her shoulders dropping as her muscles started to relax.

"It's brilliant," Rory said, unwrapping herself to let her whole body feel the damp heat. Lindsay leaned back against the wall, allowing her sheet to fall away from her.

"Aah," Lindsay sighed. "What a good idea this was, Rory."

"Just what we need to get us in prime condition for breaking the law."

"Don't say that," Lindsay groaned.

"So, tomorrow we've got to find Jack, right?"

"We've got to find him *and* figure out the best way to get him on his own so Tam can move in on him."

Rory stretched luxuriously. Lindsay couldn't help noticing the line of her small breasts tapering into her ribs, the almost imperceptible swell of her stomach, the triangle of dark blonde hair between her legs. It was oddly asexual in this context, she realised. "When will Tam and your dad get here?"

"They left Helsinki at dawn yesterday. My dad reckons they should be here tomorrow evening, provided they get decent winds."

Rory shook her head. "I can't believe they're doing this. Sailing a boat from Helsinki to St Petersburg to kidnap a wee boy. Your dad must be some guy."

Lindsay nodded. "He's sound. Doesn't have much to say for himself, but he's always been there for me. Never criticises, just accepts whatever daft thing I do. As soon as I told him why I wanted to speak to Sasha in the first place, he made me tell him the whole story. And he pointed out that my original idea of taking Jack out of the country on a train was stupid. And then he announced he had a better idea but it would only work if he came too. And that was that. *Fait accompli.*"

Rory closed her eyes and let the sweat and steam run down her face. "You don't know how lucky you are. My father is a boil on the bum of the universe. He's a drunk and a waster. I never saw the bastard from one year's end to the next till he heard about me winning the money. Now he turns up on the doorstep every few weeks, bubbling and greeting that he loves his wee lassie, and could I see my way to slipping him a few hundred quid. I tell you, I wouldn't piss on him if he was on fire, not unless I'd been drinking lighter fuel."

"I'm sorry," Lindsay said.

Rory smoothed back her dripping hair. "Don't be. I'm not. After what he did to me, he'll go to his grave without a penny of mine."

"What did he do?" It wasn't her natural curiosity that prompted Lindsay's question; it was more that she sensed Rory wanted to be pushed into revelation.

"In a minute," Rory said, pushing herself upright. "I need to cool off."

Lindsay followed her to the showers, admiring the shift of Rory's muscles as she walked. Grateful for the cold shower, she stood under the stream of water, gasping at the change in temperature, convinced she could feel her pores snapping shut.

Back in the banya, Rory ladled more water on the coals, pushing the temperature up another five degrees. "Magic," she said, returning to the bench. "So, you want to know what my piece-of-shit father did to me?"

"Only if you want to tell me."

"I came out when I was at university. Well, when I say I came out, I only came out in Edinburgh. The last people I would ever have told were my parents. I knew what his homophobic wee soul would make of it. And I knew it would break my mother's heart. She was a good woman, my mother. She worked double shifts as a cleaner all her days to keep him in money for beer and bookies. She took the beatings he handed out when he'd lost on the horses. And he lost plenty, believe me. But she never complained, she never spent a penny on herself, bought her clothes from charity shops so I could have the latest fashions. She always encouraged me to get an education, anything to avoid having a life like hers. But she was a devout Catholic and she'd never have been comfortable with the idea of a dyke for a daughter.

"Anyway, one night my girlfriend persuaded me to go to Glasgow for some lesbian benefit. I didn't want to go, but I let her talk me into it. We were staggering down Argyle Street, heading for the station for the last train back to Edinburgh, arms round each other, probably snogging every few yards. And my father walked out of some shitty dive where he'd been knocking back the pints and the whiskies and practically fell over us. Can you believe it? My one trip to Glasgow, and we walk smack bang into him. He was pissed, but not so pissed that he didn't understand what he was seeing. He called me all the names under the sun. And I just stood there. I didn't know what else to do."

Lindsay wanted to reach out and hug Rory, but in the absence of clothes, it felt too intimate a gesture. "That must have been horrible," she said, settling for the inadequacy of words.

"It wouldn't have been so bad if that had been all. But he

rang me the next day. He said he'd told my mother and she was broken-hearted. And because she was a good Catholic, she wanted me never to darken her door again." Rory's face crumpled in bewilderment. "I look back at it, and I can't figure out why I believed him. Because my mother wasn't like that. She'd have been hurt, but she'd never have rejected me. I should have realised he was lying to drive a wedge between us. He'd always been jealous of the fact that she loved me more than him. But the bottom line is that I did take him at his word. So I stayed away.

"And six months later, my mother was dead. Breast cancer. She never went to the doctor till her whole system was riddled with it. And I never knew. I never got to say goodbye. And she must have died thinking I didn't give a shit." She crossed her arms across her chest. "That's what my daddy did to me."

"I can see why you hate him. Anybody would, in your shoes."

Rory screwed up her face. "I don't think I hate him. I don't want to expend that much energy on him. I despise him, but I try not to hate him. What fucks me off most, I suppose, is that I feel like he's poisoned me emotionally." She turned to look at Lindsay, a wry smile on her lips. "I'm crap at relationships. You grow up exposed to a marriage like that and you get really cynical. I don't want to turn into my mother or my father, and the best way to avoid that is to avoid getting emotionally involved."

Lindsay shook her head gently. "You don't have to turn into either of them. From where I'm sitting, it looks to me like you've escaped that. You're a creature of your own making, Rory. You just need to let yourself love the right person."

Rory gave a bitter laugh. "You sound like my pal Sandra. 'Wait till you meet the right woman, then it'll happen.' "

Before Lindsay could reply, there was a pounding on the door. They both grabbed their sheets as Dimitri opened the door a crack. "Time for tea," he said firmly. "Then you have Russian banya."

They looked at each other, bemused. "I thought that's what we were doing," Rory said.

"Obviously Dimitri doesn't agree."

Chapter 13

Michael threw the last piece of pizza crust into the box, then methodically put the remains of his meal in a black plastic bin liner. He'd given Kevin the rest of the day off, because if he had to spend another hour listening to his mindless attempts to pick a winning horse, he'd have had to take steps to silence his sidekick permanently. Besides, there was nothing doing.

The big fucker had left in a taxi with a holdall three days ago and hadn't been seen since. He hadn't been suited up like a man going on a business trip. But what did Michael know about the way second-hand car dealers did business? Maybe they met regularly for conventions in jeans and sweatshirts and waterproof jackets. Maybe Gourlay was going off for a few days' fishing with his mates. The stress of living with a woman climbing the walls about her missing kid would drive any man to the quiet of a trout stream.

Since he'd gone, Bernie had barely left the house, other than to visit the supermarket to stock up on ready meals, whisky and fags. Patrick had sounded bored with the whole business when Michael had called in, but he wasn't for putting a stop to it. When Michael had asked if he wanted to continue, Patrick's voice had turned to steel and he'd said, "It's over when I say it's over, and not before. You'll be well looked after, Michael. I know it's not very interesting, but when the time's right, there'll be plenty for you to do."

So he'd settled in for the evening, his miniature radio tuned to a jazz station, the lights off and the binoculars sitting on their tripod in front of him. OK, it wasn't the most exciting job in the world. But Michael had seen more than his fair share of excitement over the years. He understood very well that there was a lot to be said for the dull. He shifted his position, getting comfortable in the camping chair he'd bought when they'd got their hands on the flat. Another night, another dollar.

Lindsay and Rory drained their tea cups and exchanged a slightly apprehensive look. "What's to be scared about?" Lindsay said, going for bravado.

"Right. I mean, I went to Lesbos and lived. How bad can it be?"

They grinned in complicity and emerged into the corridor. Dimitri appeared, looking disturbingly cheerful. "You are ready?" he demanded

"Ready for what, exactly?" Lindsay asked.

"The beating, the beating," he cried, enthusiastically waving his arms.

"You didn't tell me this was the S&M banya," Rory muttered.

"It was your idea."

"Maybe, but you're still going first."

They followed Dimitri back into the wooden cubicle, but he shooed Rory back out again. "Wait in sauna," he said. To Lindsay, he added, "Lie face down on bench. Take sheet off."

Then he disappeared. When he came back, he was wearing nothing but a towel round his waist and a felt hat that looked like a left-over prop from *Bill and Ben the Flowerpot Men*. He was also bearing two bunches of birch twigs. *Oh shit,* Lindsay thought. *I'm naked in a steam room with a nutter.*

First, Dimitri got the room hot and humid, then he started gently wafting the birch twigs over her body. This created an updraft, bathing Lindsay in moist air while simultaneously what felt like hot rain was pattering over her back. Then the birch twigs descended and the length of her body was covered in a blend of gentle switching and firmer strokes. Just when she was getting used to this and thinking it was really rather pleasant, the hot bundles of leaves were clamped without warning on her large muscles like a fluffy hot mustard poultice—shoulders, lower back, buttocks, thighs, calves and finally feet. Her skin was tingling with damp fire.

Then Dimitri yelled, "Cold shower, now, cold shower," and sent her scuttling off to shout out loud as she froze in the icy jets. By the time she emerged, she could tell from the exclamations that Rory was undergoing the same sweet torture. Lindsay went into the sauna, where the dry heat felt strange after the banya. She mused on what Rory had revealed earlier, thinking it sounded a little too pat as an explanation for her friend's violent allergy to committed relationships. Lindsay wondered if the real reason for Rory's avoidance of love was more to do with her mother's death. Losing the one person she'd loved and trusted in such a traumatic and treacherous way would leave anyone wary of a repeat experience, she thought sympathetically. She'd endured betrayal herself and understood only too well the scars it left behind. It would take Rory a long time to recover from something so profound.

Rory eventually joined her in the sauna. "They should have these in clubs instead of chilling out spaces," she groaned comfortably. "I can't remember the last time I felt so completely laid back."

"Better than sex," Lindsay said.

"You've obviously been doing it wrong."

Lindsay giggled. "The thing with sex is you have to expend a lot of effort to feel this good. But here, somebody else does all the work." She stretched out on the top bench, enjoying the sensation of the muscles round her spine relaxing.

A few minutes later, Dimitri banged on the door. "Your time is over, ladies," he called.

As if in a trance, Lindsay and Rory made their way back to the changing room and got dressed. "Do you know, I haven't thought about Jack Gourlay since before we had our tea," Lindsay said dreamily.

Rory gave a slow smile. "Who's Jack Gourlay?"

◆ ◆ ◆ ◆ ◆

The skies were grey over the Gulf of Finland, a force five wind blowing out of the north-west. Tam Gourlay inched his way from the galley to the hatch leading to the cockpit, cradling a mug of tea in his hands. Boats like this weren't designed for men of his size, he thought as he forgot yet again to duck under the bulkhead and caught the side of his head a glancing blow. He leaned forward and held the drink aloft. Andy Gordon bent at the knees and took one hand off the wheel to take the tea, his sharp blue eyes never leaving the gunmetal swell ahead of the full belly of the genoa sail. "Cheers," he said.

Tam clambered up the short companionway and joined Andy in the shelter of the sprayhood. "How are we doing?" he asked.

"No' bad. It makes a change, having to watch the charts all the way through the archipelago. I'm used to water I know better than the back of my hand."

"Must be a bit different, sailing a wee thing like this instead of driving a big fishing boat," Tam said.

"Aye. It's like riding a bike, though. You never lose the knack." He leaned into the wheel, his shoulders bracing against the swell. It was hard to see a resemblance between Andy Gordon and his daughter. The balding man with the broad back and the short legs was a completely different physical type, and his blunt, ruddy features gave far less away than Lindsay's open countenance. Only in the eyes was there any congruence. The same spirit that lit Lindsay from within was there in Andy Gordon's blue gaze as he scanned the horizon.

Tam sat down on the damp plastic cushion that ran along the side of the cockpit, grateful for the oilskin trousers Andy had supplied him with, even if they were six inches short in the leg. He watched the fisherman standing rock-steady on the shifting deck, marvelling at such stamina from a man in his sixties. They'd hardly stopped since they'd left Glasgow. When they'd reached Helsinki, they'd had to go straight to the Russian embassy and queue for a couple of hours to get their three-day visas. Then they'd gone to the boatyard to pick up the yacht they'd chartered from Glasgow, which Andy insisted on checking from stem to stern before he'd accept it. Andy had stayed at the wheel through most of the previous night, only dropping anchor in a sheltered cove an hour before dawn and snatching a couple of hours before they'd set off again. Tam hadn't expected to sleep, with the combination of the unfamiliar motion and his anxiety about what lay ahead, but he'd surprised himself by going spark out for over six hours. "Will you get a proper sleep tonight?" Tam asked.

Andy nodded. "We should be in clear water before too long. Then I can set the autopilot and get a few hours."

"You'll be on your knees at this rate."

"Ach, it's just a couple of nights. I can catch up when we get to port tomorrow night. And I'll have Lindsay to help me on the way back. We can split the night watch between us."

Tam shook his head in admiration. "I can hardly believe the way she's set this whole thing up. She's some lassie."

Andy's mouth twitched at the corners. "She's that, all right. Christ knows where she gets it from. Me and her mother, we've no' got an adventurous bone in our bodies. We were born in Invercross, and we'll probably die there. But ever since she was wee, Lindsay's aye been one for diving in at the deep end. And this time, I couldnae stand back and leave her to it. Not when I could do something a bit more useful than just giving her Sasha's phone number." He leaned across and checked the chart, scanning the horizon for the next landmark. "A wee touch to starboard, I think."

"I really appreciate you doing this," Tam said. "Lindsay told me you insisted, wouldnae take no for an answer. That means a lot, you know. The way you've weighed in when it's no' even your fight."

"You dinnae have to keep saying that, son. I know fine. We'll get it sorted, don't you worry. My pal Sasha, he'll see to that." He screwed his eyes up against a stray drift of spray. "Tell you the truth, I cannae quite believe I'm here myself. That lassie of mine has a way of making the world dance to her tune."

Right then, Andy Gordon's lassie was sitting in the Georgian restaurant Sasha had recommended, contemplating a dish translated on the English menu as "meat drunk on the plate." Rory, who was tucking into a grilled salmon fillet, had taken one look at the steak smothered in diced vegetables with a cream sauce and said, "I can see how it got its name. It looks just like somebody threw up over a piece of beef."

"Thanks," Lindsay said, cutting into her meat. "That'll do wonders for my appetite. But you've got to live dangerously sometimes."

Rory glanced up from under her eyebrows. "Just so long as I don't have to eat things with names like that."

There was silence while they ate their food, washed down with a chewy Georgian red wine. "It's probably better if we split up tomorrow, cover our options. Sasha can take one school while we go over to the one where Jack's most likely to be enrolled. I've checked on the map and it's quite near a metro station on the same line as the one up the street. Getting there should be pretty straightforward," Lindsay said.

"Famous last words. What are we going to do if we find it?"

"Wait and see if Jack arrives. And if he does, follow the person who brings him to school back home. That should tell us where he's staying."

"And then?" Rory pressed on relentlessly.

"I don't know. We'll have to see how it goes."

"And what if he turns up at the one Sasha's watching?"

"He'll do the same thing," Lindsay said. "Then he'll come back and pick us up. And then we'll make our plans."

"Doesn't it scare you?" Rory asked, her eyes fixed on Lindsay's. "Knowing we're about to embark on a criminal act in a country that's not noted for the even-handedness of its judicial system? Not to mention the prevalence of guns?"

"Of course it scares me. That's why I'm trying very hard not to think about the possibility of getting caught. I'm visualising the scene when Jack's reunited with his mother and I'm standing there taking the photos. It takes my mind off the alternative." It was the truth, but not the whole truth. There were other things on Lindsay's mind that had nothing to do with the fate of one small boy. But she knew she really shouldn't be thinking about them either.

"Good trick if you can manage it. But it's definitely winding me up. Shall we get another relaxing bottle of wine?"

Lindsay's expression turned quizzical. "Is the effect of the banya wearing off already?"

Rory laughed. "Listen, you don't want to go there. That banya has had some very strange side effects, let me tell you."

"Like what?" Lindsay felt the thin ice creaking beneath her words. She didn't think she was imagining the sparkle of electricity between them.

Rory held her gaze for a moment, then looked away, shaking her head. "Nothing I want to discuss in a public place." Her words were almost drowned by a noisy burst of laughter from a neighbouring table.

"Look, why don't we get the bill? We can buy a bottle of wine in the hotel bar and drink it in peace," Lindsay suggested. Rory nodded agreement.

As they strolled down the street towards the hotel, the warm evening air balmy against their faces, Lindsay was feverishly conscious of Rory's body inches from hers. It was as if she was radiating heat like the brazier in the banya. *This is crazy*, she thought. *Eight years you've been with Sophie and never once crossed the line. You're working with this woman, for God's sake. You're maybe going to be a parent. Aren't you taking enough risks already without going overboard? Put the lid on it now.* But her interior monologue had no effect on the churning in her stomach or the prickle of sweat along her spine.

They walked into the hotel and Lindsay turned towards the bar. "Another bottle of red?"

"Maybe not," Rory said. "Maybe I don't need it after all."

They didn't speak in the lift, but it was a silence that crackled with what wasn't being said. Lindsay fumbled with the key, struggling to get it into the lock. Then she managed it and they were inside the suite. "I thought I'd sleep in here on the divan, let you have the double bed," Lindsay gabbled as she flicked the switch to turn on the table lamps. She turned to watch Rory's reaction but couldn't see her eyes through the shadows.

One side of Rory's mouth rose in a knowing half-smile. "You

know, I've seen you stripped to the skin tonight. But you look a hell of a lot sexier with your clothes on."

Lindsay cleared her throat. Her voice came out half an octave higher than usual. "Delirium. That would be one of the strange side effects of the banya, right?"

The moment broken, Rory walked away and feigned an interest in the St Petersburg tourist magazine on the writing table. "Right enough," she said, her tone darker and colder. "Should you maybe phone home?"

Lindsay took a couple of steps towards Rory. "I don't want to phone Sophie."

"She'll be worried about you. Running around Russia like James Bond." There was no mistaking the coolness now.

"No, she won't. I called her on my mobile when the receptionist was booking the banya. Just to let her know we'd arrived safely."

Rory turned her head, the half-smile back in place. "She really shouldn't be worried about you, should she?" This time, the tone was regretful.

"Why are we talking about Sophie?"

"Because it puts a wall between us, Lindsay. And that's the sensible option."

Lindsay ran a hand through her hair. "I'm not good at sensible."

"Neither am I. So let's work on treating this as a 'sensible' work-shop for both of us." Rory swung round to face Lindsay and leaned against the writing table. The subtle light of the lamps cast the planes of her face into relief. Lindsay thought she had never wanted so badly to kiss someone.

"You think that'll work, do you? You think we can just ignore whatever it is that's happening here?" There was no aggression in Lindsay's questions, just a simple plea for answers.

Rory spread her hands. "What's the alternative? I want us to be able to work together. I like working with you. I don't want to fuck that up."

"Me neither. But we can't just pretend we're indifferent to each other. It's not going to go away."

"If we don't feed the flame, it'll die," Rory said.

Lindsay shook her head in frustration. "You know that's bullshit. We'll always be wondering what it would have been like. It'll be sitting there between us in the Café Virginia every bloody day. So let's get it out of our system."

Rory laughed out loud. "You know, that's probably the least seductive thing anybody's ever said to me. 'Come on, let's get it over with, one shag with you and I'll be cured,' " she spluttered.

The laughter was infectious. Lindsay couldn't help herself. All at once she was chuckling too. Somewhere in the middle of the laughter, they fell into each other's arms. Two hungry mouths connected.

Suddenly, sensible was history.

Chapter 14

Even at midnight, it was still warm in St Petersburg. Lindsay and Rory lay tangled together, the bedclothes in a rumpled heap on the floor. Unfamiliar scents and sounds drifted in through the open window, reminding them how very far they'd come. Rory ran a fingertip along the thin white line that ran down from Lindsay's right ear to the corner of her jaw. Then, with the tip of her tongue, she traced the starburst scar above her left breast, tasting the sharp saltiness of her sweat. "Tell me about the scars," she said.

Lindsay squirmed pleasurably at the sensation as Rory's mouth moved down to her nipple. "Not very romantic for post-coital conversation," she murmured.

"You want romance? You picked the wrong lover, doll. Anyway, who said anything about post-coital?" Rory teased. "I thought this was just the first interval."

"Fine by me." Lindsay ran her fingers along Rory's side, learning this unfamiliar body. After eight years with the same woman, it felt strange to explore such alien territory. She'd thought the very exoticism of novelty would provoke guilt, but she'd been mistaken. Making love with Rory had taken her somewhere outside her past experience. Wild and dark, it had shown her a bewildering new side to her own sexuality, both scary and magical. But wrong was the one thing it hadn't felt.

"So tell me about the scars," Rory persisted. "I'd never even noticed that one under your jawline before."

"They did a good job of stitching it up." Lindsay's hand strayed between Rory's thighs, but she clamped them shut and pulled away.

"Not until you tell me about the scars."

Lindsay groaned. "You're so bossy."

Rory chuckled. "Nothing like flipping the butch. You didn't mind me bossing you a wee while ago. Come on, tell me. It can't be that terrible."

"The one on my jaw I got when I tripped over a wall and landed face first on a broken bottle."

"Aw," Rory complained. "That's really boring."

"If it helps, I was being chased by a guy with a baseball bat at the time," Lindsay said, wincing at the memory.

"Now, that's much better. What about this one?" She kissed the circular scar lightly. "Wounded in a duel over a beautiful blonde? Stabbed by a jealous lover?"

Lindsay's face darkened. "I got shot by a murderous little shit who didn't take kindly to the idea of being found out by me."

"Bastard," Rory said lazily, apparently unsurprised by the notion that someone might have taken a pot-shot at her new lover. "It looks nasty."

"It didn't hit anything important. I just lost a lot of blood. And my left shoulder hurts when the weather's damp."

"Ouch. I tell you, by October, you'll be *really* sorry you left California. So what happened to the shooter?" Rory ran the palm of her hand over Lindsay's body, letting her fingers trail tantalisingly over her stomach.

Lindsay shuddered with a pleasure that took all the pain out of the recollection. "Life for murder, ten years for attempted murder on me. You probably remember the case. Penny Varnavides' murder?"

Rory nodded. "Only vaguely. She was killed a wee while before I won the money. I didn't know what I was going to do with it, so I rented a cottage on Skye for a month to try and figure out my future. I didn't touch a newspaper or listen to a news bulletin. I must have missed the trial. Which would be why I never realised you were involved in that."

"So now you know." Lindsay rolled over suddenly and pinned Rory to the bed, her knee between Rory's thighs. "Act two?"

"Mmm. I never had you pegged as a woman who would be turned on by talk of violence." Rory's voice was teasingly sexy.

"Trust me, it's not the past that's turning me on."

Nine o'clock in Glasgow, and Bernie Gourlay was alone with a glass of Johnnie Walker and a half-smoked cigarette. She'd been a prisoner of fear for so long now she had almost forgotten it was possible to entertain any other emotion. It had hit her all the harder because for years she thought she'd escaped the cold claw of terror. How stupid had that been, she told herself bitterly.

She should have known Patrick would never have resigned himself to letting her out of his grasp. But as time had passed and he hadn't materialised in her new life, she'd allowed herself to be lulled into a false sense of security. She had her fallback plan in place, so she thought. And for whole months at a time, she'd been free of the very thought of him. But now he was back, and there was no telling how bad things would get before they righted themselves. If they ever could.

It had been bad enough when she'd only had Jack to be afraid for. At least she'd had Tam's strength to draw on. But now Tam had gone off on this crazy mission to get her son back, and all she could feel was anxiety. She knew she should be proud that he loved her enough to take such insane risks for her happiness, but instead she was overwhelmed with guilt that she'd brought this nightmare to his door in the first place.

No outcome offered her any relief. If they failed to snatch Jack successfully, Tam could end up in a Russian jail. Even if he avoided that worst case scenario, she knew he would never forgive himself for letting her and Jack down. Remorse like that could be slow poison to a relationship, her presence in his life a constant reminder of his perceived inadequacy. And if they did bring him home, what prospects were there of happiness with Patrick

Coughlan on the horizon? Patrick would do whatever it took to get his own back. Neither compunction nor compassion were concepts he'd ever embraced.

Bernie crushed out her cigarette as the phone started ringing. She turned her head and stared at it. It couldn't be Tam; as far as she knew, he was on a chartered yacht somewhere between Helsinki and St Petersburg. There was nobody else she wanted to talk to, and at least one voice she definitely didn't want to hear.

She drained her whisky in one swallow and waited for the ringing to stop.

When the alarm clock drilled through her dreams at half past six, Lindsay had been asleep for less than four hours. But when her eyes snapped open, she was as alert as if she'd had a full night's sleep. Great sex would do that every time, she thought, turning her head to watch Rory struggle into wakefulness. "So, do you still respect me?" she said.

Rory yawned. "I think so. But I might have to fuck you again to make sure." She snuggled into Lindsay's side, her fingers slithering down her stomach. "Do you do mornings?"

Lindsay squirmed away. "Any other morning, but not this one. We've got work to do, remember?"

"Bo-ring." Rory planted a warm kiss on her shoulder. "OK, Splash, you win. Race you to the shower." She rolled over and jumped out of bed.

Lindsay laughed. "We've got two showers, dozo."

"Damn," Rory said, heading for the en suite.

Half an hour later, they had said goodbye to Sasha and set off down the Seventh Line towards the Vasileostravskaya metro station, fuelled only by a snatched cup of execrable coffee in the hotel breakfast room. As they passed a street kiosk selling fruit, Rory looked longingly at the peaches and bananas. "I don't suppose you could manage to buy us a couple of bananas?" she asked wistfully.

"Absolutely right. I'm keeping my powder dry for the metro station. Besides, I don't know how you can think about eating. My stomach's churning like a cement mixer."

"I always eat when I'm nervous. And believe me, I'm nervous," Rory replied. The morning was warm and humid, the sky a washed-out blue. The metro station was on the corner of Sredny Prospekt, an ugly glass and concrete structure that glared across at the McDonald's diagonally opposite. "Soviet architecture meets Western capitalism," Lindsay commented as they climbed the short flight of stairs that led into the station.

"Now what do we do?" Rory said, looking apprehensively round the foyer. On one side were automatic turnstiles coping with a constant stream of morning commuters who thrust plastic cards into the slots.

"According to my guide book, we buy a ten-journey ticket for forty roubles," Lindsay said.

"Ten journeys for a quid? Hey, I could live like a king here. On you go then, Splash. Show me how it's done."

With a feeling of trepidation, Lindsay crossed to the ticket booth where a slab-faced middle-aged woman in a polyester flow-ered dress sat glaring out at the world. Lindsay smiled and held her hands up, fingers splayed to indicate ten. Then she proffered a fifty-rouble note. The woman said something in Russian. Lindsay told her she didn't speak Russian and stretched the smile wider. The women grunted, took the note and exchanged it for a card and a ten-rouble note. "Spasibo bolshoi," Lindsay said, relieved.

Once they'd negotiated the turnstiles, they found themselves on the longest escalator Lindsay had ever seen. "This is bowels of the earth stuff," Rory muttered in her ear.

"I suppose it's got to be deep, it goes under the river."

"Hey, so does the Clockwork Orange, but you don't have to penetrate the planet's crust to use the underground in Glasgow."

The escalator deposited them in a hallway. On either side, there were rows of closed doors that resembled large lifts. The only indication as to which side of the hallway their train would arrive at were two small illuminated signs hanging from the ceiling. "It's got to be the left-hand side," Lindsay said, frowning up at the station names.

"Hey, you're really good at this funny alphabet," Rory said, impressed.

"Hardly. This is the second to last stop going north, and there's only one name on the right-hand board. Whereas there's a whole list of stations on the other one. Ergo . . ."

Rory tutted. "You'd never make it in the Magic Circle, giving away your tricks like that." As she spoke, they heard a rumbling, and the doors on their side of the hallway slid open, revealing carriages that looked remarkably spacious compared to the familiar ones in Glasgow. They boarded the crowded train and grabbed a metal pole as it pulled out of the station.

"How do we know where to get off?" Rory asked when they stopped at the next station to the accompaniment of an announcement so corrupted by static that even a Russian speaker would have been hard pressed to figure out its content.

"We count. It's the third station. Ploschad Aleksandra Nevskovo," Lindsay said, stumbling a little over the unfamiliar name. To take her mind off the nervous butterflies fluttering in her stomach, Lindsay practised her reading of Cyrillic on the handful of adverts on the carriage walls. She couldn't help smiling when, after a struggle, she finally deciphered one as being a transliteration of "internet".

They emerged at the other end of the journey in a courtyard lined with kiosks selling soft drinks and alcohol, flowers, fruit and CDs. Lindsay took her map out of her backpack and pored over it. "I think we're on Nevsky Prospekt," she said uncertainly. "If we go up here and take a left, then left again, we should end up on the street where the school is." She looked up at the corner. "At least they seem to have street signs."

Since this was the less fashionable end of the long street that sliced through the heart of the city, the pavements were relatively quiet. Most of the people who were out and about were walking briskly with a sense of purpose, focused only on their own business. To Lindsay's amazement, they ended up on Konstantinogradskaya Ulitsa at the first attempt. The street was lined with tall nineteenth-century apartment buildings and shaded with trees. They strolled along, trying to look casual as they scanned the buildings for any sign of an international school. Two thirds of the way along, the apartments gave way to a walled courtyard with tall wrought iron gates. There was nothing to indicate what went on in the rose-pink building beyond the gates and they carried on to the end of the street.

"Do you think that was it?" Rory asked.

Lindsay shrugged. "Your guess is as good as mine. I guess we'll just have to wait and see where the kids go when they start to arrive."

"We're going to look a bit obvious, standing around on a street corner," Rory objected. "Look, there's a bar on the opposite corner. With the tables outside. It looks like they're open for business. We could get a coffee and keep an eye open."

Lindsay looked doubtful. "It's too far away to be sure of identifying Jack. We've only ever seen photos of him. Kids all look the same at that age."

"Can I have a look at the map?" Rory asked. Lindsay handed it over and waited while Rory studied it. "OK, here's the plan," she said. "We go to the café and as soon as kids start arriving, I shoot off round the block so I can come into the street at the other end. You give me a minute or two, then you amble slowly up towards the school. Then we bump into each other outside the school and act like we're old friends who've just met by accident. We can stand having a blether and keeping an eye out for Jack. What do you think?"

"It's worth a try," Lindsay said. They crossed the street to the café, but just as they were about to sit down, a couple of cars pulled up outside the iron gates. Three children spilled out, followed at a more leisurely pace by their drivers. They exchanged glances, each recognising the flame of adrenaline in the other's eyes. Rory took off at a fast pace down the side street that would bring her the long way round to the other end of the street, while Lindsay began to amble slowly back towards the school.

By the time she was a couple of dozen yards away, upwards of twenty children were milling around on the wide pavement of packed earth. As far as she could see, none of them was the right size, gender or colouring to be Jack Gourlay. As another couple of cars drew up, one of the gates slowly creaked open and the children flowed through, most without a backward glance at their drivers or their mothers.

Lindsay dawdled on, then, a few feet from the gate, with no Rory in sight yet, she stooped to tie her shoe-lace. She was over-taken by three children who looked around eight years old, then by a harassed looking teenager shouting something at them in German. Reassuringly, none gave her a second glance. Lindsay caught sight of Rory in a gap between what was now a steady stream of children, and stood up, surprised by the flash of delight that sparked inside her.

They achieved the planned rendezvous a few feet from the school gates, greeting each other with every appearance of sur-prise. While they pretended to make small talk, each was keeping an eye out for Jack. It was Rory who caught sight of him first. "Don't look now," she said conversationally. "But I think that's him walking towards us. Let's act like we're going to walk back to the café."

Lindsay turned and immediately saw the child Rory had identi-fied. There was really no mistaking Jack. He looked exactly like the school photograph on top of Bernie and Tam's TV except that then he'd been smiling and now he was scowling as he scuffed the toes of his trainers along the cracked pavement. The woman who held his hand in an iron grip had the same dark hair and beaky nose as she'd seen in photographs of Bruno Cavadino. It had to be them.

Lindsay and Rory set off in the direction of the café, passing the woman and boy without a second glance, but Lindsay was close enough to the woman to hear her say in the irritated voice of adults being embarrassed by a small child the world over, "I don't care what your Papa told you, this is not a holiday and you have to go to school." As soon as they were clear of the school, Rory glanced back. "She's virtually dragged him into the playground. Looks like he's not keen. Quick, let's duck into this courtyard," she said, yanking Lindsay by the arm and pulling her into the arched entrance to an apartment block.

"What are you playing at?" Lindsay demanded, staggering to stay upright.

"Chances are she'll come back the same way and we can tail her. Otherwise we'll have to stand around on the street corner and she might pick up on us." Rory's voice was sharp with excitement. Suddenly, she leaned forward and kissed Lindsay. "I haven't had so much fun for ages."

Lindsay grinned. "Me neither. But I don't think snogging in public is a good idea in Russia," she added hurriedly as an elderly woman turned into the courtyard laden with a basket of vegetables.

They didn't have long to wait before Maria Cavadino passed the entry where they were loitering. She was walking quickly, as if she had places to go and things to do. "You go first," Rory said. "I'll follow you."

Their little procession made its way through the back streets and courtyards, finally emerging on a street about half a mile further up Nevsky Prospekt. The woman was still walking briskly in spite of the humidity. Eventually, she turned into a refurbished apartment block, complete with a doorman who resembled one of those gigantic statues of Soviet workers.

Lindsay carried on to the corner and waited for Rory to catch her up. "No way we're going to get in there," Rory said.

"Even supposing we knew which apartment was the right one."

"So what now?"

Lindsay glanced at her watch. "I'll give Sasha a call, tell him we've struck lucky. He could meet as at that nice café, then we can see how the school day pans out?"

Rory groaned. "How I love stake-outs."

"Look on the bright side. At least we've got a supply of coffee, and a toilet."

Rory grinned. "And plenty of time for you to figure out the menu."

"Why do you think I'm going to get Sasha to join us?"

Chapter 15

Andy Gordon and Tam Gourlay were trying to keep hidden from each other their apprehensions about the next stage of their journey. Tam's anxieties had been tamped down on the journey by Andy's calm handling of the boat and apparent lack of concern about navigating the complex route towards Russian waters. But as the day wore on, the thin line of the horizon had gradually swelled to reveal itself as the line of the barrage that cut off Russian waters from the Gulf of Finland. Andy had explained about the massive sea defences the Russians had constructed, which left only a narrow passage for boats to enter Russian waters via the customs and immigration channel at Kronstadt. Tam had understood the principle. But seeing the reality was something else again.

He couldn't begin to imagine the feat of engineering that had gone into its construction. Andy had told him about the plans to turn the vast dam into a ring road for St Petersburg. But as with so many grandiose Russian projects, this had ground to a halt for lack of funds. Even the barrage itself, which was supposed to prevent flooding as well as to funnel all sea traffic through one channel, had stopped a single kilometre short of the shore.

Yet more impressive than the dam was the city of Kronstadt itself, the fortifications unnervingly solid against the sky, their grey stone as forbidding as the steely waves that beat against the shore. Tam could imagine the daunting impression it must have made on the enemy. Even isolated from the city of Leningrad, its sole source of supplies, it had withstood almost three years of pounding from German guns and still remained in Russian hands, its defences largely intact. Above its grim exterior rose the vast dome of the cathedral, somehow incongruous in so obviously military a setting. "We couldn't have done this a few years ago," Andy observed. "Because it was a naval base, it was closed to civilian traffic." He looked at the chart again. "Time to get the sails down, I think."

He stayed at the wheel, shouting instructions to Tam, who crawled awkwardly around the deck desperately trying to do what he was told without causing any damage. He felt not so much like a bull in a china shop as a carthorse on a tightrope. Boats were definitely not his natural environment. But he managed to lower the sails without mishap and stumbled back into the cockpit, where Andy was studying the Admiralty chart.

"We're aiming for Fort Konstantin. See that unfinished dyke coming out from the south coast of the island? And the buoyed channel? We need to be north of there." He adjusted the course so that the bows swung round gently. Twenty minutes later, they were tied up on a pontoon, the only pleasure boat in sight.

"What now?" Tam asked, nervously fingering his passport.

"We wait for the customs to come on board." As Andy spoke, he spotted a pair of uniformed officers walk down the quay with the swagger of petty bureaucrats everywhere. He readied his own passport and the rest of the paperwork, and arranged his face into a smile of welcome as they boarded. They made an odd couple. The first was tall, blond and narrow-shouldered, his cheeks pocked with old acne scars. The other was short and swarthy, a heavy black moustache shot with silver completely obliterating his upper lip, the buttons of his tunic straining over a round little belly. The dark one said something in Russian. Andy shrugged. "Niet Russki," he said in his best Argyllshire accent. He proffered both passports and the boat's papers. The blond one reached out and began to study them while the dark one continued to ask them something in Russian.

Andy spread his hands in a shrug of incomprehension. The blond man leaned over and tapped the chart. "Where from?" he said with negligent arrogance.

Andy smiled and nodded. He pointed to the chart, drawing their route with a finger. "We came from Helsinki, through the archipelago. Then we stuck to the Sea Channel and crossed the Russian border here, near Gogland Island. That's what we were told to do by the Russian Embassy in Helsinki."

The two men conferred, the dark one sounding irritated, the blond appearing completely unconcerned. Eventually, the blond one turned to Andy. "My colleague thinks you entered Russian waters irregularly."

"Now, wait a minute, pal," Tam protested. "We just did what your people told us to do."

The dark customs official glared at Tam and let fly a stream of Russian.

"Take it easy, Tam. It's OK." Andy's relationship with Sasha had given him some understanding in the ways of the Russian world as well as smoothing their path in St Petersburg. He motioned Tam to one side and opened the lifejacket locker. He took out a bottle of VSOP cognac and placed it on the chart table. "I'd like to apologise for any irregularities," he said.

"Where to?" the blond one asked, adding something in Russian to his companion.

"St Petersburg. We're going to the Navy Yacht Club, like it says in the letter of introduction."

The dark one gave a curt nod. He produced a stamp from his tunic pocket, took the paperwork from his colleague and franked their passports and visas. Then he grabbed the bottle and marched ashore. The blond one inclined his head in gracious acceptance. "Have a safe voyage," he said.

Fifteen minutes later, the Bénéteau was nosing into the harbour to refuel and fill her water tanks. While he was filling up, Andy sent Tam to the harbour office to change their dollars into roubles. He watched him go, glad he'd been able to find something useful for the big man to do. Andy wasn't given much to flights of the imagination, but it didn't take much empathy to understand that Tam must feel on a knife-edge. He knew he'd have moved heaven and earth to get Lindsay back if anyone had snatched her from her home. Nothing would have stood in his way. And he understood that those emotions made Tam a loose cannon. He only hoped Lindsay and Sasha would have everything boxed off by the time they berthed in St Petersburg. Tam was so pent up, there was no telling what he might do if no easy opportunity to rescue Jack presented itself. And Russia was probably a dangerous place at the best of times, Andy thought. Not the sort of environment where you wanted to have responsibility for a guy like Tam on the rampage.

Not for the first time, Andy Gordon wondered what he'd got himself into. But he knew both his friend and his daughter too well to have stood idly by while they got themselves into trouble. Lindsay's original idea to get the boy out to Finland on a train had been doomed to failure, he'd known that instinctively as soon as he'd heard it. And his suggestion of doing it by sea could never have worked without him to skipper the boat. He'd had no real choice in the matter. He gave an involuntary shiver and went below deck to pump out the bilges. Keeping occupied, that was going to be the way to get through this. And luckily, on a boat there was always something that needed to be done. Plenty to keep him and Tam from pondering on the illegalities they were about to commit.

Or so he hoped.

The waitress in the café bar was starting to give them strange looks. Lindsay, Rory and Sasha had been sitting at the same table for four hours without showing any signs of moving. They'd had coffee, they'd had a couple of beers, they'd had aubergines stuffed with cheese and nuts, they'd had bowls of fish *salyanka* then they'd had coffee again. "She can't figure us out," Rory said.

"No. But she will be able to give bloody good description to the cops once they start looking for whoever kidnapped that little Italian boy from the international school," Sasha said dryly.

"We'll be long gone by then," Lindsay said with a confidence she didn't really feel.

"You hope," Rory said gloomily. As she spoke, a dozen children paired up in crocodile formation emerged from the school gates, a teacher at their head.

Even from this distance, now she knew who she was looking for, Lindsay could make out Jack. She glanced at her watch. It was a couple of minutes after two. "Action," she said, turning round to catch the waitress's eye and making the universal sign of scribbling on phantom paper to indicate she wanted the bill.

The children were walking down the street towards them. But the waitress seemed to be in no hurry. She disappeared inside at a leisurely pace. "You follow them," Sasha said. "If I don't catch up, I see you back here. OK?"

Lindsay and Rory waited till the file of uniformed youngsters had rounded the corner before they fell in several yards behind them. At the end of the street, the children crossed a narrow canal. Lindsay pulled her map out of her bag and hastily consulted it. The bridge would lead into a park alongside the Alexander Nevsky Monastery. Where else would a bunch of kids be going? "Playtime," she said to Rory as they followed.

They found themselves on the fringes of a small park. The children were running and climbing around a decrepit play area. The two women cut across one side of the park and made their way up an overgrown mound with the remains of stone terracing jutting out of the greenery. Lindsay waved an arm at the deep pink and white building nearby and read from the guide book. The church had supposedly been built on the very spot where Nevsky trounced the Swedes back in the thirteenth century.

"Let's take it as a good omen," Rory muttered. "We're too obvious here, let's keep walking."

They headed off into the shade of some trees, where the gloom made them harder to see. At exactly twenty-five past two, the teacher blew a whistle and the children lined up obediently. They headed off towards the bridge, obviously making their way back to school. "Do you think they do this every day?" Lindsay asked.

"I bloody hope so. Because it's the best chance we've got. A dozen kids running around like dafties, plenty of bushes for cover. It's tailor made for the job."

140

"We need to figure out the escape route. Let's see what Sasha has to suggest," Lindsay said, studying the map with a frown. At that moment, her mobile rang. She rummaged in her bag and unearthed it on the fourth ring. "Hello, Lindsay Gordon," she said.

"It's me." The familiar voice of her father crackled in her ear.

"Where are you?"

"About thirteen miles from St Petersburg, the wind's a nice force four or five, we should berth in a less than a couple of hours."

"No problems?"

"No complaints. It's been a braw wee sail. This boat's a bonnie mover. Everything all right at your end?"

"Aye. I think we're maybe sorted. Give me a call when you're moored up and we'll come and have a debrief."

She heard a snort of laughter. "A debrief. Aye, right enough." Then the line went dead. Lindsay smiled at the phone and tossed it back in her bag. "The boys are on their way. They'll be tied up in a couple of hours. So we'd better get a move on and check out the territory."

Two hours later, Sasha was driving them down Bolshoi Prospekt towards Lenexpo, the city exhibition and conference centre, behind which sat the basin of the Navy Yacht Club. The combination of heat and humidity was draining but in spite of that, they were in buoyant mood.

"If they do this every day, we can take the boy tomorrow," Sasha had said confidently after they'd scouted out the immediate environs of the park. "I can be waiting with the car on the far side, near Nevsky Prospekt. We will be gone before they realise anything has happened."

Lindsay couldn't help feeling a little perturbed. She never trusted easy pickings, and this all seemed to be much too straightforward.

"What's wrong?" Rory had asked her on the way back to the car.

"I keep waiting for the other shoe to drop," Lindsay said. "I can't believe how everything's just falling into our laps."

Rory shrugged. "Sometimes it goes that way."

"You'd think, having gone to all that trouble to get the boy, Cavadino would have made bloody sure nobody could get to him, though."

"Maybe he figured that bringing him to St Petersburg just made it too difficult all round. And you must admit, it's not exactly been a piece of piss to set this up. I mean, how likely is it that somebody looking for Jack would have a reliable contact in St Pete's? If your dad had been a fireman or a factory foreman instead of a fisherman, we'd have been up shit creek. Me, I'm not in the least surprised they're being a bit complacent."

It made a sort of sense. And since Rory accompanied it with a squeeze of Lindsay's hand, it performed the trick of reassurance.

They turned into the road leading to the yacht club, grateful even in the car for the shade of trees whose leaves were beginning to dry to gold and brown. A short drive brought them to a curved gateway in the pale stuccoed wall. Sasha parked and they got out. Their way was blocked by a rope slung across the entrance. To one side, a youth in grey naval cadet's uniform slouched in a wooden chair. Lindsay looked at Rory and raised her eyebrows. Rory nodded. "Love the security," she said, as they followed Sasha, who merely stepped over the rope without a word.

"Just what we need," Lindsay said. The cadet hadn't so much as flickered an eyelid at their passage.

"They are more watchful at night," Sasha said as he strode ahead apparently untroubled by the heat.

Whatever they'd expected of the Navy Yacht Club, it wasn't what they found. There were no retired Rear-Admirals in blazers with brass buttons drinking gin and tonic in the clubhouse here. Actually, there was no clubhouse. A building that looked as if it might once have housed social facilities was now a factory making sailboards. A broad tree-lined path led to the waterfront. Anyone familiar with the glossy marinas of British yacht clubs would have laughed out loud as they emerged from the trees to see half a dozen decaying wooden jetties jutting out into the basin. Tied up on the moorings was an eclectic collection of boats; a few dinghies, a couple of power boats, a handful of small sailing cruisers and one splendid racing yacht. On the furthest pontoon, Lindsay spotted a trim Bénéteau sporting a Finnish flag. On the cabin roof, Tam Gourlay sat in a folding chair, stripped down to a pair of shorts, his limbs already turning pink. Her father was nowhere to be seen.

"I see we've gone for the high end of the market here,' Rory said, kicking a tuft of dandelions in the middle of the path.

'We have no commercial marinas in St Petersburg yet," Sasha said. "This place used to be pretty smart. But after *perestroika*, the Navy didn't have money to maintain it."

"And anywhere on the water goes to shit really quickly if you don't do the upkeep," Lindsay pointed out.

"Correct. That's why they started opening it up to private visitors."

"Still, at ten dollars a night, they're not going to make enough to turn it round," Rory pointed out. They arrived alongside the boat and Tam got to his feet, a bottle of beer in his fist.

"All right, girls," he called as they boarded. Lindsay noticed Rory looked extremely wary as she clambered carefully into the cockpit.

"Have you ever been on a yacht before?"

Rory gave her a hard stare. "Oh aye. We used to go cruising every weekend in Castlemilk. Of course I've never been on a yacht."

"You never mentioned it," Lindsay said mildly.

"You never asked. Hey, Tam, how're you doing?" she called up to where he towered above her.

"What's the news?" he asked.

Lindsay introduced Sasha and Tam then asked, "Where's my dad?" She had no intention of going through the whole thing twice.

Tam pointed to a vast wooden hangar behind the dock. "He's in there, talking to some Russian about boats."

Lindsay cast her eyes heavenwards. "So, nothing new there, then. I take it this is down to you, Sasha?"

The Russian grinned. "I told him he'd find a friend of mine in there."

"I'll go and get him, then we can discuss our options," Lindsay said.

She found her father with his head in an engine, a gnarled old man standing opposite, hands on hips, a look on his face that dared Andy to work out what the problem was. "All right, Dad?" she said.

Her father straightened up. "It's that gasket," Andy said, pointing to the offending part. "You take that out, and I'd lay money you'll find a hairline crack running through it." Andy nodded a greeting to his daughter and headed for the door of the hangar. "So. Are we going to have this 'debrief' or not?"

Chapter 16

It was just after ten when Sasha dropped Rory and Lindsay off at their hotel. They'd had a council of war and laid their plans, then Sasha had insisted on taking them all out to dinner in a restaurant that boasted the worst cabaret Lindsay had ever seen in her life. The combination of tawdry costumes, Westernised versions of Russian music and a tenor with more eye make-up than Cher had been so bad it was almost good. But the food had more than made up for it, a constant procession of traditional Russian food that had left them all feeling stuffed.

The only thing that had disturbed Lindsay all evening was a look she'd caught in her father's eye. She'd been leaning over to whisper some smart remark about the dancers in Rory's ear when she'd glimpsed him sizing her up. The expression on his face reduced her to childhood. Her mother had always been a sucker for whatever line Lindsay had chosen to spin her, but Andy had always been able to see right through her. That he still had the knack to flood her with guilt infuriated her almost as much as it frightened her how easily he'd figured out that she had something to hide. Something that concerned Rory.

But he'd said nothing, and the moment had passed. The pressure of Rory's knee against hers under the table was more than enough to distract her. She'd probably only imagined it, Lindsay told herself. She was subconsciously forcing herself to feel the guilt that hadn't come naturally.

They piled out of Sasha's Peugeot. "I pick you up at eight," he said. "So don't go drinking in the bar till late."

They waved him off. Lindsay said, "Do you fancy a drink?"

Rory shook her head. "I've had enough. All those toasts. I must have drunk a quarter bottle of vodka. I can't figure out why I don't feel drunk."

"It's the way they pace it, with all the food in between. Or so Sasha says." They turned to go inside.

"He's a sweetie."

"You're not the first one to think so," Lindsay said. "There's a woman ten years younger than me in Invercross who has a wee boy the spitting image of Sasha. There's probably one in every fishing port between Newfoundland and Vladivostock."

Rory giggled. "Bad, wicked Sasha."

"Like bad, wicked Lindsay?" She stabbed the button to call the lift.

Rory looked aghast. "Me and my big mouth." They stepped inside the empty lift. "You're not like that, babe."

"You've only got my word for that. Anyway, is there any difference between one infidelity and a dozen?"

Rory frowned. "Of course there is. I should know. I'm the one who specialises in loving them and leaving them. If anybody's like Sasha, it's me."

They walked down the corridor to their room in silence. Lindsay unlocked the door, then went straight to the duty free bottle of Bowmore and poured herself a stiff measure. "Sure you don't want one?"

"I've changed my mind." Rory reached for the bottle and matched her. Lindsay sat down in the armchair, Rory on the sofa. "Do you want to knock this on the head? Draw a line under last night?"

Lindsay sipped the amber malt, letting the peaty fumes clear her sinuses. She sighed. "No, I don't. It wasn't just some one night stand, Rory. I don't do that kind of thing. It meant something to me. And I think it meant something to you too. So no, I don't want to knock it on the head. But I don't know what we call it and I don't know what we do with it."

Rory stretched out on the sofa, kicking off her shoes. "Let's get one thing straight. You love Sophie, right?"

Lindsay looked confused. "This isn't to do with Sophie."

"I know that. But you do love her, right?"

"Right."

"And you're not planning on leaving her, right?"

"I never said I was," Lindsay said, her voice defensive.

"And I'm not asking you to. That's the last thing I want. I don't do the long game, remember?"

Lindsay dipped her head in acquiescence. "That's what you said."

"But I don't want to be the Other Woman either. I don't want this to slide into some shitey hole in the corner affair where we duck in and out of bed in the afternoon and you tell lies so you can sneak off for a shag."

Lindsay winced. Rory's brutal honesty was uncomfortable, all the more so because part of her had been dreaming the impossible notion of continuing the adventure. "When you put it like that . . . So how do we go on?"

"I don't know if this makes any sense to you. But there'll be times when work takes us out of town. Either or both of us. Maybe even abroad. And then, we can be lovers."

"Out of town doesn't count?" Lindsay said incredulously. "How very male."

"I never said it didn't count. But at least it puts it in a separate box. You have Sophie, I have my little exploits, and when we can seize the moment, away from the mainstream of our lives, we do."

It did have a certain seductive logic, Lindsay had to admit to herself. "And what about if you meet somebody you want to get serious with? What happens then? 'Oh, by the way, darling, you'll have to accept my bit on the side.'"

Rory exploded in laughter. "Yeah, right, like that'll happen. Lindsay, how many times do I have to tell you? I don't do getting serious. And even supposing I did, what would change? We'd just go on being out of towners."

"And what if you wanted more than that?"

147

Rory got off the sofa and crouched down between Lindsay's knees. "I promise you I will never, ever ask for more," she said, suddenly very serious. "This is about fun. About the pleasure we take in each other. It's about a friendship that includes a sexual dimension from time to time."

Lindsay put her glass on the table and leaned forward. "Would this be one of those times?" she asked, closing in for the kiss.

"You might as well make the most of it. This time tomorrow, we could both be in a Russian jail. And I bet they don't do double cells."

Bernie put the phone down gently, staring out of the kitchen window, noticing the stray tendrils of honeysuckle that strayed over the edge of the frame, thick pencil lines against the glass. As they'd arranged, she'd called Tam on his mobile and been amazed by the extraordinary news that Lindsay had tracked down Jack. Not only that, but they thought it would be possible to snatch him back and make a clean escape. In a couple of days, she could be flying out to Helsinki to be reunited with her only child.

Now, her feelings were in turmoil. She was thrilled at the thought of seeing her son again. Her arms ached to hold him, and there was a permanent pit of anxiety in her stomach in his absence. She wanted him with her, no two ways about that. But equally, she wanted him safe.

And safe was not a state he could achieve while Patrick Coughlan knew where she was. Perhaps the time had come to tell Tam the whole story. But that held its dangers too. How would he react to the knowledge that she'd been less than totally honest about her past? Could she really expect him to uproot himself from the city that had always been his home, turn his back on a successful business and go underground as she'd once had to do? And there was always the possibility that he might insist she give Patrick what he was demanding.

That was a risk she couldn't afford to take.

There was one other possibility. She'd run away once before. Maybe she would have to do it again. But if she did, she would have to take Jack with her this time. That meant she could do nothing until he was back in her arms again. And that in turn depended on whether Tam could bring him safely out of Russia.

Nothing had changed. She was still in limbo. With a sigh, Bernie lit another cigarette and picked up the phone.

There was always a trade-off, Lindsay thought. Yesterday, their stake-out had been riskily conspicuous, but at least they'd had access to food and drink and a loo. Today, slouched in the passenger seat of Sasha's car, parked opposite the school, she felt a lot less noticeable, but it definitely scored short on the creature comfort level. Already the car was uncomfortably hot. And the conversation was considerably less entertaining. She'd always liked Sasha, but they'd exhausted all common ground the day before. Somehow, she didn't think Rory would be faring a lot better with Tam at the corner café, though at least she might get some useful info on the seedier end of the second-hand car trade. Andy was back on the boat, stowing Rory and Lindsay's luggage and making sure everything was shipshape for a speedy getaway.

The pupils of the international school had started to trickle in for their morning lessons. Lindsay kept her eyes fixed on the far end of the street, straining to catch the first glimpse of Jack. She hoped Tam would stick to the agreed plan and not try anything daft. Still, if anyone could keep him under control, it was probably Rory.

They didn't have long to wait. Lindsay saw the woman, presumably Bruno's sister, round the corner first. Jack was a couple of steps behind her. But there was a change from the previous day. Where before, the pair of them had been alone, now there was a third person in their little group. A burly man with the waddle of a weightlifter towered above Jack, his shaven head gleaming in the sunlight. A white teeshirt strained across pectoral muscles the size and shape of dinner plates and his forearms looked like ham hocks. "Oh fuck," Lindsay said. "Look. They've got a minder."

"He was not here yesterday?"

"No, I would have said."

Sasha shifted in his seat and frowned. "Maybe he is just an

escort. Maybe the woman is going shopping and he is there to take care of her?" His optimism sounded hollow.

"You're telling me people need protection to shop in St Pete's?" Sasha pulled a face. "Depends what you're going to buy."

They watched as the trio walked up the street and entered the school gates. A few minutes later, the woman emerged alone and headed back the way she'd come. "So much for the escort theory," Lindsay said bitterly.

"We need to revise our plans, no?" Sasha said, winding up his window. "You go off to the café, I'll park round the corner and join you there."

By the time Sasha joined them, the others were staring gloomily into their coffees. "Hey, Sasha. Any bright ideas?" Rory greeted him.

He shrugged. "The park is still the best place, I think."

"But that guy's enormous," Lindsay said. "There's no way we can take him on."

"Want a bet?" Tam growled.

"Don't be daft, Tam. For all you know, he might have a gun in an ankle holster," Lindsay protested. "But even if you could take him in a fair fight, the last thing we want is a ruck in a public park. We'll have the cops all over us. There's got to be a better way of doing it. Maybe Sasha can come up with something. He knows the territory, after all."

Rory stirred her coffee thoughtfully. "I don't think familiarity is the answer."

"How do you mean?" Tam asked.

"We should be cashing in on our unfamiliarity. We're foreigners. We're tourists. And we're women. Well, at least, two of us are."

Lindsay began to have a glimmering of what Rory was getting at. "We play the stranger card."

Tam and Sasha looked bemused, but Rory beamed. "Exactly."

Five to two and everyone's nerves were shredded. Sasha sat in his car at the far end of the monastery park, his fingers beating a random tattoo on the steering wheel. Tam was loitering behind a stand of bushes on the edge of the play area, smoking frenetically, trying to look as if he was casually appreciating the beauties of nature. Rory and Lindsay were sitting in the corner café, bill paid, sipping at the dregs of the glasses of wine they'd ordered to give themselves Dutch courage.

Lindsay anxiously checked her bag, making sure they had what they needed. "God, I hope this works," she said.

"You and me both. Because we're the sitting ducks here. Once we get on that underground train after the snatch, we're rats in a trap."

"Thanks, Rory, that's what I really needed to hear." Lindsay gulped the last of her wine and grimaced at its sourness.

Rory, who had taken the seat facing up the street, straightened up. "Hey, Splash, it's showtime."

"Is the Terminator with them?" Lindsay asked.

"Walking right beside Jack." Rory leaned across the table and clasped Lindsay's hand, momentarily earnest. "Whatever happens, you know I wouldn't have missed this for the world."

Lindsay smiled. "Let's see if you're still saying that in an hour's time."

They waited till the crocodile of schoolchildren had rounded the corner before they followed. Everything was identical to the previous day, except for the presence of Jack's bodyguard. Down the street, across the bridge, into the park, then the children erupted into carefree play. Lindsay and Rory hung back, watching and waiting. The minder had taken up station on the fringe of the playing area, about twenty yards from where they knew Tam was lurking. He didn't take his eyes off Jack, who was running around in a game of tig with three other boys. Whenever Jack went more than half a dozen yards from him, the minder moved to keep him in range. The teacher had her back to them, watching half a dozen children playing a wild game of football.

"Let's go for it," Lindsay said, watching how Jack's game was taking him closer to Tam's hiding place. They walked across the grass, Rory with the guidebook, Lindsay with the map, pretending to argue about where they should be going, stopping a couple of times to look around helplessly. As they drew level with the minder, Lindsay suddenly swerved towards him, Rory trailing in her wake, doing her best to put herself between the man and the object of his attention.

"*Spasibo*," Lindsay began. "How do we get to the Tikhvin Cemetery?"

The man frowned and said something in Russian, sidestepping to bring himself closer to Jack. Rory moved nearer to him, doing the dizzy blonde. "We're lost," she said, giving him the dazzling smile that Lindsay knew only too well was a killer. "The Tikhvin Cemetery?" She pointed to the guide book.

The bodyguard frowned and glanced down at the page.

"*Kladbische*," Lindsay said helpfully, thrusting her phrase book under his nose. *Stay, Tam, stay,* she urged him mentally. It was still too risky.

The bodyguard's face cleared and he said, "*Da, Tikhvin Kladbische.*" But instead of giving them directions, he pushed between them and shouted. "Jack. Come now."

Lindsay's heart sank as Jack slowed to a halt and glared at the minder. "I'm playing," he said defiantly.

The bodyguard covered the few yards between them in seconds. He grabbed Jack's hand. "Stay with me." Then he turned back to Rory and Lindsay. He pointed to the far end of the park. "Go there, to end of street. Then right." He smiled.

Lindsay forced a smile in return and said, "Come on, Rory." She headed towards the bushes where Tam was hidden. "Abort," she said conversationally as they approached. "Stay out of sight, Tam," she added more insistently.

They rounded the bushes and found Tam crouched like a coiled spring. "Fuck it, I'm going for it," he growled.

"Don't be stupid," Lindsay said. "You'll blow the whole thing if you try it now." She took out her mobile and dialled Sasha's number. "Sasha? Abort. We'll see you back at the boat."

She turned back to find Rory and Tam engaged in furious argument. "He's my son," Tam said mutinously.

"We've all stuck our necks out to get this far, Tam," Rory said. "You've got no right to put everybody else at risk. We'll figure something else out for tomorrow. But today's a bust. Leave it."

"She's right," Lindsay said. "We need to figure out a better way of doing this. But we can't do it now. Come away, Tam," she added, taking his hand. "There's no sense in you getting arrested."

"Or worse," Rory pointed out.

The argument was settled by the blast of the teacher's whistle, summoning her charges back into line for the walk back to school. Tam's head dropped and he pulled away from Lindsay, trudging despondently towards the far exit where minutes before Sasha had been waiting.

Chapter 17

There was no need to take the Metro now. Lindsay flagged down a passing taxi on Nevsky Prospekt and managed to communicate their destination. They arrived back at the boat to find Andy and Sasha with tumblers of whisky in their fists. The atmosphere of depression was palpable.

Lindsay poured drinks for the rest of them while they recounted the disastrous operation. Afterwards, they slouched in the cockpit in gloomy silence. It was Sasha who opened the discussion. "We have one more chance, no?" he said.

"That's right," Andy said. "We've only got three-day visas. That means we need to be back at Kronstadt by lunchtime the day after tomorrow. So, realistically, if we don't get the boy tomorrow, we'll have to leave empty-handed."

"No fucking way," Tam stated, pounding his fist against the bulkhead. "Youse can do what the hell you like, but I'm not leaving without Jack."

Lindsay felt a headache beginning at the base of her skull. "That would be one way of making sure neither of you leaves Russia for quite a while," she said tartly. "Look, can we skip the heroics and get down to brass tacks? Obviously, we need a better diversion if we're going to get Jack away from his minder. Any ideas?"

No one spoke for a moment, then Rory said, "Rather than

directly approaching the minder, maybe we should try to think up something that would draw everyone's attention away from the kids?"

"Like what?" Tam demanded.

"I don't know. Maybe Sasha and Andy could pretend to have a fight?" Rory suggested.

"Who'd drive the getaway car then?" Lindsay objected.

"You could. Or I could," Rory said.

"You'd get lost," Sasha said.

"We could practise the route tonight," Lindsay countered.

"I need to be with the boat, Lindsay," her father said. "What if somebody calls the police, and we cannae get away? What happens then? You're stuck with the boy and no way of getting out."

"I can sail the boat," Lindsay said.

"I'm no' disputing that," Andy said. "But all the paperwork is in my name. They Russian bureaucrats, they're not going to wave you through if your papers aren't in order, are they, Sasha?"

The Russian shook his silver head. "He's right, Lindsay. It's too risky. We could all end up in jail that way."

"Have you got a better idea, then?" Tam challenged. Sasha shrugged.

"You know, I think we're making this all too complicated. Keep it simple, that's always the best way," Andy said. They all looked at him in surprise.

"How do you mean, Dad?"

"I wasnae there this afternoon, so I'm just going by what you've all said. But from the sounds of it, this minder's a pro. Would that be right?"

Rory nodded. "He knows what he's doing."

"Right. So at the first sniff of any kind of diversion, his first instinct is going to be to protect the lad. It doesnae matter how clever we get, he's going to do his job. So there's no point in us trying to be smart. We've just got to tackle it head on." Andy's voice was quiet, but Lindsay knew from experience that his low-key approach disguised a stubbornness that nothing would shift. Whatever her father's idea, she had a sneaking suspicion that would be what they ended up doing.

"So, what are you saying, Andy?" Tam leaned forward, suddenly alert.

"Keep it simple, like I said. We've got Sasha waiting in the car, like before. But this time, we wait till the kids are running about, then Tam just walks through the park, picking a line that'll bring him close to where Jack is. Then he just grabs him and makes a run for it. You two," he pointed to Lindsay and Rory, "your job is to buy Tam some time. You wait by the path till Tam passes you, then you get in the minder's road. Trip him up, make him go the long way round, whatever. Just slow him down long enough, then disappear yourselves." Andy sat back and the others looked at him in stunned astonishment.

"It'll never work," Lindsay said. "They're bound to have told the bodyguard to look out for Tam. He'll recognise him."

Sasha cocked his head to one side, considering Tam. "Maybe not if we get rid of the beard and chop the hair off and put him in an FC Zenit shirt..."

"You really think we can hold him up for long enough to let Tam get clear?" Rory asked.

Andy shrugged. "I don't know. I've never seen the guy. But from what you said, he sounds like a weightlifter. They're no' built for speed."

Tam gave a harsh bark of laughter. "And you think I am?"

"It's amazing what the human body's capable of when it comes to your bairns," Andy said. "You'll do just fine, Tam."

Tam held out his huge paw to Andy. They shook. "That's settled, then," he said.

Lindsay and Rory exchanged a bewildered look. "Outflanked by the old man," Lindsay said, shaking her head, half-amused and half-terrified at the thought of what her father had just let her in for.

"We should go back to the park, make sure we all know the ground," Sasha said, swallowing the last of his whisky. "Andy, you must come too, give us an extra pair of eyes."

As they walked back to Sasha's car, Lindsay managed to detach her father from the group and hung back with him. "Tam's really wound up," she said. "I think you need to get him off the boat. He's going stir crazy on there. Is there any chance that you and Sasha can take him out and get him pissed tonight? Maybe the two of you could stay at Sasha's?"

"What about the boat?" Andy asked, casting an apprehensive look back at the Bénéteau.

"I'll stay on board with Rory. We've checked out of the hotel, remember? We can't go back, it'll only draw attention to us. And after we snatch Jack, the cops will be looking for two British women behaving suspiciously. We need to keep a low profile."

"And you two want the place to yourselves, eh?" Andy asked severely.

"It's a small boat, Dad. We're all going to be cooped up there for long enough as it is. But I'm not suggesting this for my sake. Tam needs to let off some steam before he blows up."

Andy stopped and stared hard at his daughter. "That better be the real reason, Lindsay. I've seen the way that lassie looks at you."

"Aye, well, Dad, if wishes were horses, beggars would ride," Lindsay said, using anger to hide her guilt. "Please yourself."

She began to walk away, but Andy put a hand on her arm. "I'll do what you suggest," he said. "Don't let yourself down, Lindsay."

Her father's words echoed in her head hours later as she made up the double berth in the forepeak cabin for her and Rory to share. Was she letting herself down, or was she finding the road back to herself, a road that had been obscured by the forces of habit and affection? It was a question that had no easy answer. She tucked the sheet in under the thin foam mattress as Rory called, "Dinner is served, madam."

Lindsay finished off and joined Rory in the cockpit, where she'd arranged a picnic with the food they'd bought from a small grocery store near Sasha's apartment. There was ham and red caviare, a sweating block of yellow cheese, various flavoured yoghurts, black bread and, improbably, a baguette. They'd supplemented this with bananas, peaches and tomatoes from a nearby kiosk, and a couple of bottles of Georgian red wine recommended by Sasha.

"Looks good," Lindsay said, leaning across to kiss Rory on the mouth.

"I don't know if I can eat much," Rory said. "I never realised you could feel the boat moving even when you're tied up like this."

"You'll get used to it." Lindsay grinned. "Either that or you'll be seasick."

"Gee, thanks," Rory said, cutting off a chunk of bread and smearing it with caviare.

"Just remember it's always better up on deck," Lindsay said. "Poor Sophie gets sick as a dog when she's below. That's why she never used to come on overnight trips with me."

"Did you used to sail in California, then?"

"I learned to sail almost as soon as I could walk. When we were in America, I had a half-share in a thirty-six foot Baltic."

Rory shook her head. "That means nothing to me."

"It's a classic yacht. A colleague of Sophie's found her languishing in a boat yard and he persuaded me to go in with him. It took us the best part of a year to get her seaworthy, but it was worth it. I had some great sails in that boat. I really miss her, especially on a night like this, sitting on the water and just soaking up the peace and quiet."

"So, are you going to get a boat back in Scotland?" Rory asked, uncorking the wine.

Lindsay shook her head. "I can't afford it."

"That's a shame."

"I'll just have to try and hitch a ride crewing for some of the rich bastards who keep their boats up in Invercross. They're always desperate for an extra pair of hands."

Rory grinned. "Either that or we'll have to make lots of money selling stories."

"Maybe." Then a sudden thought stabbed her. "Except I might have another mouth to help feed." She managed to remain in denial about the prospects of parenthood ever since the plane had taken off from Glasgow, but now it was there between them, a monkey on her back that wouldn't stay caged.

Rory reached across and squeezed Lindsay's hand. "Hey, maybe you should try the lottery."

Lindsay burst out laughing. "I think you've used up enough luck for both of us there."

Rory winked. "You mean, you don't think you'll get lucky tonight?"

Lindsay made herself a cheese and tomato sandwich. "I intend to take full advantage of tonight. It could be our last chance for a while."

Rory frowned. "But we're going to be on the boat for another couple of nights, surely?"

"Yeah, but so will my Dad," Lindsay pointed out. "Call me a coward, but that is not going to make me feel relaxed and sexy."

"Duh, silly me. You think he'd tell Sophie?"

Lindsay sighed. "No, I don't think he would. I just don't want him to know that there's anything *to* tell Sophie. It's easier all round."

Rory leaned against Lindsay. "Well, we'd better eat fast, then."

"I thought yesterday was bad, but this is hell," Lindsay muttered to Rory as Tam disappeared inside the bar in search of the toilet.

"If it gets any hotter, Tam's going to spontaneously combust," Rory agreed. They were sitting at a pavement table at a bar on a side street between the international school and the play area. From the safety of his car, Sasha had watched Jack and his minder arrive at school a couple of hours before. He'd stayed put just in case they left early, but so far, Lindsay's mobile had remained silent.

The air was heavy with humidity, the sky coppery and oppressive. It was the sort of day when a thin sheen of sweat covered every exposed piece of flesh, making bodies adhesive. The weight of the weather served only to accentuate the discomfort and drag of hanging around.

Waiting alone with Rory would at least have held an element of pleasure. But with Tam added to the mix, it was grim. He couldn't keep still. When he wasn't smoking, his fingers danced incessantly on the table top. He made Lindsay check her phone every five minutes, just to make sure she hadn't missed a vital call. He kept running his hands over his newly naked chin and the half inch of hair that was all that remained of his thick auburn mop, as if he couldn't quite believe he was still in his own skin.

What was worse was that his nervousness was contagious. Lindsay had started the day feeling fairly calm, but she was growing more and more edgy with every passing minute. "He's doing my head in," she complained.

"He can't help it," Rory said. "He's scared. And if there's one thing a macho Scottish male can't acknowledge, even to himself, it's being scared. So he's hiding it behind impatience. Try and relax, Lindsay." She leaned across to massage Lindsay's neck between her fingers and thumb.

"Oh yeah, right. Relax. That'll work. How am I supposed to relax?"

Rory smirked. "Think of something pleasant. No, actually, skip that. Think of something wildly, extravagantly, sexily fabulous. You shouldn't have to search far back in your memory..."

In spite of herself, Lindsay smiled. Before she could reply, Tam came lumbering back to the table. With his new look and his blue Zenit shirt, nobody from Glasgow would have recognised him. Lindsay herself had had to do a double take when he'd appeared at the boat earlier with her father and Sasha. A bodyguard who'd only seen a photograph would have no chance.

"How long now?" he asked, dropping like a stone into his chair.

Lindsay checked her watch. "Fifteen minutes."

"Right. Gonnae get me a vodka?" he asked her.

"Are you sure that's a good idea?" Lindsay said.

"I need a drink, OK? It didnae do me much harm last night, did it?"

She couldn't deny that. According to Sasha, they'd been drinking vodka till well past midnight, but none of them had a hangover in spite of Tam having reportedly collapsed in a senseless heap on the floor of Sasha's living room. She signalled to the waitress and ordered a vodka, counting out the roubles to pay so they wouldn't have any delay when the time came to move.

When the drink came, Tam swallowed it in one. "Right then," he said. "I'll wait here till I see the kids passing the end of the street. You two better head off, get into position."

160

They stood up. Now the moment was upon them, Lindsay felt curiously solemn. It had to work this time. There would be no third chance. And if they failed, she'd have to deal with the fact that she had let the genie out of the bottle. She realised that, having come this far, Tam could never return empty-handed to Bernie. Impulsively, she gave him a quick hug and kissed his smooth cheek. "Good luck, big man," she said.

He nodded, beyond words, adrenaline and alcohol flushing his pale cheeks. Rory gripped his shoulder. "We'll get it right this time."

They walked off briskly, barely reaching the corner when Lindsay's phone rang. Sasha told her the children had left the school gates, heading in the right direction. He was going to drive straight to the far exit to wait for Tam and Jack. Dry-mouthed, Lindsay passed the message on to Rory, who nodded grimly. In silence, they entered the park and ambled across the grass to the shrubbery where Tam had hidden the previous afternoon. It ran almost to the edge of the path where Tam would attempt to escape with Jack, providing the perfect spot for them to ambush the minder.

As they took up position, a low growl of thunder grumbled in the distance and the sky seemed to darken. Lindsay looked heavenward with a look of dawning delight. "I think we're in for a thunderstorm," she said, hardly able to believe the evidence of her senses.

"Oh, great, just what we need when we're about to go sailing," Rory said.

"Never mind that. If it hits now, we've got the perfect diversion."

Rory got the point and gave a low whoop of delight. "You're right!" Suddenly she started bouncing up and down, waving her arms and dancing in a little circle.

"What are you doing?" Lindsay said, bemused.

"Rain dance." Rory grinned. "Can't hurt, can it?"

Lindsay shook her head, amused in spite of herself. She peered through a jigsaw gap in the bushes and caught sight of the children arriving in the park. Already they were running free. Today, Jack seemed to have joined the game of football, though he was

161

noticeably less frantic that the others in his pursuit of the ball. Another peal of thunder, this one louder than the last, caused a momentary pause in play, but they carried on instantly.

A few minutes later, she caught sight of Tam, strolling casually towards the children. "Oh, smart move," she said softly as he took a line that would bring him to the edge of play. When the ball drifted towards him, he brought it under control and moved into the game, passing it to one of the children. He waved casually at the teacher, and carried on making his way through the players, gradually working nearer and nearer to Jack. One of the boys kicked the ball to Tam and he dribbled expertly towards his stepson. For a moment, it looked as if he would feint past him. Then at the last minute, Tam stooped low, scooped Jack into his arms and took off. As if on cue, the thunder crashed again, a jagged bolt of lightning split the sky and the heavens opened.

Rain sheeted down, adding to the confusion of noise and blurring the rush of movement. Jack was screeching like a banshee, hammering his fists against Tam's shoulder as Tam pounded across the field towards the path. Hot on his heels, the bodyguard had sprung into action, roaring something incomprehensible as he went. The cries of playing children had suddenly turned into screams of panic.

Now Tam was running faster than Lindsay would have believed possible, in spite of the struggling child in his arms. Clearly, Tam's disguise had Jack fooled as much as his minder. He was giving chase, but as her father had rightly surmised, his body was built for strength, not speed, and although he was unencumbered, he wasn't gaining ground fast enough. "I think they're going to make it," she said. "You ready?"

Rory nodded, poised on the balls of her feet. Still peering through the bushes, Lindsay caught sight of the teacher. She was frantically gathering her pupils together, her face blanched as a turnip, her mouth still a round O of shock. Then suddenly Tam was thundering past them, his breathing ragged and painful. "Now!" Lindsay shouted.

Rory stepped into the path, closely followed by Lindsay. The bodyguard was bearing down on them. He tried to swerve at the last minute to avoid them, but Rory kept on walking, driving him towards the grass. He thrust an arm out, pushing her out of the way, but the edge of his foot skidded on the wet grass and sent him sprawling.

He scrambled to his feet, spitting what had to be curses at Rory, and hurtled on after Tam. But the distance was too great. There was no chance he could catch them now, Lindsay thought with satisfaction. "Act nonchalant, look a bit bemused, as if it's all nothing to do with us," she said, steadying Rory and steering her down the path in the opposite direction, taking advantage of the confusion to depart the way they'd come without a backward glance.

As soon as they had cleared the park, they picked up speed, cutting briskly down a side street to the Obvodnogo Canal. Within five minutes, the ugly concrete box of the Moskva Hotel reared up before them. There was no sign of pursuit, and they began to breathe easier as they crossed the busy intersection in front of the hotel and walked into the Metro station. Jubilation welled up inside Lindsay, but she took care to show none of it.

In silence, they rode the Metro to the end of the line then set off towards the Navy Yacht Club from a different direction. Now they were finally able to release some of their tension, laughing in pure delight as they relived the rescue, indifferent to the rain streaming down their faces. They had only walked a couple of hundred yards when Sasha's car drew up alongside. Holding her breath, Lindsay gave him a questioning look.

Sasha grinned and gave her the thumbs-up sign. "All aboard. They wait for you. All you have to do now is get the boy out of the country."

According to Sasha, Tam had barely made it to the car ahead of the bodyguard. "I had engine running and back door open," he said. "Tam threw the boy in and dived on top of him. Poor Jack, he was squealing like a pig, he wouldn't believe it was Tam at first. Anyway, I shot off before Tam even got the door closed. Just as well I did, because the bodyguard was close enough to hit the boot with his fist as I pulled away."

"Did he get your number?" Lindsay had asked, worried for her

163

father's generous friend.

Sasha had tapped his nose with his index finger. "No matter if he did. I got plates from a scrap yard, six o'clock yesterday morning."

They'd never have done it without Sasha, Lindsay realised. She and Rory had been so gung-ho, so convinced they could cut a swathe through whatever Russia threw at them. But they'd been hopelessly wrong. She had to wonder if back in Glasgow, even at some deep subliminal level, the reason she'd been so eager to get involved in Bernie and Jack's problem had been about impressing Rory. Or even about getting Rory on her own, in a foreign environment, in a strange light where recklessness might look like romance.

At the Navy Yacht Club, they ran through the sheeting rain to the boat. Andy, Tam and Jack were below in the steamy cabin, mugs of hot chocolate in their hands. Jack barely looked up as they arrived. He was snuggled into Tam's side, talking nineteen to the dozen about his experiences. The tracks of his dried tears snaked down his cheeks, a vivid reminder of the terror he must have felt when Tam snatched him. "And when Papa went away, I was left with Zia Maria and she made me go to school, and it was horrible, and she wouldn't let me phone Mum, even though Papa promised I could," the boy prattled on. "I hated it. I wanted to come home, but Zia Maria said I had to stay until Papa came back. It was supposed to be a holiday," he added, self-righteous disgust in his voice.

Rory sat down on the bench seat and let out a huge sigh. "We made it."

"So far," Andy said cautiously. "Lindsay?" He gestured towards the cockpit with his head. "A word."

"You need me," Lindsay protested. "Nobody else can sail the boat with you. And in weather like this, you need another pair of hands."

Andy shook his head stubbornly. "They're going to be looking for two British women. You said that yourself. While I was sitting here waiting for you, I realised it was madness to try and take you both out on the boat."

"So I've got to stay behind? Are you sure you're not just trying to keep me and Rory apart?" Lindsay's blood was up now, the adrenaline rush of the snatch reasserting itself as anger.

"Should I be?" Andy said calmly.

"Well, Dad, you should know by now that if you want me to do something, the best way is to tell me I can't. And you should also know better than to stick your nose in my business."

"We're a family, Lindsay. Your business is my business. You should be thinking about Sophie."

Lindsay gave a harsh bark of laughter. "Yeah, right. Like Sophie thinks about me when she makes her decisions. Dad, you don't know the half of it. Everybody always assumes I'm the difficult one. Well, just for the record, it's not always me. OK? Now, let's get this boat under way. We're wasting time we can't afford to spare."

"You're not coming, Lindsay. I've already spoken to Sasha. There's a train out this afternoon. We'll meet you in Helsinki. Just put your own feelings to one side for a wee minute and think about the boy's safety. We're going to have enough questions asked about why Tam looks different from his passport. Not to mention why we've got somebody extra on board."

"OK. So you two go back alone with Jack. Rory and I will get a flight out," Lindsay said stubbornly.

Andy shook his head. "Like I said, they're going to be looking for two British women travelling together. You need to split up."

"So let Rory fly out and I'll stay with the boat. You really could use another pair of hands. And having an extra person on board makes more sense if it's your daughter, doesn't it?"

Andy shook his head. "We thought about that. Sasha doesn't think Rory's confident enough to handle the independent travel."

"It's my story, Dad. Not Rory's."

They glared at each other, impasse reached. Just then, Sasha's bulk appeared in the doorway leading down to the cabin. "Your father is right, Lindsay. I know it's hard, but you're too smart not to see he's right. One of you has to stay behind." He glanced at his watch. "You could be on the quarter to five train to Helsinki."

Lindsay closed her eyes and exhaled noisily. She knew when she was beaten. The boat wasn't going anywhere while they were both on board, and they couldn't afford to let the time drift away from them if they were to make good their escape from Russian territory. She turned away and gazed across the marina to the expo centre. "Get Rory up here," she said.

Sasha called below and moved into the cockpit to let Rory up the companionway. "What's going on?" she asked, her expression puzzled.

"The boys think we need to split up. Because the Russians will be looking for two British women, after our attempt yesterday. So one of us goes with the boat and the other gets the train to Helsinki."

Rory looked stunned. "That's not what we planned."

"Plans sometimes have to change," Sasha said. "It is too dangerous to have you both on the boat."

Rory nodded, seeing his point instantly. "OK. I'll take the train. It makes more sense for Lindsay to stay with the boat, she can help Andy."

Andy smiled in relief. "Thanks, Rory." He raised his eyebrows at Lindsay. "That all right with you?"

Lindsay shook her head ruefully, knowing when she was defeated. "Give me your keys, Sasha. I'll walk Rory to the car. We've got a bit of business to sort out."

They said goodbye in the shelter of a dripping tree that overhung the Peugeot, clinging to each other, neither willing to admit the desperation they felt at this sudden severance. "I'm sorry it's turned out like this. But we'll have a night in Helsinki," Lindsay murmured, nuzzling the soft skin beneath Rory's ear.

"Provided we all make it past the Russian customs."

"We'll make it," Lindsay said, with a confidence she was slowly beginning to feel. "And at least I'll get my copy written on the voyage without you to distract me." She kissed Rory's mouth, trying to imprint it on her memory so she could summon it at will.

They stepped apart and Rory opened the car door. "Safe journey," she said.

Lindsay nodded. "See you in Helsinki."

Chapter 18

The 32ft Bénéteau began to bounce a little on the heavy swell that was rolling in from Kronstadt towards St Petersburg. Lindsay had finished stowing her possessions and was lying back on the bunk in the forepeak cabin, trying to compose her intro and not be distracted by thoughts of Rory speeding through the streets of St Petersburg towards the Finland Station. She was interrupted by a bang on the cabin door.

"Lindsay?" It was Tam.

"You're OK, I'm decent."

The door to the tiny V-shaped cabin opened and Tam leaned in. "Andy wants you up on deck, just to run through what we've got to do at Kronstadt."

She followed him up to the cockpit, where Jack perched on a bench, dwarfed by a scarlet lifejacket that was clipped on to the boat. Andy Gordon never took chances on board. Tam sat down next to the boy, who immediately snuggled under his encircling arm. Neither seemed any the worse for their nail-biting escape, Lindsay thought.

Her analysis was interrupted by Jack. "When will I see my mum?" he asked plaintively.

"In a couple of days. We've got to sail all the way to Finland first. But we'll phone her just as soon as we get you smuggled through the customs," Lindsay said.

Jack looked apprehensive. "What's 'smuggled', Dad?"

"It's like hide and seek. You have to hide and stay really, really quiet for ages. Not a whisper. Because if you make a noise and we get caught, they might put me and Captain Andy and Lindsay in the jail. And we don't want that, do we?"

Jack's grin said he didn't quite believe what he was being told. "Then I wouldn't have anybody to take me back to my mum."

"Correct," Tam said. "So you have to listen to what Captain Andy tells you and do exactly what he says."

"Where are we going to stow him?" Lindsay asked her father quietly.

Andy tugged at the brim of his salt-stained San Francisco 49ers cap. "A wee boat like this, there's not an awful lot of choice. There's not even a sail locker. About the only option is to put him in the under-berth storage and cover him up with clothes. I hope the wee bugger doesnae suffer from claustrophobia."

"And that the Russian customs aren't having a bad day," Lindsay added darkly.

"Aye, well, there's still a couple of bottles of decent brandy to cheer them up a wee bit," Andy said. "Do you want to take the helm while Tam and I get things sorted down below?"

Lindsay couldn't help the thrum of excitement that ran through her as she took the wheel and felt the pull of the boat under her hands. There was nothing quite like sailing, she thought, scanning the set of the sails and glancing at the chart to check her course. Even in a swell like this, there was a tranquillity that was irresistible. No sounds other than the hiss of the hull through the water, the occasional slap of a wave and the crack of a sail.

These steely northern waters couldn't be more different from the blue dazzle of the Pacific. The rain had stopped and the sky was clearing now, but the weather here could turn on a sixpence, and there were treacherous currents aplenty to confuse the unwary sailor. Lindsay inspected chart and compass again, making sure she was sticking to the course her father had pencilled in. Kronstadt was fast approaching. Another fifteen minutes, she reckoned, though she'd have to change tack.

Andy's head appeared in the hatch. "How are we doing?"

"Ten, fifteen minutes. Do you want her back?"

Andy shook his head. "I think it might be better if you bring her in."

"Why?" Lindsay asked, slightly apprehensive about berthing an unfamiliar boat on a mooring pontoon.

"Well, see, Sasha explained this to me. The stamp in your passport says you came in on a plane. They might get a wee bit funny about you going out on a boat, but if you're actually sailing her, it looks more natural." Andy climbed up the companionway. "I'll do the sails when you're ready."

"Did you get Jack hidden away?" she asked.

"He's crawled right into the forepeak. He's a brave wee bugger, I'll give him that. Tam's just arranging your bag and your clothes so he cannot be seen."

For the rest of the journey into Kronstadt, anxiety kept all three adults locked in their own thoughts. The silence was only broken by Lindsay's instructions to her father. Eventually, they tied up and sat waiting for the customs inspectors. This time, it was a long half hour before they finally appeared.

As Andy had warned, they were suspicious of the fact that Lindsay had flown in and was leaving by boat three days before her visa ran out. And when they saw the contrast between Tam's passport photo and his current appearance, it was clear this wasn't going to be a straightforward passage. Neither of the officials spoke English, so there was another delay while an English speaker could be tracked down and brought to the boat.

First, he demanded an explanation for Lindsay's behaviour. "Why are you coming by plane and going by boat?"

"I wanted a little longer in St Petersburg than I would have had if I'd come both ways on the boat." She smiled, attempting innocent reassurance. "I wanted to see the Hermitage and the Russian Museum. And Pushkin's House. Too much for a couple of days."

He pored over her papers. "But you have return flight from St Petersburg," he pointed out.

"I know. It's silly really, but it worked out cheaper that way. A single fare would have ended up costing me more than the return. It was a special deal from the airline." It was bullshit, but it was

169

the kind of bullshit that might just be true, she thought.

"Why are you with these men?" the official asked.

"The older man, he's my father. And the other one is my boyfriend." Lindsay hoped they wouldn't start asking her leading questions about Tam. It was a risky line to take, but one that made more sense than any other.

The official studied her papers again and finally nodded. "OK. But your boyfriend, he doesn't look like his picture."

Lindsay gave an exasperated sigh. "He looks ridiculous, doesn't he? It was so hot in St Petersburg, he decided to have his hair cut and his beard trimmed. But the barber didn't understand what he wanted, and he ended up looking like this."

Tam tried to look sheepish. "I said I wanted to get rid of my hair because it was too long in the heat, and before I knew it, the guy was shaving me as well. I tell you, I'm going to suffer when I get back to Glasgow."

The official frowned. "You will suffer? How will you suffer?"

"How do you think? Everybody's going to laugh their heads off when they see me looking like this," he said. He shook his head. "I can't believe I let this happen to me."

"You can't believe it?" Lindsay said. "I can't believe I've got to walk around with somebody who looks like a moronic thug."

The customs official gave a thin smile. "Please do not tell anyone this is happening in Russia. It is not good for our reputation. Now, I must look at boat."

Eventually, an hour and a half after they had moored, they were free to go, two bottles of cognac and a carton of Marlboros lighter.

Lindsay almost wept with relief. It was only as they hoisted sail, leaving Kronstadt behind, that she realised how taut she had been holding herself. Tam hurried below decks, and she could hear him calling to Jack. The pair of them emerged on deck a few minutes later, the boy giggling in delight at being released from his damp and uncomfortable prison. They all hugged each other, grinning like fools. Andy reached into the chart locker and produced a flat half-bottle of whisky, taking a swig himself before passing it round.

"Christ, I wouldnae like to go through that again in a hurry," he said, hugging his daughter. "See you, Lindsay? You're nothing but trouble."

Tam took his mobile out of his pocket and suggested to Jack that they ring Bernie. The boy agreed eagerly.

"You'll maybe be wanting to phone Sophie before your mobile goes out of range." Andy said to Lindsay.

She shook her head. "I'll wait till we're safe on dry land."

Kevin was snoring softly in the camping chair when Michael dug him in the ribs. "Looks like we've got some action," he said, already on his feet and heading for the door. Kevin stumbled to his feet and hurried out of the flat after Michael, who was taking the stairs two at a time.

By the time they hit the street, the taxi that had pulled up outside Bernie's flat was driving off. "Shit," Michael cursed, running for the car he'd hired using the false driving licence Patrick had supplied him with. Kevin was barely aboard when they screeched out of their parking space and raced after the taxi. "She was carrying a suitcase," Michael said as he turned right in the wake of the cab, earning a blast of the horn from the car he'd cut across.

The taxi had stopped at the traffic lights, and he breathed a sigh of relief. Michael slowed down, allowing another car to slip in between them. They turned in convoy on to Great Western Road and headed out towards Dumbarton. "Where the hell is she going?" he wondered aloud.

"You think she's doing a runner?" Kevin asked apprehensively.

"Who the fuck knows? Maybe they've found the kid and she's going to fetch him? Either way, we better not lose her." He concentrated on keeping a safe distance between them and the taxi. They drove on out through Drumchapel and Clydebank, then turned off towards the Erskine Bridge.

"Isn't this the way to the airport?" Kevin asked.

Surprised that he knew that much, Michael nodded. "I think so."

Kevin's guess proved correct. The taxi dropped Bernie off at the departures entrance. "Get out and follow her," Michael said. "I'll park the car."

Five minutes later, he hurried into the terminal, apprehensively scanning the check-in queues. He spotted Kevin first, leaning against a wall, pretending to read the paper. "Where is she?" he demanded.

Kevin indicated the direction with a jerk of his head. "KLM. She's in the queue for the Amsterdam flight."

"She could be going anywhere," Michael said through clenched teeth as he clocked Bernie. There were only a couple of people in front of her now. Somehow, he had to find out her destination. It wasn't going to be easy; she was looking around constantly, her face a mirror of his own anxiety. But he didn't have a choice. Patrick wasn't a man to whom you could say, "I bottled out." He watched for a little longer, until the man ahead of Bernie handed over his passport and tickets.

"Wait here," Michael said. He noticed a stand containing film developing envelopes and grabbed one in passing. The counter next to the one where Bernie was waiting was empty and he ambled over there without a sideways glance. He leaned on the counter and began slowly filling in the required details on the envelope.

He'd timed it well. Bernie stepped up to the counter, placing her bag on the luggage belt. "Good afternoon," the man on the check-in desk said, reaching for her paperwork. He looked at the tickets, then added, "Your bags will be checked right through to Helsinki, you don't have to worry about them in Amsterdam."

It was all he needed to hear. Michael walked off towards the destination board. The KLM Amsterdam flight was due to leave in a little over an hour. He crossed to the KLM ticket counter and smiled at the woman tapping something into her computer keyboard. "Excuse me," he said. "Is there any chance of me getting to Helsinki this afternoon?"

"I'll just check for you, sir." She hit a few keys then frowned at the screen. "I'm sorry, sir. The connecting flight to Amsterdam is full." She clicked her mouse. "I can get you there first thing in the morning, but this afternoon's impossible."

"There's nothing at all? Not even business class?"

She shook her head. "I'm sorry. The flight's full and I've already got three people on standby."

He wanted to smash her stupid computer over her empty head, but instead, Michael simply turned on his heel and walked away. He pulled his mobile out of his pocket and called the familiar number. "It's me," he said when Patrick answered. "We've got a problem. Our target is at Glasgow Airport. She's going to Helsinki. And I can't get on the flight."

"Why didn't we know about this already?" Patrick demanded. "She must have gone to the travel agent or something?"

"She's not been near a travel agent. I've been on the bitch's tail every time she's been out of the house. She could have booked it on the internet or over the phone or anything," Michael protested.

"Well, this is a fine mess," Patrick said, his voice poisonous. Michael had never heard him show his anger so obviously and it was unnerving.

"What do you want me to do?" he asked.

"There's fuck all you can do, is there?" Patrick sighed.

"We could meet every flight from Helsinki into Glasgow," Michael said. "She's got to come back sometime."

"You think so?"

"Well, either her or the husband. You don't just walk away from a house full of furniture and stuff." As he spoke, Michael knew there was a hole in his logic. If he had a vengeful Patrick Coughlan on his tail, he might be tempted just to walk away from his life and everything in it.

"See what you can do, then," Patrick said grudgingly. Michael's ear tingled as the phone was slammed down at the other end. With a deep sigh, he headed back towards Kevin. He'd already had enough of Glasgow Airport. But it looked like he'd be seeing a lot more of it over the next few days.

Rory stared out of the window of the St Petersburg-Helsinki train. She'd caught the Sibelius express with scant minutes to spare, rushing aboard with scarcely time to thank Sasha for all he'd done for them. He stood on the platform of the Finland Station, waving as the train shrugged into motion.

Rory settled into her seat and took a paperback from her bag. It sat in front of her, unopened, as she looked out across the landscape, seeing nothing. All she could think of was the confusion of feelings that had rampaged through her since she'd said her unexpected farewell to Lindsay. She felt bereft. There really was no other word for it, she realised with painful clarity. She'd never felt that about a lover before. Always, she'd been in charge of the comings and goings; always, she'd been in command of her feelings.

Only once had she experienced this sense of abandonment. Gazing across the Russian landscape, Rory finally understood something about herself. She'd fought to keep the women in her bed out of her heart because she knew only too well what it felt like to be left utterly, to be stranded on the shore when the person you loved had disappeared over an unseeable horizon. She'd never recognised before that she had been building barricades to save herself from being forsaken as her mother had forsaken her.

But Lindsay had somehow crept behind the fortifications and laid claim to the part of herself she had never relinquished before. Rory even understood how it had happened. In the past, she'd always assumed control. She'd been the one who had taken care of business, looked after the details, made things happen. But the moment she had agreed to come on this crazy adventure, she had handed the reins over to someone else and in doing so, she had ceded more than she had realised.

Fuck it, I love her. It was the one thing she had promised she would not let happen, and it had ambushed her. Instinctively she knew that if she let it, this time it could work. But that wasn't the deal. Lindsay wasn't free. And Rory wasn't in the business of busting up other people's relationships. She wasn't about to cast herself as the Scarlet Woman of the West End.

There was only one solution. If she couldn't sleep with Lindsay without letting love come between them, she'd just have to do without her. They'd have their night in Helsinki, because it was just too complicated to explain to Lindsay what had changed. Then they'd go home and it would naturally come to an end. And in a couple of weeks, once the dust had settled, Rory would give Lindsay the brush-off. She'd find the words to let her down easy.

Anything rather than tell the truth.

Fuck it, I love them both. It was the one thing Lindsay had promised herself she wouldn't let happen, and it had ambushed her. *I did this on purpose*, she thought, bracing herself against the deck as the evening dwindled towards night. All those risks, all that recklessness; it had all been about pushing herself so far away from Sophie that there was no way back, to the other side of a chasm where love wasn't strong enough to bridge the distance.

Somewhere in her heart, Lindsay had granted victory to the idea that there would be no future for her and Sophie once the baby was born. On a conscious level, Lindsay didn't have the courage—or the conviction—to make a clean break. So without bothering to discuss it with the rest of her, her subconscious had decided to take steps to drive her away before she had to play out the depressing, long-drawn-out decline and fall of their relationship.

Rory had been the perfect diversion from the straight and narrow. Rory made her laugh. She made her feel accomplished and talented again. She even made Lindsay feel sexy, which had been balm to a soul that felt it was taking second place to a syringe full of sperm in the attraction stakes.

Any other time, Lindsay would have been satisfied with those fillips to the ego. But this time, she had wanted to walk out on the high wire and to hell with a safety net.

Well, she was paying the price now. Her eyes were on the sea, but her vision was of Rory. She sailed on automatic pilot, her mind constantly replaying the past few days and inventing alternate futures she knew could never happen.

For the irony was that now she understood the mechanism behind her love for Rory, she could no longer play the game out as Blind Man's Bluff. It was like a magic trick; once you knew how it worked, it couldn't fool you any longer. Knowing what Machiavellian tricks her mind had been conjuring, she couldn't pretend fate had taken things out of her hands and left her its helpless victim.

She had to go back to Sophie and do her best to make it work. She'd let herself love Rory, and it was going to hurt like hell to keep that as her dirty little secret. But keep it secret she must. Rory hadn't asked for love and didn't want it. Admitting to it would hurt everyone.

But mostly, it would hurt Sophie, who had done least to deserve it. "Time to grow up," Lindsay growled, checking the compass one more time and correcting her course accordingly.

Sophie stretched her legs out on the window seat and leaned against the wall. She wondered where Lindsay was and what she was doing now. They'd spoken briefly the previous evening, when Lindsay had told her of the failed attempt to rescue Jack. She almost wished Lindsay hadn't made the call, for anxiety had kept Sophie awake most of the night.

Partly, she was anxious for Lindsay, afraid that her lover would blunder into some disaster that would keep her from home for an unimaginable time. But mostly, she was anxious for them both. The worst of the phone call was not what they had said, but what they had been unable to say.

Sophie was under no illusion about how hard she was driving Lindsay. If she had felt any choice in the matter, she would have backed off. But no one who had not felt the inexorable demand for a baby could begin to understand its overwhelming hunger. It informed every minute of her waking life. It was like a constant, discordant background music to every action and thought. It was implacable and inescapable. It had hit her like a tidal wave rising out of a calm ocean, and it had battered her ever since.

It had cast her uncommon decency and fairness to the winds. Sophie had lost herself to this imperative that had turned her into a baby factory. She didn't like it. In fact, mostly she hated this invasion. But it was undeniable. The only thing that would calm the turbulence was a baby. All she could do until then was cling to the wreckage and pray she would survive.

The big question in Sophie's mind was whether Lindsay would find a lifeboat and set sail without her.

Chapter 19

The sun was still shining as they went about, ready for the approach into the harbour at Helsinki. The weather had meant near perfect sailing for the past three days, and the atmosphere on board had been surprisingly light and playful. Andy seemed to have relaxed once they had cleared Kronstadt and Lindsay made the most of the rare opportunity to share quality time with her father.

Lindsay sat in the bows, legs dangling over the side, enjoying the cooling spray that tickled her skin. "Lindsay, can you put a couple of reefs in the mainsail?" Andy shouted from the cockpit.

Lindsay scrambled to her feet and made for the mast, noting that Tam was putting his weight into the winch that furled the big genoa sail. It was nearly over. In a matter of minutes, they'd be tying up at the quay and the proper journalistic work would begin. Rory had called from Helsinki to say she had already negotiated a deal with one of the Scottish tabloids for the full story of Jack's rescue and his reunion with his mother, while Lindsay had written the copy, leaving out her and Rory's part in the drama. All they had to do now was take some photographs with the digital camera, garner some quotes from Bernie, Jack and Tam and insert them into the story. They could transmit the whole package from Helsinki and it would be in the papers within hours of them returning to Scottish soil.

Lindsay leaned against the mast and put a hand up to shield her eyes from the late afternoon sun. They were still too far from the quay to distinguish any individual, but she felt sure Rory and Bernie would be there waiting. Tam had called Bernie at her hotel in Helsinki an hour earlier, warning her of their approach. Then he'd phoned the airport to confirm they were all on the next day's flight to Amsterdam and then onwards to Glasgow. It was going to be some celebration, Lindsay thought. And then home to Sophie. Which would be a different kind of celebration. It didn't make a lot of sense to her, but in spite of all that had happened with Rory, a large part of her was still looking forward to getting home, still eager to be reunited with Sophie.

At her father's instruction, she lowered the main sail completely, feeling the throb of the engine through the fibreglass hull. The harbour loomed ever closer, till at last Lindsay could make out two figures standing on the quayside. "Jack," she called excitedly. "I can see your mum. Can you see her?" She pulled the small digital camera out of the pocket of her shorts and took a few shots of Tam holding Jack up so he could see Bernie. The look of sheer delight on the small boy's face was a reward in itself for the anxieties of the past week. His grin split his face from ear to ear, and he was waving both arms in a salute.

They'd barely come alongside when Tam plonked Jack ashore. Mother and son sprinted towards each other, Lindsay's camera bearing witness to every stride. Tears streamed down Bernie's face as she gathered her son into her arms and crushed him to her breast. Lindsay couldn't hear their words, but that was as it should be. Some things were just too personal.

She looked up and caught Rory's eye. The electricity between them made her feel suddenly weak in the knees. To hell with good resolutions. They could wait for tomorrow.

The "fasten seat belts" sign illuminated above their heads as the plane began its approach to Glasgow Airport. Lindsay glanced across the aisle to the line of three seats where Jack sat sandwiched between Tam and Bernie. Tam was glowing with delight and pride, but Bernie was more subdued. Lindsay couldn't quite figure her out. The woman should be overjoyed to be reunited with her son. But there was something off key in her response, just as there had been at their first encounter.

Lindsay couldn't quite put her finger on it, and she hadn't had the chance to discuss it with Rory, since Andy had pointedly sat between the pair of them on the flight. But it was as if behind Bernie's delight there was a lurking and continuous edge of fear. Maybe she was simply anxious that Bruno Cavadino would react badly to being thwarted. Whatever it was, it was eating her up from within. She must have lost a stone in weight since they'd first met, Lindsay thought. Her clothes were hanging loose on her, and her face had gone from pleasantly full to gaunt.

Oh well, there was nothing she could do about it, she told herself. Her involvement was over now. She and Rory were the visiting firefighters who parachuted in, did what they had to do and walked away, leaving people to get on with their lives. She didn't imagine they'd be seeing Tam and Bernie again after the follow-up stories to the rescue. The time they'd spent together had been intense and had produced a false sense of intimacy. But in her experience, once the dust had settled, the subjects of such intense scrutiny usually withdrew sharply afterwards, almost embarrassed by the extent to which they'd let strangers into their lives. It was the nature of the game, and it didn't really bother her. She understood the difference between real closeness and its simulacrum.

To Lindsay's surprise, Sophie was waiting for them at the airport. She tried to hide the awkwardness she felt introducing her to Rory, camouflaging it behind their farewells to the Gourlays, who were heading for the taxi rank. Tam engulfed her in a hug. "I'll never be able to thank you enough," he said. "What you've done for us, it's nothing short of a miracle. Any stories I come across, they're yours."

Bernie's farewell was more formal. She hugged Jack to her and extended a hand to Lindsay, then Rory. "I appreciate what you did. It took real guts. Thank you."

Then they were gone. "I better go and get myself a taxi too," Rory said.

"Don't be silly," Sophie said. "Lindsay told me you live near us. I'll drop you off."

Lindsay realised she'd been right to think that what had seemed so simple and straightforward in St Petersburg was fraught with discomfort and danger here in Glasgow. It wasn't that she feared Rory would say or do anything that would give their secret away. It was more that having the pair of them in such close proximity made her feel confused, and confused wasn't ever the best way to steer a sensible course. "You'll stay with us tonight, Dad?" she asked as they loaded their bags into Sophie's car.

"Of course he will," Sophie said. "You're not thinking about driving home tonight, Andy. I won't hear of it. There's a leg of lamb roasting in the oven, you'll have dinner and a good night's sleep before you even think about getting behind the wheel of your Land Rover."

Andy grinned. "You'll get no argument from me on that score. Lindsay, you get in the front with Sophie, I'll be fine here in the back with Rory."

He really does know, Lindsay thought. And not because of anything he'd witnessed between them. He knew simply because he knew his daughter too well for her own good. And she minded. Not because he would ever say anything to Sophie; he was far too fond of the woman he regarded as his daughter-in-law ever to hurt her like that. But because she valued his good opinion, and knew that he couldn't understand what had impelled her into behaviour he would only ever interpret as disloyal and disreputable. Nothing, she reminded herself, ever happened in a vacuum.

They dropped Rory off at her flat and headed home. It was, Lindsay thought afterwards, one of those rare, apparently perfect evenings. The food was delicious. Sophie was relaxed and mellow, Andy was in fine form, full of tall tales and tittle-tattle about the inhabitants of Invercross. Lindsay herself was simply happy to be home, her first major story under her belt and the sense that for the first time since she'd come back to Scotland, the prospects looked bright.

Just after ten, Andy yawned and stretched. "Well, I'm away to my bed. It's been a long day. Good night, girls."

He left them in the flickering light of the candles that gleamed against the rich wood of the dining table. The wavering flames cast a flattering glow on Sophie's skin, emphasising the brightness of her eyes and the sparkle of the silver strands that shot through her curls. "You look particularly beautiful tonight," Lindsay said, surprised at the sudden flare of desire she felt for her lover.

Sophie smiled. "And it doesn't occur to you to wonder why that might be?"

"If I said the candlelight is flattering, that would spoil the moment," Lindsay teased. "I suppose it's because I haven't seen you for the best part of a week."

Sophie shook her head. "Try again."

Lindsay struggled. There was nothing obvious; no new hair-style, no tinted eyelashes, no sunbed tan. "A clue?"

"What makes women bloom?"

Lindsay's stomach flipped and settled with the dead weight of a stone. "It worked?" she said, feeling the ground beneath her feet plummeting away from her.

"It worked. I'm pregnant."

Lindsay was waiting outside Café Virginia when it opened the next morning. After her father had left, the house had felt too claustro-phobic to contain her. She'd gone for a short run, her ankle still too fragile for anything sufficiently cathartic. Then she'd showered and taken the bus into town, reluctant to meet Rory outside a work context.

She needn't have worried. By half past eleven, there was still no sign of her business partner. Lindsay felt faintly disconsolate. Her story on the rescue of Jack Gourlay had made the splash and spread of the *Standard* and she wanted to share her moment of glory. She also wanted to lay her head on the table and weep because Sophie's news had left her in the grip of a profound panic that threatened to engulf her. She couldn't deny that a small part of her rejoiced for Sophie's triumphant delight, but mostly she was scared of what this would mean.

181

It was so early. So much could still go wrong. Sophie could easily miscarry. There could be a problem with the foetus. Then there were all the things that could turn nasty during pregnancy. Sophie might be blooming now, but there was no guarantee that would last. And then, if she somehow made it to term, birth was still such a bloody, dangerous business. Lindsay didn't even want to look at what lay beyond birth. How could she be a parent when she couldn't even organise her own life in a sane and sensible fashion? What would she do if Sophie stopped loving her?

None of it bore thinking about.

So Sandra Singh's arrival felt like a small gift from the gods. Sandra plonked herself down opposite Lindsay and wrestled her cigarettes out of her bag. "Hiya," she said. "I see Splash Gordon's back with a vengeance," she added, prodding the pile of newspapers on the table. "Nice one."

"It's always encouraging to get a good show," Lindsay admitted. "Especially when it involved taking as many chances as this one did. Though we did have a lot of fun in between the scary bits."

Sandra raised her eyebrows. "So I hear. Rory and I went out clubbing last night. She told me all about it."

"Ah," said Lindsay.

"Don't worry, she's not a blabbermouth. But we're best pals, we tell each other everything. And it stops there. Your secret's safe with me." She shook her head as her coffee arrived. "My, but you like to live dangerously."

"Sometimes you just have to get on the rollercoaster," Lindsay said. "Life's hardly worth living if you don't take the odd risk."

Sandra spooned sugar into her coffee and stirred it. "Maybe. But I can't help thinking it might have been better all round if you hadn't got on this particular fairground ride. I don't think it's passed its health and safety inspection. And I hate to see anybody get hurt needlessly."

Uh oh, Lindsay thought. *The gypsy warning from the best friend. Break her heart, I'll break your legs.* "I hear what you're saying, and I think your concern is commendable. But there's no reason why anybody should get hurt, Sandra."

182

"That's easier said than done. There's more to Rory than meets the eye, you know."

Lindsay's smile was entirely spontaneous and it lit her eyes. "I think I'd worked that one out for myself. Sandra, trust me. I'm not going to break her heart."

Sandra gave her an odd look. But before she could say more, Rory herself appeared, looking hangdog and hungover. "What the fuck was I drinking last night?" she groaned as she eased herself into the booth.

"You ended up on tequila slammers with wee Ian Harvey," Sandra said. "That was after five gin and tonics, two Zombies, several bottles of that disgusting lemon alcopop and a rum and Coke."

Rory groaned. "I wish you hadn't told me that. Now I know it's going to get worse before it gets better."

Annie dumped a cappuccino in front of her and shook her head in disgust. "You need a Bloody Mary," she said.

Rory shuddered. "No, don't. Remember we've got a Human Rights Act now."

"Look, Lindsay got the splash and spread," Sandra said, waving the paper in front of her.

Rory managed a wan smile. "That should put you back on the map, babe. Me, I wouldn't have touched the story, but you were right to go with your instincts."

Sandra finished her coffee and her cigarette. "I'm out of here," she announced. "I've got to meet some guy at the modern art gallery. Apparently he makes sculptures out of sex toys. Which probably means he'll win the Turner Prize next year."

They watched her leave in silence. Then Rory looked blearily at Lindsay. "You're awful quiet for a woman who should be celebrating her return to the big league. Is it just out of respect for my hangover? Or is there something I should know about?"

"There is something. But it's not what you think," Lindsay added hastily, seeing the hurt spring up in Rory's eyes. "This is not about us." She ran a hand through her hair. "Sophie's pregnant."

Rory's eyebrows arched. "Is she sure?"

"She's a fucking obstetrician, Rory. Of course she's sure," Lindsay snapped.

"OK, OK, don't take it out on me." She reached across the table and covered Lindsay's clenched fist with her hand. "How are you feeling about it?"

Lindsay sighed. "I don't know. Scared, mostly. It's like everything in my life is going to change, and I have no idea how. I feel like I've got no choices, no control over what happens next. And I've just got to go with it."

"Sounds about right to me. Because you're not about to leave her, are you?"

"No, I'm not. I know you're the last person I should be saying this to, but I love her. I can't face the thought of losing her."

Rory shook her head. "Who else would understand that better than me? Of course you're scared. Anybody in your shoes would be. She's sprung this on you, backed you into a corner and given you no choice about something that is totally life changing. But you've got nine months to get your head round the idea. And for what it's worth, I think you'll make a great parent."

"Thanks. Look, can we talk about this another time? I just wanted you to know, but I think I'm still in a state of shock."

"Sure." Rory rubbed her eyes then yawned. "I'm supposed to be meeting Giles for lunch. Do you think I'll live that long?"

Lindsay grinned. "Probably. I'm going to stay here and plough through the local papers. And maybe a punter will bring me a wee titbit of a story, given that we've been away for the best part of a week and there must be something somebody's dying to tell us."

Rory stretched and yawned again. "Oh God, I'd better go." She slid out of the seat and turned to go.

"You really shouldn't have got so drunk," Lindsay said, amusement in her voice.

Rory glanced over her shoulder. "You shouldn't have made me miss you." She poked her furred tongue out at Lindsay. "Only joking. But it was worth it for the look on your face."

Only joking? Lindsay thought. She fervently hoped so. Because the only way she was going to be able to keep her own divided emotions under control was by convincing herself that Rory did not, would not, could not feel the same turbulent surge of emotion and desire that had her in its grip. Believing that, Lindsay could stick to the conviction that revelation would only lead her to rejection. Keep it light, that was the way to deal with it.

How hard could that be?

Patrick Coughlan stared at the newspaper spread across his desk. He'd been relieved when Michael had called him the previous evening to report that Bernadette had turned up at Glasgow Airport with the boy and her husband and that they'd gone straight home. The couple of days she'd been out of his reach had made him edgy and tense, something which both his staff and his perpetually embittered wife Mary could attest to. Knowing she was back where he could put his hand on her whenever he wanted to was satisfying.

But he'd been horrified by Michael's call suggesting he get hold of a copy of that morning's *Scottish Daily Standard*. He'd sent one of his counter girls straight down to the big newsagent's in town to pick up a copy. And there she was, plastered all over the paper again, complete with the dramatic story of her husband's rescue of the boy from a Russian park. The man clearly had more balls than brains, Patrick thought. He supposed he should be grateful to Tam Gourlay for doing his work for him, because there was no denying that any threat to the boy was what kept Bernadette firmly in line.

But Patrick was far from happy. He had a sneaking suspicion that Bernadette was trying to outflank him. Perhaps she thought that if she kept herself in the public eye, it would make him back off.

She couldn't be more wrong, he decided grimly. If she wanted to play this game out in the full glare of the media, so be it. He'd give them something to write about. Something she couldn't argue with. Something that would surely make her hand over what was rightfully his. Something very special indeed.

Rory groaned. "It's not nice to mock the afflicted, Giles," she complained, warily sipping the glass of brandy he'd insisted she drink.

"I'm not mocking, Rory," Giles said. "I'm telling you the truth. Madonna and Guy are absolutely not buying a house in Drymen."

"Oh well, you lose some and you lose some." But even through her bleariness, Rory could tell there was more that Giles wasn't telling her. There was a twinkle in his eye that suggested there was more to come. "What?" she said. "You're not telling me the whole story here."

Giles nodded. "Well spotted. Your tip did check out, in the sense that I managed to find three top notch estate agents who finally admitted that yes, they'd been showing properties to Madonna. So I got on to her people, and they were adamant that I was mistaken. So I gave them a list of dates when my contacts said that Madonna had been in Glasgow looking at Scottish estates. And her PA came back with a list of other places where she'd definitely been on those dates."

Rory had perked up at the sniff of a mystery. "How very curious," she said.

"So while you were in Russia, I made some other calls and I found an estate agent in Perth who had been approached by someone purporting to be representing Madonna. They'd made arrangements to view an estate near Gleneagles. So I turned up with a pic man and we fronted up the alleged Madonna and her PA, who had, incidentally, stayed the previous night in a suite at Gleneagles at the estate agency's expense." He paused for effect.

Rory leaned forward. "And? Come on, the suspense is killing me."

Giles grinned. "'Madonna' turned out to be an unemployed actress from Edinburgh. She and her mate had hit on this scheme for getting freebies from estate agents. They've been swagging nights in luxury hotels, free meals, limos, the lot, from these estate agents desperate to flog their prestige properties to a celeb client. A lovely little con, really."

Rory burst out laughing. "Gotta love it," she said. "So what happens now?"

'We're running the story across six and seven tomorrow."

"And what about the women? Are the agents going to have them prosecuted for fraud?"

Giles shrugged. "I suspect the estate agencies will let it lie. It makes them look too silly if they go to the cops. So, although it didn't quite stand up, we ended up with something even better."

"You know, that story is the best hangover cure I've come across in ages." She raised her glass. "You made my day, Giles."

"All part of the service. Now, tell me all about Russia."

Chapter 20

Lindsay's prediction had come true. Just after the lunchtime rush, a middle-aged man with cropped hair and the smartest leather jacket she'd seen in a long time eased into the booth opposite her. "Are you Rory McLaren?" he asked.

"I'm her business partner. Lindsay Gordon. Anything you were going to tell Rory, you can tell me."

He looked slightly dubious. "I don't know. The friend who told me I could trust Rory, he didn't say anything about you."

Lindsay gave him her most reassuring smile. "That's probably because we've not been working together very long. Look, I understand your reluctance, and if you want to come back another time when Rory's here, I'm not going to be offended. But you're here now. You might as well do what you came for."

"I need to be sure you'll keep me out of this," he said. "It could cost me my job if it comes back on me."

Sensing a thaw, Lindsay nodded. "You don't have to worry about that. I've been keeping confidential sources under wraps for years." She pulled a self-mocking face. "It's got so my girlfriend complains I won't even tell her where I get my gossip from."

Forty minutes later, Lindsay was in possession of the bare bones of a story that she thought could be dynamite. Her source was a Senior House Officer at a city hospital, and he was concerned because surgical equipment designated for single use only was being employed several times. "It's not hygienic, and with some pieces of equipment, it's just not safe," he'd told her. "We've already had a couple of near-tragedies on the operating table, and it's only a matter of time before somebody dies." He'd given her several leads to follow up, and she was looking forward to bottoming the story.

By the time she'd finished writing up her notes of the interview, it was too late to start work on the investigation. Rory still wasn't back from lunch, and Lindsay guessed she might have taken her hangover home to bed. She might as well take an early cut herself. On the way home, she stopped to buy a huge bouquet of designer flowers for Sophie, secure in the knowledge that the *Sentinel*'s coverage of the kidsnatch story would mean she could pay for it out of her own pocket.

Although she was home before five, Sophie was there before her, feet up in the living room, a pile of papers on her lap. "Good to see you're taking care of yourself," Lindsay said, presenting the flowers with a flourish.

"They're beautiful," Sophie exclaimed, pulling Lindsay down so she could kiss her. "Thank you. I decided to bring some work home with me because I was feeling a bit sick. Of course, it passed as soon as I got back here, so now I feel like a fraud."

"You're pregnant, you've got to look after yourself," Lindsay said gruffly, leaving the room to put the flowers in water. When she came back, Sophie had put her work to one side.

"How was your day?" she asked.

"Did you see the *Sentinel*?" Lindsay asked, placing the vase on the floor in front of the fireplace.

Sophie's hand shot up to cover her mouth in an expression of horror. "Oh, Lindsay, I'm sorry. It completely slipped my mind."

Trying not to show her disappointment, Lindsay shrugged. "No big deal. It's not like you've never seen me get a splash and spread before. Besides, it wouldn't do your street cred any good in the university to be seen reading the tabloid press."

"I'm really sorry, love. I know it was important to you, I should have remembered."

Lindsay perched on the arm of the sofa. "Well, at least my business partner noticed. And was impressed."

"I'm glad. She seems like a nice kid, Rory."

"Hardly a kid, Sophie. She's been in the game a good few years, she's running a freelance business that's successful enough for her to be able to give me a job."

"I guess it's a sign of old age, when the journalists start to look like children," Sophie said, trying to make light of it.

"I told you we were too old for this parenthood business," Lindsay said, not entirely joking.

"You underestimate yourself, Lindsay. And besides, a child will keep us young."

Lindsay winced. "I'm not sure I want to be young. Rory came in this morning with the hangover from hell. You should have seen her. I swear to God her face was green, and the whites of her eyes were somewhere between pink and yellow. She'd been out clubbing with her pal Sandra till all hours. It sounds like they drank a distillery between them. I think I do old better."

"Well, that's hardly a mature attitude to business, turning up in a state like that. It's not exactly going to inspire confidence in the sources or the customers."

"Come on, you know how drinking still goes with the territory here in Scotland. Rory's perfectly capable of doing what she needs to do, regardless of how much she's had to drink or how little sleep she's had." Even as she spoke, Lindsay realised how protective she sounded. *Careful*, she warned herself.

"I didn't realise that working with Rory meant you had to become her staunch defender too," Sophie said, a spike of malice in her voice.

"Feeling a bit hormonal, are we?" Lindsay flashed back at her.

"Don't turn it back on me, Lindsay. This is your reaction we're talking about."

"Well, you don't even know her, and here you are, sitting in judgement on her. You've no idea what she's like."

Sophie cocked her head on one side. "So what is she like?"

"She's very smart, she's good company, she's very funny and she's totally professional. Believe me, we were in a couple of tight spots in Russia, and she was absolutely on the ball. I can't think of anyone I'd rather have had in my corner."

"So I gathered from your conversation over dinner last night. Rory this, Rory that, Rory the next thing. You sounded like a teenager with a crush."

Lindsay stood up abruptly and walked across the room to the window. "Now you're talking rubbish. Come on, Soph, we'd just come back from a really dangerous job, running on adrenaline. Of course I had to decompress, talk it out of my system."

Sophie raised her eyebrows a fraction. "And that's all it was?"

"I'm not even going to dignify that with a reply," Lindsay said, forcing outrage into her voice. She didn't quite know how it had happened, but she was out there on the thinnest of ice, hearing it creak under her words. She'd never believed in lying to Sophie and she didn't want to start now.

"It's not like you to be lost for words."

"Well, maybe that's a sign I'm finally acquiring the maturity I'm going to need if I'm going to be a parent."

"If?"

Lindsay sighed. "OK, when."

"You don't sound very certain."

"I'm certain."

"You sure Rory would approve of her new employee embarking on parenthood?"

"This has got nothing to do with Rory. You know I love you. I wouldn't be here if I didn't."

"Suddenly we're on to love? Where did that come from, Lindsay? Why are you hiding behind declarations of love? More to the point, what are you hiding?"

Lindsay shook her head in frustration. "I can't talk to you when you're in this kind of mood. I'm going to cook the dinner."

"Never mind dinner." Now Sophie was on her feet, moving to cut off Lindsay's route to the door. They faced each other, a couple of feet apart. Sophie tried to keep the fear that had burned in her for days out of her voice. "We need to talk about this. I know when you're hiding stuff from me, Lindsay. Are you sleeping with her?"

Lindsay's eyes widened in shock. She'd never had any problem with avoiding the truth when bullshit was the route to nailing a story. But she had never looked Sophie in the eye and delivered absolute falsehood. "This is stupid," she said, trying to find a way round the question.

"Answer the question, Lindsay. Yes or no. Are you fucking Rory?" Sophie's face was white, her whole body tense as a gun dog on point. She'd forced this moment of truth and she couldn't back away from it now, whatever the cost.

Lindsay closed her eyes momentarily. "I slept with her."

The words hung in the air, vibrating with a terrible life of their own. Sophie gasped, then slapped Lindsay so hard her ears rang. Lindsay recoiled, her hand automatically going to her scarlet cheek. "You bastard," Sophie said in tones of utter contempt. "You absolute bastard. I'm sitting here, going off my head because I don't know if I'm pregnant or not, and you're escaping from your life, shagging some bimbo in St Petersburg."

"Look, that's not how it was," Lindsay said, groping fruitlessly for a response that wasn't a wretched cliché.

"That's exactly how it was." Tears stung Sophie's eyes and she turned away to prevent Lindsay seeing her pain.

"You make it sound like I had it all planned out." Lindsay put out a hand to Sophie, who shrugged it off violently.

"Well, didn't you?"

"Of course I didn't. Jesus, Sophie, what do you take me for?"

Sophie turned back, eyes blazing. "I take you for a coward, Lindsay. Hedging your bets. 'If Sophie's pregnant, hey, that's OK, I can just run off into the sunset with Rory.'"

"You're so wrong," Lindsay said desperately. "What happened between me and Rory was not about you."

"No, it was all about your perennial bloody selfishness. You don't like your life? Trade it in for a different model. That's what you've always done."

"That's bullshit."

"Is it? Think back to when we got together. You didn't like the way Cordelia was making you feel so you cheered yourself up by diving into bed with me."

Lindsay stepped back as if she'd been slapped again. "That's not

192

true. You think we'd still be together if you'd been nothing more than a diversion? Come on, Sophie, you know that's not how it was."

Sophie shook her head. "No, Lindsay, I don't know how it was. I thought I did, but that was when I thought I knew you. Only, the person I thought I knew wouldn't have betrayed me the way you have, so I can't trust anything I believed about our relationship now. The fact that you're shagging Rory turns everything on its head. Nothing means what it did before."

Lindsay shook her head, trying to find the words to ease Sophie's hurt. "Nothing fundamental has changed, Sophie. You're still the most important person in my life. Yes, I slept with Rory. I won't pretend it was just a bit of fun because that would insult all of us. But it was in a different dimension to what goes on between you and me. You're the one that I love. I've never doubted that, not for a minute. I'm not about to trade my life in for something else. I couldn't leave you."

Sophie flushed a deep scarlet, anger flooding her face. "How dare you? You stand there and tell me you're sleeping with some-body else and I shouldn't be worried about it because it's in a different dimension? And you're very kindly not going to leave me? Well, that's really big of you. So, what are you planning on doing? Moving Rory in here? Dividing your nights between the two of us?"

Lindsay held her hands up, palms outward in a placatory gesture. "Look, it happened. It's not going to happen again."

"You seriously expect me to believe that? When you're spending more time with her than you are with me?"

Lindsay ran her hands through her hair in a gesture of helplessness. "I made a mistake, OK? I won't be repeating it. We can get over this. It doesn't change the way I feel about you."

"It bloody changes the way I feel about you," Sophie shouted. "You just expect me to forgive and forget? I don't think so."

Lindsay hung her head. "I'm sorry."

"Well, you took your time to get the apology in. Too little, too late, Lindsay. We always agreed we would be monogamous. It was basic. It was who we were. You can't break something so funda-mental and expect everything to go along like it did before. This is it, Lindsay. It's over."

"You don't mean that."

"I've never meant anything more. Get out. Just get out of my sight, out of this house."

"This isn't the way to deal with this, Sophie. We've got to talk about it. I love you." Lindsay felt the ice break under her feet, felt herself falling, swallowed by the black cold of Sophie's rage.

"No, you don't. You bastard, you only love yourself. Don't you get it? There's nothing to talk about. Not any more. Just get the fuck out. Now!" She reached for a heavy pottery bowl on the nearby table and threw it at Lindsay with all her strength. "Get out!"

Lindsay dodged the missile and backed towards the wall. The dish clattered to the floor and split into smithereens on the pol-ished wooden boards. "Listen to me," she pleaded, on the edge of tears herself now. "I love you."

In reply, Sophie picked up an African soapstone carving. As her arm came back, Lindsay dived for the door. "And don't fucking come back," Sophie screamed. The ornament hit the wall with a sickening thud.

Dazed, Lindsay stumbled for the front door, grabbing the satchel that held her laptop and her wallet. She closed the door behind her then leaned against the solid wood, hot tears spilling down her cheeks. Not for the first time in her life, she thought her heart would break. But this time, she had nobody to blame but herself.

Chapter 21

It was raining, of course. A bleak, dismal rain that sheeted out of a sky gone prematurely grey. After she'd stopped shaking, Lindsay had climbed into her car and stared unseeingly at the distorted world through her windscreen. How could she have blown it so badly? Why couldn't she have dredged up enough journalistic skill to lie for once? Or at worst, having been honest, why couldn't she have found the words to explain to Sophie what she herself knew—that whatever she felt for Rory, it was irrelevant because it didn't change one iota of her feelings for Sophie?

Instead, she'd provoked the sort of explosion that would leave a permanent crater in her life. Even if she could persuade Sophie to take her back, it would always be there, a hole in the road for unwary feet to stumble into. Not that she had any confidence that she could worm her way back under Sophie's guard. Sophie might be the most generous and warm-hearted person Lindsay had ever known, but when she felt betrayed, she was adamantine. She didn't so much bear a grudge as stuff it and wall-mount it in a prominent position. The despair that Lindsay felt then was no self-indulgence; it was realism.

She leaned her head on the steering wheel and moaned softly. The thing she couldn't get her head round was that in spite of the fact that the pain inside her was as fierce as a physical injury, she didn't actually wish undone what had happened between her and

Rory. Was that simply what Sophie had characterised as her perennial selfishness? That she wanted to have her cake and eat it? Lindsay thought not; she really wasn't greedy in that way. She still couldn't escape the notion that the feelings she had for Rory were too important to let them go by her. The paradox was that, equally, they weren't worth losing Sophie over.

She turned the key in the ignition. Sitting in the rain wasn't getting her anywhere. But then, where could she go? She didn't have any close friends in Glasgow any longer. She certainly wasn't going home to her parents, to face the reproach in her father's eyes. And she couldn't really afford to check into a hotel. There was only one real option, but pursuing it would be the most reckless of all her recent risk-taking. If Sophie found out she'd gone straight to Rory, she really would have burned her bridges.

Bernie sat by her son's bed, reading him a chapter of *Harry Potter and the Goblet of Fire.* Nothing measured up to the comfort of having Jack home again. Tam had called to say he was going out for a drink with a client, he'd be home soon after seven. Then they'd all be under one roof again, the way it should be. She didn't blame Bruno for what had happened, not really. He only wanted the best for Jack too. But she couldn't help being grateful for having Jack by her side. Even if that wasn't the safest option. But she'd think about that later. For now, it was enough just to luxuriate in his presence.

The ringing of the phone broke into her calm like a brick through a greenhouse. She jumped up hastily and ran through to the kitchen. "Hello?" she said cautiously.

"You've been leading me a merry dance, Bernadette."

Patrick's voice chilled like walking into a butcher's freezer. "It wasn't my fault," she blurted out.

"So you say. Look, I'm running out of patience. You had no right to behave the way you did to me. I was always generous to you and yours, Bernadette. And now I want what's mine."

"I know you do," she whispered. "I know."

"Tomorrow, then? I'll meet you when you take the boy to school."

"No," she said sharply. "No."

"You're telling me you won't hand over what belongs to me?"

"I can't." The phone slipped from her fingers and fell back into the cradle. She knew that hanging up on Patrick Coughlan might be a disastrous move. But she couldn't take his voice for a second longer.

She couldn't live like this. She had to do something. Slowly, she picked up the phone and dialled Lindsay's mobile number. But before it could connect, she replaced the receiver. She couldn't afford to ask for help this time. She had to figure out an escape route alone.

Rory opened her door, looking ten years younger than she had that morning. "Hey, Splash, come in," she said instinctively. Then she took in Lindsay's appearance. "What's the matter?" She pulled her into a hug without waiting for a reply.

At first, Lindsay said nothing. It was enough just to be held. Almost anyone would have done. But this was Rory, she reminded herself as soft lips nuzzled her neck. She took a deep, shuddering breath and said, "I'm homeless."

Rory leaned back so she could check whether Lindsay was joking. But there was no mistaking the sincerity in the red-rimmed eyes. "You'd better come and sit down and have a drink and tell me all about it." She took her hand and led her through to the kitchen.

Lindsay slumped in a chair and said nothing while Rory poured them both a whisky. "She threw me out." She swallowed half her drink in a single, eye-watering gulp.

"Do I need to ask why?"

"She asked me a straight question. I tried to dodge it, but she kept on at me." Lindsay looked up, her face asking forgiveness. "I'm sorry, but I can't do barefaced lying to people I love."

Rory tried not to let her consternation show. "So you told her we've been sleeping together?"

197

Lindsay sighed. "I tried to explain, how it wasn't about her, but she wasn't exactly in the mood for listening. Look, I'm sorry to land on you like this, but I don't have anywhere else to go. Can I stay here for a couple of nights, just till I get myself sorted out?"

"Of course you can. Stay as long as you want. No strings. Just don't answer the phone, that's all."

"What? You don't want me to put your other women off?" It was a pathetic attempt at humour, but at least she was trying.

"No, moron. I don't want you to wreck your chances of getting it back together with Sophie. If she calls here, I'll just tell her I've not seen you outside work. Of course, if she turns up at the door with a breadknife, you have to come to my rescue."

"That would be so beneath her dignity," Lindsay said sadly.

"Well, that's a relief. Look, I'm sorry I got you into this mess. This wasn't part of the master plan."

"Don't be sorry. I'm not. I don't regret one minute of what happened between us. I just wish it hadn't blown up like this."

"Me too. I wouldn't hurt you for the world," Rory said, suddenly very serious.

Lindsay rubbed her hands over her face. "What a fucking mess. I handled it so badly."

"I don't think there's a good way to handle the moment when you tell your lover you've been shagging somebody else," Rory said dryly. "Not if monogamy's the deal."

"Maybe not. Maybe your friend Sandra should have issued the gypsy warning before we went to Russia."

Rory frowned in confusion. "What do you mean?"

"Sandra gave me the hard word this morning. You know? 'Don't go breaking her heart.' That one. She should have spoken sooner. Maybe I'd have paid attention if I'd thought you and me getting together was on the cards."

Rory felt puzzled. It wasn't like Sandra to interfere in her love life. Unless she had figured out that Rory was getting in too deep. Rory couldn't imagine how Sandra had realised something she herself had only acknowledged the night before. "Well, it's too late for that now," she said. "And speaking of late, I'm supposed to meet Sandra for a curry in twenty minutes. Come on, we'll drown our sorrows in vindaloo."

Lindsay shook her head. "I'm not in the mood. Either for curry or for company."

Rory considered for a second. "OK. I'll give her a bell, tell her I need a rain check. I can see her any time."

"No, don't be daft. I'll be fine. You go out and enjoy yourself. I'm better on my own, honest."

"Are you sure?" Rory really didn't know what to do for the best, but she was inclined to take Lindsay at her word. She hadn't noticed her being backward in making her needs known in their short past, and she didn't see why that should have changed just because her emotions were in turmoil.

"Aye, I'm sure."

"I'll just show you where things are, then." Rory gave Lindsay a whirlwind tour of the flat. "My office, use the desk if you want to plug your laptop in, there's a modem connection on the wall. Bathroom, help yourself to smellies. Spare room..." She looked a question at Lindsay, who shook her head ruefully. "Thought not. OK, here's the mistress bedroom. House rule is I sleep on the left." She turned and pulled Lindsay into her arms. "I know it's a fucking mess," she said softly. "But it'll get sorted."

"You sure about that, are you?"

Rory grinned wickedly. "Trust me, I'm not a doctor. Listen, I'm off. I might be late, don't wait up, OK? I'm perfectly capable of waking you up when I need you..." She kissed her hard on the mouth, her tongue flickering along the inside of her bottom lip. "Take care, OK?"

Then she was gone. Left to herself, Lindsay mooched back to the kitchen and refilled her whisky glass. It felt strange being on Rory's territory without her, as if she were an intruder. At least Rory hadn't treated her bust-up with Sophie as an opportunity to move in on her. She'd obviously meant what she'd said about this being a friendship with sex as an added extra. *What a pity I can't manage to be that sanguine myself.* Faced with the events of the evening, Lindsay couldn't resist the dark truth that somehow, she was managing to love two people simultaneously. And it was ripping her up.

She flicked through a couple of magazines but she couldn't settle. She needed to offload the disaster on to someone else. If there was nobody available in the flesh, she'd have to make do with email to bridge the distance and the time lag between herself in Glasgow and her friend Roz in California.

Lindsay unpacked her laptop and went through to set it up on Rory's desk, as instructed. She had to push a pile of papers to one side to make room, and a glossy brochure slithered to the floor, revealing what looked like a poem written in Rory's familiar hand. Curious, Lindsay glanced at it, not meaning to spy. But the title caught her eye and she couldn't resist.

Russian for Beginners

There is a word missing.
Between the wishy-washy and the helter-skelter,
there exists nothing.
Avoid the dizzy plunge of the word that, once spoken,
cannot be ignored,
the four-letter word that shocks
much more than "fuck",
and what remains?
"Fond" is for maiden aunts and pussy cats,
a faint insult lurking in its shallows.
"Care" is better, but still too burdened with the freight
of obligation.
But sometimes,
"love" is just too big,
too soon,
too terrifying to presume.
So we resort to foreign tongues,
hiding fear behind an unfamiliarity
whose very strangeness makes declaration safer.
Ya tebyeh lublu.

Lindsay read it through twice, not quite wanting to believe the freight of meaning held captive in those twenty lines. She was surprised on so many levels; that Rory would resort to poetry; that

Rory knew even one word of Russian, never mind three; but mostly that it looked as if Rory was being as cagey about her emotions as Lindsay was herself.

So where exactly did that leave them?

The rain was lashing the Clyde coast, making navigation difficult, especially when the destination was no official harbour. But the small motor boat chugged on through the waves that threatened to swamp it, eventually nosing into a small sheltered cove south of Wemyss Bay. The helmsman flashed his leading lights on and off a couple of times and a reply came immediately from the shore in the form of a powerful torch beam that cut a narrow slice in the black shoreline. The boat made for the light on the shore, the engine throttled back as far as it could be and still allow for forward passage. The bows ground on shingle and the helmsman immediately put the twin propellers into neutral.

Above the scratchy beat of waves dragging at pebbles, he shouted to the man in the bows, "That's as near as I can get her. If you jump for it, I'll pass you the stuff."

Patrick Coughlan was out of his element on the water, but he swallowed his unease and clambered over the safety rail then let himself fall into the water. The sudden arrival of solid ground under his feet made him stagger. He'd expected the drop to be farther. He looked back up and saw the helmsman looming above him, a heavy holdall dangling over the gunwale of the boat.

"Hang on a minute," he called. Turning towards the shore, Patrick bellowed, "Kevin, get your arse over here."

The torch beam split the night again, illuminating Patrick up to his thighs in freezing water. Then he was cast into shadow once more as Kevin moved between the light and the boat. "I'm here, Patrick," he said.

"Grab this bag, will you? And don't get it wet," Patrick instructed, lurching away from the boat towards dry land. He aimed for the torch, losing his feet a couple of times in an ungainly scramble up the pebbled beach. "Jesus," he said as he drew level with Michael. "I hope you've got a towel in the car." He shook Michael's hand.

"Good to see you," Michael said.

"Everything we need is in the bag." They watched Kevin struggle out of the water towards them, the holdall clutched to his chest. "Are we all set?"

Michael nodded. "It won't take me long to put it together. Tomorrow morning, you said?"

"No time like the present. It's time Bernadette realised she can't hold on to what doesn't belong to her."

The trio headed towards the top of the beach, where the hire car was waiting. "What was it she took from ye, Patrick?" Kevin panted.

"You'll know soon enough, son." The geniality in Patrick's voice surprised Michael. Either Patrick was very confident of success, or else he was so focussed on the next step that he wasn't looking at the big picture. Either could lead to carelessness of a kind of which Michael had never suspected Patrick capable.

He hadn't been worried about the operation before. But now he was.

Rory drained her bottle of beer and signalled to the waiter for another. She raised an eyebrow and Sandra shook her head. "I'm OK for now."

"By the way," Rory said, her drink replenished. "What was all that about this morning? Giving Lindsay the hard word about not breaking my heart?"

Sandra looked baffled. "What?"

"She said you were doing the protective best friend bit. You know. Warning her off hurting me."

Sandra laughed so loud the couple at the next table in the Indian restaurant pursed their lips and looked away. "Talk about getting hold of the wrong end of the stick. I was warning her, right enough. But I was warning her about you. Trying to stop *her* from getting serious, getting her heart broken by the queen of the one-night stand."

"Well, thank you, Sandra," Rory said sarcastically. "Just what I needed."

Sandra gave her a long, considering stare. "My God, you've fallen in love."

Rory's glare should have been heat enough to light the cigarette Sandra pulled from her packet. "Your words, not mine."

"Maybe. But that doesn't make them any the less true, does it? Oh Rory, poor you." Sandra leaned across and patted Rory's hand. "All those women who would have given their right arm for a relationship with you and you couldn't give a damn about any of them. And then when you do fall, it's right into the middle of the briar patch."

Rory gave Sandra a tired smile. "Something like that. It's just too complicated, Sandra. I don't want to be the reason for her splitting up with Sophie. Because she's not ready to leave her yet, and she'd always blame me deep down."

"That's quite an insight for somebody that makes a cult out of not doing relationships."

"The spectator always sees more of the game," Rory said.

"So you haven't told her how you feel?"

"Of course I haven't." Rory's distress was obvious to Sandra, even through the tone of irritation. She sighed. "It's chewing me up, all this pretence. I've never felt like this about anybody before, Sandra. I never let myself. But Lindsay just slipped under my guard." She closed her eyes. "It's so fucking hard."

"I know," Sandra said. "So what are you going to do about it?"

Rory gave her a steady look. "Keep on lying. What else can I do?"

"You could always try telling her."

"She doesn't need that right now. And frankly, neither do I. Just let me get through this in my own sweet way. Get it out of my system and get back to normal."

"Oh, Rory," Sandra said. "I'm so sorry."

"Not half as sorry as I am." Rory made a self-mocking snort of laughter. "I should be happy, shouldn't I? The woman I love is in my bed, waiting for me to come home and make mad, passionate love to her. And instead, I can't think of anything worse."

Chapter 22

Bernie grabbed the two slices out of the toaster as they popped up and slathered them with butter. She put one in front of Jack and leaned against the counter, munching the other herself, waiting for the kettle to boil for a second cup of tea. Tam tucked into his scrambled egg and mushrooms, chattering away to the boy about their plans for the weekend.

"We could go to the football, if you fancy it," he said. "I can get tickets for the Jags, no bother. What do you say, wee man?"

Jack smiled through a mouthful of toast. "Brilliant," he said. "Can we go swimming on Sunday?"

"We'll see," Bernie said. "Just because you've been to Russia doesn't mean you get spoiled when you come home."

Jack laughed, knowing he would get his own way. He usually did with his mother. Suddenly, his expression changed to one of consternation and he pointed at the window. "Tam, look behind you," he said urgently.

Tam swung round, all senses alert. But there was nothing to be seen. When he turned back to the table, however, his last mushroom had mysteriously disappeared, and Jack's mouth looked suspiciously full. "Wait a minute," he complained.

Jack swallowed hard. "Too late, you missed the mushroom thief."

Tam laughed and leaned over to rumple the boy's hair. "Some

places, you'd get your hands cut off for that."

"Are you taking me to school in the car today?" Jack asked, pulling away from Tam's hand.

"You know Tam only takes you when it's raining. And it's not raining this morning. I'm walking you." Bernie told him. "If you don't get some exercise, your legs will wither away and fall off."

"You're making that up," Jack said.

"No, she's quite right, son," Tam confirmed, a serious look on his face. He wiped his plate with his last piece of bread and stuffed it into his mouth. "I need to get on my way. I'll see youse tonight." He jumped up and grabbed his jacket off the back of the chair, leaning down to kiss Jack on the top of his head. He swung Bernie into his arms and planted a smacker on her lips. "Have a good day," he said over his shoulder as he hurried out.

"Are you glad to be home?" Bernie asked Jack as he drank down his milk.

He looked up at her, white moustache stretched into a smile. "You bet," he said. "You can't read what the Russian Pokemon cards say."

It took a moment for Lindsay to realise where she was when she woke. The bed felt wrong, the light was wrong, the background hum of the street outside was definitely wrong. Then memory swam into focus and the previous evening was there in the front of her mind, inescapable. She turned her head to check the other side of the bed. Rory lay sprawled on her stomach, her head turned away from Lindsay, her breathing almost inaudible. It was the only thing that didn't feel wrong, although Lindsay knew it was the one thing that should be incompatible with her desperate desire to see Sophie, to talk to her, to try to get things straight between them.

She hadn't heard Rory come home. Not surprisingly, the emotional drama of the previous evening had left her drained, and the several whiskies she'd worked her way through in the course of the evening had set the seal on a deep sleep. Secretly, she was glad Rory had let her slumber on. It would have been too easy to take the wrong sort of comfort there. It wasn't what had happened between Lindsay and Sophie that would have made it wrong; it was her new understanding of what Rory truly felt for her.

Lindsay slipped out of bed, trying not to disturb Rory. She scooped up her clothes and headed for the bathroom. Twenty minutes later, she was showered and dressed. Her first instinct was to head for home, to force Sophie to talk to her. It was still early enough to catch her before she left for the university. But that wouldn't get Lindsay anywhere. If she was going to stand any chance of persuading her lover that they still had a future, she'd have to wait for the first flare of Sophie's anger to subside. Better to find something more constructive to do with her time.

She left a note for Rory in the kitchen: Woke early. I've gone into the Sentinel office—I promised Bernie and Tam a set of photographs, I thought I'd go and sort it out with the picture desk. See you in Cafe V. later. Love, L. There was a lot more she wanted to say, but a scribbled note wasn't the appropriate medium. Maybe later, on the nearest they had to neutral territory, in the café.

The *Sentinel* office was still quiet when she walked on to the newsroom floor. Twenty to nine in the morning, and only the assistant news editor and a few reporters were at their desks. A couple were reading the opposition, and a third had a phone to his ear, doing the police station calls. Lindsay recognised him from her own days as a news hack and sketched a wave as she crossed to the picture desk. "Are you Gerry?" she asked the chubby, balding man flicking through the morning papers.

He looked up, appraised her as low value and returned to the *Herald.* "Aye, I'm Gerry," he said. "Who's asking?"

"We've spoken on the phone. I'm Lindsay Gordon," she said. "The Russian kidsnatch?"

Now she had his attention. "Oh aye. Nice pix. What can I do for you, Lindsay?"

"I wanted a set of the snaps, for the punters."

He nodded. "No problem. Can you hang on a wee bit till some of the team crawls in? Then I'll sort you out."

Lindsay nodded. "No problem. I'll find a quiet corner." She

moved over to the reporters' area and sat down at a vacant desk, grabbing a couple of papers as she went. She had just opened *The Guardian* when the phones all round started ringing. Five or six of them, all at once. Even after the duty staff picked up, there were still a couple trilling out, including the one in front of her. Lindsay picked it up. She could always take a message.

The breathless voice on the end of the phone was like a time machine. Suddenly she was back at the sharp end, a young reporter who still believed that the great stories would arrive down a crackly phone line, delivered with almost incoherent urgency. She'd learned differently since then, but this time she was listening to the exception that proved the rule. "Is that a reporter I'm speaking to?" the voice said, the words tumbling over each other in its eagerness. An elderly man, by the sounds of it.

"I'm a reporter, yes," she said calmly, automatically reaching for the pile of scrap paper on the desk and raking in her bag for a pen.

"There's been an explosion. A car bomb, by the looks of it. You should see it, it's hellish. Flames shooting up, black smoke, the whole shebang."

Startled into alertness, Lindsay said, "Where about are you speaking from?"

"My house."

"Where's that?"

"Kinghorn Drive. North Kelvinside.'

Cold fear gripped Lindsay. It couldn't be. It had to be a coincidence. "And you say a car blew up in the street?"

"That's right, hen. I was sitting at the window, eating my All Bran. Fellow that lives just down the street on the other side, I saw him come out the door. Got intae his Jag and boom! The whole lot went up."

"I'll need to take your name and address," she said, on automatic pilot now. She scribbled down the details then got off the phone. They'd need to speak to him later for eyewitness quotes. But that would keep. She jumped to her feet and hurried towards the newsdesk, suddenly aware that everyone else was doing the same thing.

Everybody was speaking at once. "Car bomb...West End...cops aren't confirming...ambulance on their way...Where's Kinghorn Drive?"

Lindsay cut through the noise. "Kinghorn Drive is where Bernie and Tam Gourlay live. The Russian kidsnatch family."

Andy, the assistant news editor turned to her, his face blank. "You saying this is something to do with your story?"

"I don't know. It's just a funny coincidence, that's all. My caller said the car was a Jag. And Tam Gourlay drives a Jag."

Andy fiddled with his stringy pony tail. "Are you free to do a shift for us? Only, I think you should go out with the first car, take a pic man."

"I think so too," Lindsay said grimly.

Kinghorn Drive was like a war zone. A pall of greasy black smoke hung in the still, damp air, trapped by the high canyons of the sandstone tenements. Already, police crime scene tape cordoned off the epicentre of the blast, keeping back the ghoulish spectators drawn to disaster like herring gulls to landfill. Lindsay let the photographer lead the way, pushing through the crowd until they could get no closer. She stared uncomprehendingly down the street where, about fifty yards away, a blackened chassis was all that remained of what she feared was Tam Gourlay's Jaguar. The cars that had been parked on either side were twisted and crumpled from the impact, their window glass shattered in sparkling shards across the road. Sniffer dogs strained at the leash as their handlers systematically swept the area. A distorted voice through a loudhailer was asking people to evacuate the buildings without panic. Anxious residents were still emerging in ones and twos, escorted away from their homes by solicitous police officers.

It was impossible to take in. Lindsay knew she should be going through the motions, finding eye witnesses and accumulating copy. But all she could do was stand and stare. As she watched, an ambulance threaded its way down from the far end of the street and stopped yards short of the bombed-out car. She watched as the door of Tam and Bernie's flat opened and two policemen emerged, almost carrying Bernie between them. A woman officer followed, Jack a cowering bundle against her chest.

Professional responsibilities forgotten, Lindsay gave into purely human instincts. She ducked under the tape and sidestepped the flak-jacketed cop who tried to stop her. Picking up speed, she made it to Bernie's side just as they reached the ambulance. "Bernie," Lindsay gasped. There was no response.

A police officer tried to move her to one side as they loaded Bernie in through the rear doors. "I'm a friend of the family," Lindsay insisted.

As if to back her up, Jack raised his head and caught sight of her. He held his arms out towards her and screamed, "Where's Tam? I want Tam." He wriggled free of the policewoman and threw himself at Lindsay, who automatically folded him into her arms and stroked his hair.

The ambulance attendant stood impatiently by the doors, waiting to close them. "Look, either get in or move away. This lady's in deep shock, she needs to see a doctor."

Lindsay had no intention of hanging around to argue with the police. She struggled up the steps of the ambulance, made awkward by her burden, and collapsed on the seat opposite Bernie. "Bernie," she said softly. "Bernie, I'm so sorry."

This time, there was a reaction. Bernie looked up and mutely held her arms out to her son. He dived on to her lap and buried his face in her shoulder. The ambulance moved off, blue light flashing, the occasional two-tone blurt of the siren clearing their path. Bernie kissed Jack's hair, then stared bitterly at Lindsay.

"I as good as killed him," she said, her voice a strained whisper. "The day I let him into my life, I as good as killed him."

Lindsay shook her head. "You mustn't think that. Why should it be anything to do with you and Jack?"

Bernie looked at her as if she was stupid as well as culpable. "Poor, poor Tam. Never had an idea what he was getting into."

"You mustn't blame yourself. Tam loved you; he wanted to be with you and Jack. That was all he cared about." Lindsay didn't know what was going on here, just that she needed to keep Bernie talking.

Bernie shook her head in wonder. "I thought it was safe. But I was wrong, God help me, I was wrong. I told him, you stood there and listened to me telling him. But the pair of you got your teeth into it, and that was that. I should have stopped it before it started. I should have thrown you out my house."

"Are you seriously saying you think Bruno made this happen?" Lindsay didn't want to sound like a cop or a hack, but she couldn't ignore the obvious implication.

"I'm seriously saying if you and Tam had let things be, he'd still be alive now." Her voice wobbled, but still the tears didn't come. Bernie rocked to and fro, clutching her whimpering son to her, her eyes like stones.

Lindsay told herself it was shock and hysteria talking. The notion that an Italian diplomat would even consider a car bomb a reasonable weapon in a childcare dispute was not only bizarre, it was ludicrous. There had to be another explanation. But what could it be?

Before she could probe further, the ambulance shuddered to a halt and the doors swung open. "Go home, Lindsay," Bernie said roughly. "Stay away from things you don't understand." She swung round and carefully clambered out of the ambulance, leaving Lindsay to stand and stare after her.

Among the cars, taxis and ambulances that drove in and out of the Western Infirmary, the Vauxhall Vectra parked in the disabled bay didn't warrant a second glance. Michael Conroy sat in the driver's seat, cleaning his nails with his penknife. Kevin leaned against the passenger door, frowning in concentration as he watched people come and go through the Accident and Emergency doors.

A taxi pulled up and Patrick Coughlan emerged, glancing quickly around before he climbed into the rear seat of the Vectra. "Neatly done, boys. At last."

"I still don't see why," Michael said.

"That's why I'm where I am and you are where you are, Michael," Patrick said, the geniality of his tone doing nothing to hide the steel beneath. "Now, boys, I want you to make sure that where the bitch and the boy go, you go too. See that you let me know what's happening."

210

Without further ado, Patrick got out of the car and walked off towards the street. As soon as he was a safe distance away, Michael shifted in his seat and scowled. "It's not right, this. It's too personal. And personal leaves traces."

"I don't hear you saying that to your man," Kevin said.

Michael jabbed his knife blade into the newspaper folded on the dashboard. "I want to go home in one piece."

Lindsay walked out of the A&E entrance and leaned against the wall. Since she couldn't use her mobile inside, she'd already dictated her copy from a payphone in the waiting area, which had turned out to be a bad idea. She took out her mobile and called the newsdesk of the *Sentinel*, to check there were no queries on what she'd already sent. "Hi, Andy. It's Lindsay."

"You still at the hospital?" he demanded.

"They threw me out. One of the cops overheard me filing copy on the phone and that was that. They had me out the door so fast I left skidmarks."

"Bastards. At least you got some good quotes off the grieving widow. Nice one, Lindsay. So what's the real story on Tam Gourlay? You've just spent three days on a boat with him, you must have got some sort of idea what the big secret was."

Lindsay frowned. "As far as I know, there is no story. He was just a second-hand car dealer. A pretty straight one, by all accounts."

"No such thing," came the cynical response. "There must have been a sideline."

"Not that I know about."

"Well, what about the wife?"

"What about her?"

"She's Irish, isn't she? Car bombs, that's very IRA."

Lindsay couldn't believe she was hearing this. "Just because Bernie's Irish, that makes her husband an IRA target?"

"Don't shoot the messenger. I'm just passing on the off-the-record from the cops. So far, it looks very like one of the republican factions. So stick with the wife. See what you can find out."

"Andy, I'm not going to get near Bernie now. As soon as the

doctors are finished with her, the cops are going to be all over her."

"Never mind. Just stick with it."

"Fine," Lindsay sighed. So much for the new life. She'd barely been back in the game five minutes, and already she was stuck with exactly the kind of pointless task that had made her despair of the job all those years ago. Not only that, but she was homeless.

Where, she wondered, was the rewind button?

Chapter 23

Café Virginia was half-empty, the lunchtime rush still some way down the line. Two young men gazed soulfully into each other's eyes like a pair of Labradors. A few singles read the papers and drank coffee. Annie was polishing glasses to the sound of Horse closing her eyes and counting to ten, and Rory stared gloomily at a bottle of Rolling Rock. Giles Graham slid into the booth opposite her.

"Terrible news," he said.

Rory nodded. "I keep getting flashbacks of the three of them on the plane. They were so bloody happy."

"At least he wasn't taking the lad to school."

"Fucking Pollyanna."

"Thank you, vicar. Where's Lindsay?"

"I have no idea," Rory said. "She was going into your office first thing, I'm assuming she got caught up in the story. I tried ringing her a wee while ago, but the mobile was switched off."

Just then, Lindsay walked through the door and headed straight for the back booth, pausing only to ask Annie for a large whisky. She dropped to the bench next to Giles. "Hell of a business. I just wanted to say I'm really sorry," he said before she could speak.

"It makes no sense," Lindsay said wearily. "They're saying it looks like the IRA, but that makes no sense whatsoever. Tam

Gourlay was one of the least political animals I've ever met."

"The unofficial line is, 'Bernie's Irish'," Giles said.

"Oh great. That's all right then," Rory said with savage irony. "That makes it clear, logical and justifiable. Fucking slab-faced bigots."

"You don't think it's anything to do with Jack's father? Revenge for snatching him back?" Giles asked.

"He's an Italian diplomat, not the Mafia. I know it's tempting to say the two things must be connected, but I don't see how," Lindsay said. Annie placed a glass in front of her and she sipped at it immediately. "Besides, it's not exactly going to help his bid for custody, is it?"

Rory frowned. "Maybe it is to do with Bernie. Maybe she does have a secret past life connected to the IRA. Remember how edgy she was right at the start, how reluctant she was to go for publicity? And I thought she was really off-key in Helsinki. Her reaction was complicated, you know what I mean? It was more than just being thrilled to bits about getting her son back. You never know. What if she was on the run, and the story exposed her?"

Lindsay pondered for a moment. "You know, you might just have something there. You're right, she hasn't been behaving naturally since that first night when Tam took us back to meet her. I wonder if she does have a past..."

"There's only one way to find out. Hit her while she's down," Giles said with chilling logic.

Lindsay winced. "Even if I wanted to, I don't think the cops will let me anywhere near her. I was supposed to be keeping an eye on her for the *Sentinel*, but I called the newsdesk back and told them I had something more important to do. Life's too short for sitting around on stories that are going nowhere."

"Giles is right, though. We're not going to find out the truth unless you get Bernie to talk. And we need to find out what's really happening here, Lindsay. Because we were there. We were in the firing line. We set up the sting that got the boy back. And if this is about revenge, we need to know if we're going to be the next targets."

214

Lindsay's eyes widened. "I never thought about that." A frisson of fear cramped her chest.

"Well, think about it now. I've never had any desire to be a heroic martyr for the cause of journalism. If I need to get on the next plane to the nearest faraway place, I want to know about it."

Lindsay gave a wry half-smile. "Leaving me to face the music, huh?"

"Don't be daft," Rory scoffed. "Paying single-room supplements is such a waste of money."

They exchanged a look that for once contained no hiddenness. Lindsay swallowed the dregs of her whisky and stood up. "I'm out of here. See if I can find a way under Bernie's guard. Talk to you later." She stood up and leaned across the table to kiss Rory's cheek. "Take no prisoners."

Giles watched her leave then raised his immaculate eyebrows at Rory. "Sandra says . . ."

"I don't give a bugger what Sandra says," Rory interrupted. "It's not going to happen."

Giles shook his head sadly. "You'll never forgive yourself."

"That's my problem." Rory stood up. "Now, if you'll excuse me, I've got to go and point out to David Keillor the error of his ways."

"You're turning Keillor over again?"

Rory nodded. "He's on the take from CCD. Lindsay nailed the evidence, now it's time for the showdown. I might as well try and produce something that'll cheer us both up. There's nothing else on the horizon that's likely to do that."

Lindsay didn't go straight back to Kinghorn Drive. She wanted time to think, so she caught a bus as far as Kelvingrove Park, then slowly meandered up towards the university. She got as far as the corridor where Sophie's office was, but realised she had no weapon in her armoury that would pierce Sophie's defences yet. There was no point in confrontation for its own sake, and no prospect of an encounter that could even begin to heal the damage between them. Lindsay couldn't afford to let herself believe there was no possibility of bridging the breach, but she couldn't for the life of her imagine the strategy that would achieve it. Still, the thought of failure made her want to curl up in a ball and howl like an abandoned puppy.

With a sigh, she turned away and continued on her way to Kinghorn Drive. The area cordoned off by the crime scene tapes had shrunk to the immediate area around the explosion. Inside it, a team of white-suited Scene of Crimes officers were on hands and knees, collecting and bagging everything they could find. A clutch of journalists was still huddled in one corner, waiting for something to happen. Lindsay made her way over to them. "What's going on?" she said.

A BBC reporter shrugged. "Not a lot. We're waiting to see if the wife's going to make an appeal."

"Is she back at the house?" Lindsay was surprised.

"The cops brought her back about an hour ago. Apparently she insisted on coming home. They tried to talk her out of it, but she wouldn't have it. So we all came back here from the hospital. It's a waste of time. There's no way she's going to talk. Not today."

"Aye," Lindsay said. "Probably not." She eyed the scene. She couldn't see how she was going to get anywhere near Bernie. Her front door was flanked by two officers in full riot gear. Time for some lateral thinking.

She melted away and walked back up to the florist on Hyndland Road. "Can you make a local delivery this afternoon?" she asked.

The woman glanced at the clock. "Shouldn't be a problem. The van'll be back any minute now."

"I want a large bouquet of lilies," Lindsay said, giving the delivery details.

"Any message?"

"I'll write the card myself." The florist offered her a selection of gift cards, and she chose one with a simple spray of forget-me-nots in one corner. I know how you're hurting. I've lost someone I loved, I understand the pain. But we need to talk about what's really going on here. Just between us. Then maybe we can stop it. Ask the cops to bring me in. Deepest sympathy, Lindsay.

She wasn't convinced it would work. But it was worth a try. As she was about to pay, she had a sudden thought. "Have you got any yellow roses?" The florist pointed to a bucket in the corner. "A dozen, please. And can you deliver them too?" She chose another card, giving this message even more thought. You've always known I'm an asshole. But it never stopped you loving me. I want to spend the rest of my life with you, I never meant to put that at risk. Talk to me? Please? Love, Lindsay.

She didn't think for one moment it would change anything. But at any rate it showed she wasn't ignoring the situation. And at least Sophie was still within her reach, not like poor Tam Gourlay, lost to Bernie forever. Now she had to make sure she wasn't going to go the same way.

Jack sat on the floor, playing Nintendo with terrifying concentration. His whole world had shrunk to a tiny screen, the work of his fingers all he had space to think about. The headphones cut out any sound that might catapult him back into reality. Bernie was curled up on the sofa opposite, unable to take her eyes off him. She knew she was still in shock. She could feel nothing except a fierce desire not to let Jack out of her sight. The place in her heart occupied by Tam was frozen solid. Sooner or later it would melt and she would drown in the floodwaters of grief, but that hadn't happened yet.

It wasn't that she hadn't taken it in. She knew full well what had happened. She knew the how and she knew the why. The knowledge felt like a brooding bird of prey, perched inside her, biding its time before it ripped her heart out.

And she would deserve it. All of it and more.

The policewoman they had insisted must stay with her put her head round the door. "I'm sorry to intrude, Mrs. Gourlay. But there's a gentleman on the phone for you. He says he's family, that you'll want to talk to him? He said his name was Patrick."

Bernie's heart lurched in her chest. The bastard would know they'd be monitoring her calls. He'd say nothing that would sound even slightly off key. But he'd want her to know that he was still there, inescapable as death. "I'll be right there," she said.

All she had left now was her son. All she could do was try to protect him.

Ten minutes later, Lindsay was sitting on a wall in Kinghorn Drive sharing a tube of Smarties with a local radio reporter who looked young enough to be her son. "See my boss? The guy that owns Radio NMC? He knew him," the lad said proudly.

"What? Tam Gourlay?"

"Aye. They were at the school together. Stayed pals, like. Used to go fishing up Loch Lomond. He cannae believe it. I had to do an interview with him, like, this morning? He was just devastated. Couldnae make sense of it at all."

"Has he got any theories?"

The lad looked self-important. "Mistaken identity. My boss reckons they got the wrong target. See, the Grand Master of the Orange Lodge, his name's Gourlay. John Gourlay. And he drives a Jag that's near enough identical to the victim's. That's the line we're going with, anyway."

"Could be," said Lindsay. *Biggest load of bollocks so far,* she thought, wishing Rory was there to share the moment. *I've got to stop thinking like that,* she admonished herself. If she was going to make it back with Sophie, she was going to have to train herself out of the habit of yearning.

Before she had to endure any more nonsense, the florist's van drew up at the edge of the cordon. An elderly man got out, carrying a lavish bouquet, and spoke to the nearest police officer. The cop took it and crossed to Bernie's door. It opened to reveal a uniformed woman officer, who accepted the flowers and closed the door firmly behind her.

Time crawled past. Lindsay chewed the skin round her nails, wondering what was going on inside Bernie's head. Eventually, the door opened again and the WPC who had taken in the bouquet spoke to one of the officers on guard. He nodded and stepped to the gate. "Is one of you Lindsay Gordon?" he shouted down to the waiting journalists.

Lindsay pushed herself off the wall and waved a hand. "That's me." Ignoring the outraged complaints from her fellow journalists, she pushed her way through and ducked under the tapes.

"I'll need ID," the officer in the gateway said. Lindsay dug her driving licence out of her wallet and waited while he scrutinised it. "Hang on a minute," he said, turning away and muttering into his personal radio. She wondered what would come up in any records search. She didn't have any criminal convictions, but she'd had some uncomfortable brushes with the law over the years. She speculated whether that information was stored on the Police National Computer, or if it was tucked away in some obscure Special Branch file.

Whatever his control told him, it clearly wasn't bad enough to prevent them letting her near Bernie. He glanced over his shoulder, nodded curtly and said, "OK, on you go."

The WPC was right inside the door, waiting for her. She opened the living room door and ushered Lindsay in, then left them alone. The curtains were closed and the room was dim in the light of a couple of table lamps. Jack was locked into his computer game, while Bernie seemed fixated on the cigarette she was smoking. Neither looked up when she entered. Lindsay crossed the room and kneeled down at Bernie's feet, taking her free hand. Bernie raised her head then and met Lindsay's sympathetic gaze with a bleak, empty stare.

"I do know what it's like," Lindsay said softly. "Years ago, my lover died. You feel guilty just for surviving. Never mind the hole they leave in your heart."

"Are you here as a journalist or as a friend?" Bernie asked roughly.

"I'm here because I'm part of this. Tam made me a part of this, and I need to know what's really going on."

"Oh God." Bernie shivered and pulled her hand away, covering her eyes. Lindsay got up and sat next to her, putting an arm round her shoulders. It was time to start pushing, but she didn't want to lose the fragile contact she'd established.

"Bernie, I know there's stuff you haven't told me about. I don't think you told Tam about it either. And he's paid the price, hasn't he?"

Bernie shrugged Lindsay's arm off. "Who the hell gave you the right to sit in judgement on me?" She glared at her.

"You did. When you let me put myself in the firing line right beside Tam. I don't know what's going on here, but if you want to put an end to it before anybody else dies, you better start talking to somebody. And since my neck's already on the block, it might as well be me."

Lindsay felt the long sigh shuddering through Bernie. "I don't know if I can." She looked down at Jack and her shoulders dropped in resignation. "I can't do this by myself any longer," she groaned. "He's not Bruno's son."

Lindsay frowned, trying to make sense of this bolt from the blue. "Not Bruno's? Then what ...?"

"You want the truth? Well, listen," Bernie said, her voice gathering strength from her determination finally to share her burden. "I grew up outside Belfast. On a farm. The man who owned the farm was called Patrick Coughlan. He was a rich man, a bookie in Belfast. But we all knew that he was a lot more than that. Strangers were always turning up at funny times of the day and night. That was one of the reasons why his marriage was so unhappy.

"Everybody knew Patrick and Mary hated each other. They say it started because she couldn't have children. And Patrick being a strict Catholic, he couldn't divorce her. Anyway, when I turned sixteen, Patrick offered me a job in Belfast, in one of his betting shops. I was glad of it, for there's not a lot of work back home. And he used to drive me back to the country at weekends. And he paid me a lot of attention. And like you do, I became his mistress. And because I was young and stupid, I fell pregnant. 'Never mind,' says Patrick. 'You'll have the baby in a nursing home in England, and me and Mary will adopt the child.'" Bernie looked beseechingly at Lindsay as she lit another cigarette.

"I couldn't let that happen. I couldn't give a child of mine to that hellish marriage. And I didn't want my child growing up thinking the IRA was a fine and noble career for a man."

"Jesus," Lindsay breathed.

"I had some money saved, and I knew where Patrick kept his

emergency stash. So I took off. I got the boat to Stranraer and the train to Glasgow, and found myself a hotel job. I'd only been there for a fortnight when I met Bruno. He fell for me, and I let myself be carried along with the flow. He wanted to marry me and he was handy."

"So did he believe Jack was his son?"

"At first. It wasn't hard to persuade him." She gave a derisive snort. "You know men. They like to think they're all stud bulls. But eventually he figured out the truth. The marriage was in ruins by then anyway." She sighed again. "I should have known Patrick would find me one day. I've always lived with the fear of it."

"So what happened? How did he find you?"

"I've no idea. He started phoning me a couple of weeks ago. He said he wanted me to get used to the idea of Jack living with him. So I did the only thing I could think of to protect Jack."

Suddenly, light dawned in Lindsay's brain. "You set the kidnap up with Bruno!"

"We made the plans a long time ago. Just in case. I couldn't think of anything else, and I knew Bruno would take good care of Jack. But I underestimated what Tam would do for love of the boy."

Lindsay's mind was racing now, far ahead of Bernie's story. "So when we grabbed Jack back again, Patrick killed Tam?"

Bernie nodded. "As a warning to me not to thwart him. He phoned here this afternoon. He wants Jack. What am I to do, Lindsay?"

Lindsay felt about six miles out of her depth. "You could tell the police?"

"Tell them what? I haven't a shred of evidence. I don't know where he is. The police have never been able to stop him doing exactly what he wanted to. Why should they start now? You think they can do anything? Patrick's not some toerag. He's respectable, rich, and he's never been nailed for anything more than a speeding ticket. Sure, the security forces know he's 'RA, but they've no evidence. He's got more than Tam's blood on his hands but they've never been able to lay a finger on him."

"Then you're going to have to do a runner again."

Bernie shook her head hopelessly. "I can't. He's having me watched. He knows my every move. When I go in, when I go out. He phones to let me know. He said he'd phone me tomorrow with instructions for the hand over. If we try to get away, he says he'll have me killed and snatch Jack anyway." Suddenly, her composure cracked and fat, heavy tears spilled from her eyes. "What am I going to do?" she sobbed.

Lindsay took a deep breath. "Well, we'll just have to think of something."

Chapter 24

The flat was clearly off limits now for Michael and Kevin. Everybody who lived in Kinghorn Drive would come under suspicion, everyone would be questioned, and it would only be a matter of time before the police got round to finding out about the two Irishmen in the vacant flat. Chances were that the estate agent would already have put two and two together and volunteered the details of his own venal stupidity.

This left Michael with the problem of how to carry out Patrick's orders without taking too many risks. He'd stayed out of jail throughout the troubles simply because he was good at figuring out the odds and staying on the right side of them. He wasn't about to change his ways now. And so his first move had been to send Kevin back to the B&B to await further instructions.

It had been easy enough for a while after Bernadette had returned. There were enough sightseers for him blend in. But the gawkers had thinned out now. Probably away home for their tea, like good wee civilians, he thought with contempt. However, their desire to fill their bellies didn't help him one whit. Eventually, he'd called Patrick and made a suggestion.

So when Lindsay was picked out of the pack and shown through a front door he'd become all too familiar with, Michael was standing only yards away from her, a camera round his neck and a camera bag at his feet. He hadn't known the lad who had delivered the equipment to him on the corner of Great Western Road, but he supposed it had cost Patrick a bob or two to kit him up with something good enough to pass muster as a press photographer's gear.

It was the perfect disguise. Nobody gave him a second look. In the clannish world of news journalism, strangers stayed that way until and unless they made themselves one of the crowd. If you wanted to stay aloof, fine. All it meant was that you would be cut out of any sharing the pack decided to do with what meagre pickings they'd got.

He couldn't believe it when Lindsay materialised in front of him, carving a line through the crowd and walking straight in. He knew from what he'd read in the paper that she'd been at the heart of the operation to recover Jack Gourlay from his kidnappers. He didn't think Patrick would be pleased to find her in the thick of it again.

Michael walked a few yards away from the crowd and called Patrick. Quickly, he outlined what he'd just seen.

"Fucking bitch," Patrick grumbled. "We're nearly done here. I don't want outsiders interfering. This isn't the time for playing games."

"So what do you want me to do?"

There was a pause. "Follow her when she comes out. Persuade her to keep her nose out of our business."

"How persuasive would you like me to be?"

"She's a woman. They frighten easily. What she saw this morning should be enough to keep her mouth shut, provided you give her a little encouragement."

The phone went dead. Michael allowed himself a small smile. It would be a pleasure.

Sophie locked her office door with a sense of relief. It had felt like the longest day of her life, and all she wanted to do was go home, unplug the phones and try to make up for some of the sleep she'd lost the night before, tossing and turning and crying over someone who simply wasn't worth it.

She'd almost made it to the lift when she heard her secretary call her name. Sophie thought about pretending she hadn't heard, but couldn't bring herself to be so rude. Lucy was hurrying towards her with a hand-tied bouquet of yellow roses. *My favourite, damn you, Lindsay.* "These have just come, Professor Hartley. I thought you'd want to take them home with you." She thrust the flowers eagerly at her boss.

Sophie's first reaction was to stuff the flowers in the fire bucket. But that would only provoke more departmental gossip than the bouquet itself. She forced a tired smile and accepted the offering. "Thanks, Lucy. See you in the morning." She struggled to press the call button for the lift, but Lucy reached past her and helped out.

"There you go," she said cheerfully. "You're obviously a very lucky lady," she added.

"Sorry?"

"The flowers. Somebody must think a lot of you. A dozen roses. That's special." Lucy sketched a wave and headed back down the corridor.

Not special enough, Sophie thought grimly. She'd half-expected to be showered with phone calls, even to see Lindsay waiting hangdog outside her office when she'd arrived that morning, but there had been nothing. She wasn't sure how to interpret that. On the rare occasions when they rowed, Lindsay always went over the top when it came to mending fences, as enthusiastic for reconciliation as she was for everything else she cared about. Did her silence mean she was secretly relieved to have found a fire escape from parenthood and Sophie? Or was it that she realised that this was one time where she had overstepped the mark so utterly that all normal routes to appeasement were shut off? Or was she simply too busy having fun with Rory?

Sophie ripped open the envelope stapled to the cellophane. Reading Lindsay's words, she couldn't resist either the half-smile or the prickle of tears that accompanied them. "You are an asshole," she said softly.

She wasn't ready to forgive. Not by a very long way. But for the first time since Lindsay's admission had slashed at her heart, Sophie was prepared to consider that forgiveness might be a remote possibility.

Lindsay walked along Great Western Road in the gathering shadows of early evening, oblivious to the traffic flowing past her in a stuttering stream. Her head was whirling with questions and options, trying to process the full implications of what Bernie had told her. She had the vague glimmerings of an idea that might just get them all off the hook, but it was a long way from something that could be graced with the term "plan".

Without thinking, she took the turn that would bring her back home. She was twenty yards down the street when she remembered that this wasn't home any longer. Lindsay groaned out loud and turned on her heel, marching back the way she'd come, crossing over to cut through the Botanic Gardens to Rory's flat. That was another thing she was going to have to deal with. She couldn't keep staying at Rory's. It had been almost possible before she'd found that poem. But knowing the truth about Rory's feelings had changed everything.

Head down, preoccupied with enough troublesome thoughts to occupy half a dozen heads, Lindsay turned into the entry for Rory's close. As she opened the door, she suddenly heard running feet behind her. Lindsay swivelled to see what was going on.

Two men emerged from the shadows of the trees that shrouded the street. They were going so fast when they hit her that they barged her into the mouth of the close, the door banging shut behind them. Before she could react, they had crowded her against the inside wall. In the dim light, she could tell them apart. One was small and ferrety, the other looked about as friendly as a peregrine falcon who's just spotted breakfast. The ferret stepped back and brought his fist crashing into her stomach. As she doubled over with the pain, Lindsay felt him grab her hair and yank her head back, cracking it against the cool tiles of the wall.

Lazily, the falcon let her see the blade of his knife before he placed the point in the hollow of her throat. She could feel some thing trickle, but had no idea if it was sweat or blood. Lindsay knew all about fear. And this, she understood, was one of those times when being scared shitless was the only sensible option. When he spoke, his voice was the nasal drawl of Belfast. "We've got a wee message for ye, bitch."

Terrified as she was, she couldn't bring herself to be craven. "That would be from Patrick?" she managed to croak.

The falcon withdrew the knife and for a split second she thought she'd won some ground. But he nodded to the ferret, who smashed his fist into her stomach again. She felt as if her lungs had shot into her throat and she fell into a spasm of retching and coughing, limp as a sleeping child in the ferret's grasp. Her head swam and she lost track of time for a few seconds. When she tuned in again, the falcon's knife was at her throat once more.

"Like I said, we've got a wee message for you. Keep away from Bernadette and the boy. Or else you'll get what Gourlay got. Only, more slowly."

Suddenly, the door behind them opened. Through the groggy haze of pain, Lindsay recognised Rory's familiar silhouette. Before she could shout a warning, Rory dropped her shoulder bag and screamed, "Police officer! Drop the knife!"

Taken by surprise, the falcon's knife hand shifted away from Lindsay's neck. From a standing start, Rory took a flying karate kick at him, screeching like a demented Amazon. She connected mid-thigh and, caught off balance, he tumbled to the ground, his knife clattering into the shadows.

In the confusion, the ferret released Lindsay and turned to make a move on Rory, whose momentum had taken her beyond him. As he moved towards her, she feinted to one side, then dropped into a forward roll, knocking his feet from under him. He crashed to the ground howling as Rory righted herself and landed a kick in his ribs.

Lindsay couldn't stand up any longer and she crumpled to the ground just as the falcon tried to get at Rory. His feet tangled in her legs and he crashed into the wall of the close. "Jesus," he swore, spinning round and heading for the door. "Fucking come on," he yelled, yanking the door open and making for the street. The ferret hobbled after him.

"Fucking bitches, the pair of ye," he shouted as he made the safety of the street.

Panting, Rory crouched down beside Lindsay. "Are you all right?"

"No. But I'd be a lot worse if you hadn't turned up." Her final words were swallowed in a paroxysm of retching coughs. Rory cuddled her close, stroking her sweating forehead.

"That wasn't a mugging, was it?" she asked gently.

"No, it was a warning."

Rory tried to keep the jagged edge of fear out of her voice. "Just as well I did the women's self-defence course, eh?"

Lindsay nodded weakly. "Police officer, eh? Smart move."

"I thought so."

"Do you think we could go upstairs?"

Rory thrust her shoulder under Lindsay's armpit and helped her struggle to her feet. "I suppose it would be too much to hope that those two Neanderthals were Sophie's hired muscle?"

In spite of herself, Lindsay choked out a laugh. "Oh God, if only."

Lindsay lay on the sofa, swathed in Rory's fluffy bathrobe, her hair damp from the bath. On the table in front of her stood a bottle of whisky and a jug of water, flanked by two glasses. Lindsay wanted a drink, but she knew it would hurt too much to reach for the glass. She'd been on the receiving end of violence before, but that didn't make it any easier to deal with. Fear kept reverberating through her, as she knew it would for days, maybe weeks to come. A dark street would make her sweat until she managed to replace its connotations with something more powerful, more pleasurable. But that was in the future. For now, she had to cope with the flashbacks and the palpitations that came with them.

"And I still say you've got to walk away from it," Rory said firmly as she walked in from the kitchen with a plate of sandwiches.

"And let that murdering bastard get his hands on Jack? It'd be signing Bernie's death warrant. My way is the only way to make sure Patrick doesn't come after the kid. Plus he might just get the idea that he'd be a lot safer if I was off the planet too. So I've got to do it. And I need help."

Rory shook her head. "He wouldn't come after you." There was no conviction in her voice.

"How can you say that after what happened this evening? Rory, this guy blew up Tam Gourlay in the middle of a residential street in the morning rush hour for the sole reason that he was pissed off with the man. If he thought I could finger him, he wouldn't think twice. So are you going to help me or not?"

"Lindsay, I want to help. But I'm a journalist, not an urban guerrilla."

"Have you got any better ideas?"

Rory shook her head.

"Look, forget I asked, okay? I'll work something out. And pass me that whisky, would you?"

Rory picked up Lindsay's glass and perched on the sofa arm next to her. "OK, I'll help. I can't let you do this by yourself."

"Can't *let* me?" Lindsay was only half-joking.

"The shape you're in, I can afford to call the shots." Rory stroked the back of Lindsay's neck tenderly. "Hey, what's life without a few risks?"

"You can afford to say that, you won the lottery. This is worth doing, you know. You won't regret it. I promise."

"I have a feeling you've used that line before," Rory said. "Bet it wasn't true then, either. The one thing that still bothers me—apart from my new career as accessory to blackmail—is that it's not just you and me that's involved here."

"Bernie won't be a problem. She'll do anything to keep Jack safe." Lindsay shifted along the sofa, wincing, then patted the cover beside her. "Come and give me a cuddle. But gently," she added apprehensively as Rory slid over the edge of the arm to bounce on to the seat.

"If this is going to work, we need another body," Rory pointed out a few minutes later.

"I know. Anybody in mind?"

"I know just the man," Rory said.

"Does it have to be a man?"

"Don't tell me you're one of those lesbians that don't like men?" Rory teased.

"Oh, I like some of them fine," Lindsay said. "I just wouldn't trust them to hold the dog while I went for a pee."

"Well, I trust Giles."

"Giles Graham?" Lindsay said incredulously. "You've got to be joking. He'd get his suit creased."

Rory shook her head. "You underestimate him. He used to be in the Territorial Army, you know."

"That's meant to be a recommendation?"

Rory snuggled into Lindsay's side, taking care to avoid the area she knew was going to be a multi-coloured bruise by morning. "Giles is one of the good guys. Besides, he owes me. I know where the bodies are buried."

"An unfortunate metaphor," Lindsay said. "OK, Giles it is."

"So when are you thinking about swinging into action?"

Lindsay sipped her whisky and stared into the middle distance. "Not tomorrow. There's too much to get organised. The night after, I think. Bernie reckons she can stall Patrick until then, she'll tell him she can't get away from her police protection."

"Can you squeeze another twenty-four hours out of him?" Rory asked. "Only, I know Giles is going out of town tomorrow on a job. And we need time to make sure we know exactly how we're going to carry it off."

Lindsay considered. One more day wouldn't make any difference. Bernie could always plead fear and demand police protection for a bit longer. "I don't see why not. It'd give me more of a chance to recover. And I need to go up to Argyll before then."

Rory's curiosity was pricked. "You're not thinking about bringing your dad in on this?"

Lindsay shook her head. "No way. But there's something I need to sort out first."

"Tell," Rory demanded.

"No. A woman has to have some secrets, you know." Lindsay rumpled Rory's hair. "Thanks. For everything."

Rory snorted derisively. "What? For buggering up your life? You're going to have to talk to Sophie, you know. You've got to get things sorted out between you."

"What? Fed up of having me under your feet already?"

"Stop hiding behind facetiousness. You don't belong with me, you know that."

Lindsay took a slow, considering sip of her whisky. "It's not quite that simple, though, is it? We both know that in different circumstances..."

Rory pulled away and stood up, moving to the armchair opposite. "But we can only play the hand we've been dealt, Lindsay. And the bottom line is that you still love Sophie and that's too important to throw away for a maybe."

"I think it's already more than a maybe for us, don't you?"

Rory flinched, clearly uncomfortable with Lindsay's insight. "Look, I've been doing some thinking today. I don't think we should sleep together any more." Her eyes pleaded with Lindsay not to push for a reason.

But Lindsay couldn't close it there. "Why not?"

"It's not that I don't want to. I do, I really do, and that's the problem. If it were just a fling, just a shag, like it was supposed to be, that would be fine. But it's not. It has emotional content for us both. And so it's pointless, because your heart's still tied to Sophie, which is how it should be. And if I can't have everything, I don't want anything. Except your friendship. If that's still on offer." The words dragged out of Rory, words she'd never spoken before, and every one an effort.

They stared at each other for a long moment, both gripped by the inevitability of Rory's argument, both pierced by the poignancy of the decision that they knew they'd already taken. "Go and talk to her," Rory said softly. "Go and fix it."

"Maybe not tonight, eh? I'm feeling a wee bit fragile."

"Yes, tonight. You'll feel worse tomorrow, once those muscles have stiffened up. And it's not like you're going to get a good night's sleep, is it? Do it now, before you start figuring out another set of excuses. Besides, I've got some copy to write. I fronted Keillor up this afternoon. He tried to bluff his way out of it, but we've got more than enough to go with."

Lindsay managed a wan smile. "Well done. What a team, eh?"

Rory sighed. "Aye. What a team, right enough. So, come on, Splash, get some clothes on and go and see Sophie."

"There's no point, you know," Lindsay said, edging forward and working her way into a standing position.

"Of course there's a point. Apart from anything else, you need some clean knickers."

Chapter 25

When the doorbell rang, Sophie was curled up in front of the fire in her dressing gown, talking to her stomach. She got up and looked out of the window. No sign of Lindsay's car. The bell trilled out insistently again. Whoever it was obviously realised she was home and wasn't giving up without a fight. It was trademark behaviour. "Lindsay," she sighed wearily.

Her first thought when she opened the door was that Lindsay was holding herself very strangely, as if she were primed to take a blow. Her face was tense, but with pain as much as anxiety. "What happened to you?" Sophie said without preamble.

"It's a long story. And it's really not important. I need to talk to you, that's what's important."

Sophie shook her head. "A dozen roses doesn't buy you access. I don't need to talk to you, Lindsay. And I don't want to." She moved to close the door.

"At least let me come in and pick up a few things. I can't keep wearing the same clothes forever." Lindsay was trying to sound appealing, but apprehension kept slipping through.

Sophie stood back, opening the door, then walked away to the living room. Lindsay followed. "Your knicker drawer is not in here," Sophie pointed out.

"Sophie, please don't shut me out."

"What, like you didn't shut me out when you were shagging

Rory?" Sophie struggled to keep her face under control. She was determined not to show Lindsay how deeply hurt she was.

"I'm sorry. I've behaved badly and you don't deserve that."

"I know I don't. Which is why you'll never get the chance to repeat it. I'm not going to let you talk your way back into my life. It's over, and you better get used to the idea." Sophie turned away dismissively. She sat down and picked up a discarded medical journal from the table, flicking through the pages without seeing a word.

"Please," Lindsay said. This time, there was no disguising the pain in her voice. "Look, I did a stupid, stupid thing. I never meant to hurt you and I can't begin to tell you how sorry I am for what I've done. But you can't throw everything away just because I made one dumb mistake."

"Watch me," Sophie said. "Lindsay, sleeping with someone else doesn't come into the category of mistake. Mistake is when you put black socks in with a white boil wash. Mistake is when you put salt instead of sugar in the custard. This was not a mistake. It was a calculated bit of pleasure-taking and to hell with the consequences. Well, here are the consequences. And if you don't like them, that's tough. You should have thought about that before you seized the moment with the blonde."

Lindsay walked round the sofa to face Sophie. "I know I did wrong. But please. I want us to be together. You said you wanted us to be a family. That's what I want too."

Sophie barely glanced up. "You think I want to bring up my child with a liar and a cheat?"

"I'm not a liar," Lindsay protested. "If I was a liar, you'd be none the wiser."

"OK, I'll grant you that. But you're a cheat. And I could never trust you again. Which is the bottom line."

Impulsively, Lindsay dropped to her knees. She almost passed out with the pain that flashed across her ribs. She folded her arms protectively over her abdomen and gasped. "Oh fuck."

Sophie couldn't help herself. In an instant, she was on the floor beside her. "Lindsay, what is it? What's wrong?"

Lindsay leaned against the sofa, her face grey and sweating. "I got beaten up, OK? It's none of your business, remember?" Somehow, she pushed herself upright and slumped into the seat. "I'll be fine in a minute. Then I'll go." She closed her eyes, waiting for the nausea to pass.

When she opened them again, Sophie was still kneeling on the floor, unable to hide her concern. "How did you get beaten up?" she demanded.

"Sticking my nose in where it wasn't wanted. I seem to be doing that a lot today." She got to her feet unsteadily. "You're all I ever wanted, Sophie. I'll never forgive myself for forgetting that, even for a moment."

Sophie watched as Lindsay staggered across the room. She listened to the sound of drawers opening and closing, then slowly got to her feet. *Only Lindsay could refuse to trade on having had the crap beaten out of her,* she thought with rueful affection. She met Lindsay in the bedroom doorway, carrying a gym bag. "I'll arrange to come for the rest of my stuff when I've sorted myself out with somewhere to live," she said, her voice dull.

"Don't do anything hasty," Sophie said. "Give me some time, Lindsay. Call me next week, OK?" The spark of hope that flared in Lindsay's eyes was hard to resist, but Sophie was determined not to cave in so easily.

Lindsay nodded and reached out a tentative hand to Sophie's belly. "You take care now. Take care of both of you."

"Don't worry about us. Just try and stay alive, Lindsay. Don't piss anybody else off between now and then."

She couldn't quite unravel the curious expression that crossed Lindsay's face. "I'll do my best," she said.

Patrick Coughlan paced the floor of his room. One Devonshire Gardens was reputedly the finest hotel in the city, but its luxury was wasted on him tonight. He'd thought that Tam Gourlay's death would settle Bernadette's hash once and for all. But she was acting as if she still had rights. Well, if she was relying on her journalist pals this time, she'd be in for a rude surprise. According to Michael, the Gordon bitch wouldn't be so keen to muscle in on his business a second time.

But that still left the problem of the boy. Bernadette had conceded that she would have to hand him over, but she claimed she couldn't make the arrangements while she was still under police protection. He could see the force of that, but it worried him all the same. She'd already tried to thwart him with that stupid kidnap ploy, and he supposed he should be grateful to the Gordon bitch and her sidekick for making sure Bernadette hadn't got away with it. She'd better not try it again.

He sincerely hoped she'd learned her lesson. Killing gave Patrick no pleasure. He had always regarded it as a necessity, no more, no less. Bernadette had once meant something to him, it was true. But unlike many of his fellow countrymen, Patrick had no streak of sentimentality. If killing Bernadette was what it took to bring his son home, then he would have no compunction about ordering it done.

He wanted the boy with him. His absence had smouldered like heartburn since the day Bernadette had disappeared. Patrick had only just got used to the joyous idea of finally being a father when the bitch had snatched it away from him. She couldn't have known the pain she'd dealt him. Being a father to his own boy was the pinnacle of his ambition, and she'd wantonly deprived him of the chance to do the most decent thing he was capable of. There hadn't been a day when he hadn't wondered where his son was, whether he took after his father, what he liked and disliked. Without knowing the first thing about his son, Patrick loved him with a fierce passion. Bernadette had had no right to steal that from him.

One way or another, it would all be over soon.

Sophie rubbed her temples. She'd woken with a headache and it seemed determined to hang around. Possibly it was a symptom of pregnancy; more likely, it was a symptom of Lindsay. Luckily, she had a fairly quiet day ahead, the morning devoted to writing up some research in her office.

When the knock came at her door, she expected a colleague or a student. But in response to her weary, "Come in," she was astonished to see Rory McLaren walk in. "Actually, don't bother," she said. "Just turn round and leave."

"Five minutes," Rory said. "That's all I'm asking."

"That's five more than I'm prepared to give you." Sophie glared over her glasses. "I thought Lindsay was big enough to fight her own battles."

"She doesn't know I'm here. She'd kill me if she knew I was. You should know that." Rory's air of amused exasperation struck a chord with Sophie in spite of herself.

"So why are you here?"

"Two reasons. First, to apologise. And second, to intercede."

Sophie frowned. "Five minutes. No more." Rory moved towards the chair that faced Sophie. "No point in sitting down, Rory. You're not going to be here that long."

Rory stopped in her tracks, looking awkward. "OK. Right. Look, I should never have slept with Lindsay. I don't make a habit of trespassing in other people's lives."

"It's hard to imagine how I could care less about your habits. And frankly, it's not you who shouldn't have slept with Lindsay. It's her who shouldn't have slept with you."

"What happened, it was my fault. I made all the running. She was pissed and a long way from home." Rory looked at the floor. "I took advantage because I wanted her."

"She could have said no," Sophie said, not giving an inch.

"She could have. But she didn't. A moment of weakness, that's all it was. And we were both clear it wasn't going to happen again." Rory looked up and met Sophie's hard-eyed look with a half-smile. "And if she wasn't such a fool to herself, that's where it would have ended, with you none the wiser."

"You think it's foolish to be honest?"

Rory's eyebrows quirked upwards. "When all it does is bring everyone concerned a shitload of grief? Hey, Sophie, it's obvious that whatever I say, you're going to pick a fight with, and I can't blame you for that. Can we just get to the bottom line? Lindsay loves you. And I think you love her. If you let one colossal act of stupidity fuck that up, I think you'll both regret it for a very long time. Apart from anything else, every kid deserves two parents who love each other."

Sophie glared at Rory. "She told you I'm pregnant?"

"Of course she told me. She was thrilled. I know she wasn't very keen on the idea to begin with, but when she realised it was a reality, she was over the moon."

"Now I know you're full of shit."

"It's true," Rory protested. "That's a big part of why she's so upset now. Take her back, Sophie. She needs you." She glanced at her watch. "That's my time up. I won't keep you any longer." She turned away and made for the door.

Sophie chewed her lip. As Rory reached for the door handle, she said, "She's very lucky to have a friend like you. It's more than she deserves."

Rory flashed a smile over her shoulder. "We're both more than she deserves. And also rather less." Then she was gone.

Sophie stared at the closed door for a very long time. She recognised love when she saw it. And she was afraid that Lindsay might do exactly the same. The night before, she'd come close to offering an olive branch to Lindsay. But perhaps it was already too late for them both.

Lindsay sat on a crumbling dry stone dyke that had once formed part of a sheep fold. Her ribs ached, there was a lump on the back of her head the size and texture of a fillet steak and her whole body was stiff. She'd slept badly, struggling to find a comfortable position in Rory's spare bed, and her eyes felt gritty and sore. Sitting in a car all morning hadn't helped. But she was here now, which was the main thing.

She'd parked on a forestry road about quarter of a mile up the hill, well hidden from anyone down the glen, and now she was biding her time. Her father's boat wasn't at the quay, which meant he was out fishing and would be gone for a few hours yet. Her mother, she knew, would leave the house within the next hour or so and walk the mile into town to perform her daily circuit of the three village shops. Fresh rolls, milk, a few vegetables, maybe a bit of meat, whatever she needed for that day's meals. Getting the messages and the local gossip would take her out of the house for long enough for Lindsay to collect what she needed.

She perched on the wall, pulling the collar of her fleece closer to keep out the chill wind coming off the hill. Even on a grey day like this, it was hard not to be seduced by the harsh beauty of the landscape. The grass was fading as winter approached, nibbled close by Duncan Campbell's hardy mountain sheep, hefted to the hill and spared the foot and mouth cull that had devastated flocks further south. The village crouched below, grey harled cottages hugging the shoreline like a string of runners waiting for the starting pistol to throw themselves pell mell across the rippled grey steel of the quiet sea. She could identify every one of the buildings, though these days Lindsay couldn't say for certain who all the inhabitants were. At least three of the cottages had fallen to week-end visitors, and the old folks of her youth had been replaced by new faces she didn't always recognise.

She wouldn't swap with them for anything, in spite of her attachment to the land. She couldn't live here. She'd known that since her early teens. She needed wider horizons, different responsibilities.

She needed Sophie. *Please God, let her relent.* It was no consolation to realise that if Sophie refused to consider a reconciliation, Rory was waiting in the wings. Whatever her feelings for Rory, it wouldn't diminish the pain of losing Sophie.

Lindsay was spared any further introspection by the appearance of her mother at the end of the path leading from the family home to the main road. She watched her as far as the first house in the village, then Lindsay cut across the field and into the trees. She drove down to the house and let herself in. Fifteen minutes later, she was cruising down the main street, mission accomplished. She couldn't just turn round and drive back to Glasgow, however. Inevitably, someone would have clocked her car and a report of her presence would make its way back to at least one of her parents. The last thing she wanted was her father wondering what she might have been doing there. She spotted her mother outside the minimarket, chatting to a woman bent almost double over her walking frame. Lindsay recognised her primary school teacher as she parked and crossed the street.

Miss Macintyre caught sight of her and tapped her mother on the arm. "Here's your Lindsay," she said.

Mrs. Gordon turned round, surprise on her face. "Lindsay! What a nice surprise."

"I'm on my way to Tarbet," Lindsay lied easily. She'd never had any problem keeping things hidden from her mother. It was an irony she was alive to that morning. She exchanged a few pleasantries with Miss Macintyre then led her mother back to the car.

"You look tired," Mrs. Gordon said, reading the lines of strain round her daughter's eyes.

"I didn't sleep very well. I tripped on the stairs and hurt my ribs." Half a truth was better than none.

"Have you got time to stop for your dinner? I've got some lovely prawns back at the house."

Lindsay shook her head. "I just thought I'd stop and say hello. I'll drop you back home, then I'll need to be going."

"You'll have time for a cup of coffee." It was a statement, not a question.

Lindsay smiled. "That'd be nice."

"So how's Sophie keeping?" her mother asked. Lindsay's heart sank. Maybe coffee wasn't such a good idea after all.

Bernie stood on a chair and took the suitcases down from the top of the wardrobe. She wanted to believe that Lindsay's plan would work. But she needed insurance. If Patrick couldn't be neutralised, then she would have to go on the run again. It would be harder with Jack in tow, but without him there would be no point.

She would pack a couple of bags, just the essentials for the two of them. She'd stow them in the boot of the car. Then if things went wrong, she could just hit the road and head south. Hull would be a good place to leave from. They could cross the North Sea to Holland and make their way down to Italy. She'd learned basic Italian when she'd been married to Bruno. It wouldn't be too hard to find a decent job in some big anonymous city where Patrick and his thugs would never find her. Bruno would help, she was sure. After the initial acrimony of the divorce, he'd proved a surprisingly good friend. She supposed that was because he'd grown to care about Jack.

But in her heart, she didn't want to run. She wanted to stay here in this house where she'd been happy with Tam. She wanted to mourn at his funeral. She wanted to grieve in peace, without having to look over her shoulder all the time. Bernie sat down heavily on the bed and let the tears flow. "Oh, Tam," she sobbed. "What am I going to do without you?" Misery and remorse seized her and she rolled on to her stomach, pounding the pillows with her fist.

She was lamenting not only what she had lost but the knowledge that she could never again take the risk of allowing someone to love her. That was what had cost Tam his life. Under no circumstances could she gamble with another's. From now on, it was her and Jack against the world.

Chapter 26

Giles stared at Rory. "Why me?" he asked plaintively.

"Because I trust you."

"What about Sandra?"

Rory snorted derisively. "Would you let Sandra loose on something that needed split second timing? She'd probably chip her nail varnish or get distracted by some trainee accountant with a cute bum."

Giles smiled in spite of his discomfiture. "I see your point. But really, is this sensible?"

"Of course it's not sensible. But the thing I've realised about Lindsay is that once she decides she's going to do something, she won't be diverted. And if she tries to do this single-handed, it'll never work. I'm doing it purely for business reasons, because I don't want anything bad to happen to her." Rory avoided his eyes, not wanting him to see too much.

"And you're asking me to help because you know I don't want anything bad to happen to you," Giles said, reaching across the table and patting her hand. "Purely for business reasons, of course."

"Hey, where else would you get all the best stories? But the real reason I want you on board is that if it all goes horribly wrong, Julia can use her influence to get us off the hook," Rory said, deflecting his seriousness with flippancy. "So, are you in or are you going to make me ask Sandra?"

Giles shook his head, wondering at his own stupidity. "I'm in."

"Thanks, Giles. I appreciate it. Now, this is what you have to do." She ran through the details of the plan once more, making sure he was clear about his role. "Can you see any flaws in it?"

"Apart from the general insanity of trying to blackmail an IRA capo? No, not a thing. It all makes perfect sense," he said sarcastically.

"Lindsay will pick you up at half past seven. And we'll take it from there." Rory stood up and gathered her things. She took a theatrical look around Café Virginia. "I've loved these days," she said. "Do you think if I don't make it back, they'll put a blue plaque on this booth?"

"More likely a health warning. 'Sitting in this booth may provoke the illusion that you are Don Quixote.' "

Rory grinned. "Bring on the windmills."

Lindsay checked over the electronic equipment one last time. "I've put new batteries in everything, there shouldn't be a problem," she said. She studied Rory carefully, knowing the margin for error was small and needing to be sure of her. "You OK about this?"

Rory nodded. "Let's get on with it before my bottle goes completely."

Lindsay picked up a small radio mike with a crocodile clip and a loose wire dangling from it. "This is the radio mike. Not exactly state of the art, but it does the business. I'll have the receiver in my car, linked up to a tape recorder."

"So where do I wear it?"

Lindsay couldn't resist a wicked grin. "Experience has shown that for women, the best place is attached to your bra."

"So much for keeping your hands off my body." Rory stood up and unbuttoned her blouse, trying to keep it as matter of fact as she could. "How much do I need from Coughlan, do you think? Is it enough if he acknowledges he's Jack's real father?"

"You have to get him to admit to being involved with Tam's

murder. That's the only insurance policy that's worth anything. You get that, then you get clear."

Rory nodded. "Then you phone him and tell him that if anything happens to Jack or Bernie—if a pigeon so much as craps on their car—the tape goes to the police. And the papers." Rory opened her blouse and gave a wry smile. "All yours," she said.

Lindsay picked up the mike and stepped towards Rory. In spite of her best intentions, she couldn't avoid a nostalgic frisson of desire. Trying hard to stay businesslike, she delicately slid the mike inside the bra so it nestled neatly against Rory's left breast. Rory gave an involuntary shiver as Lindsay's hand brushed her skin. "Sorry," she muttered.

"Don't be," Lindsay said softly. She laid her hands on the soft skin stretched over Rory's collarbone. She frowned slightly, her eyes filled with sadness. "I..."

Rory put a finger on her lips. "Don't say it. I know. Me too, for what it's worth."

Lindsay nodded and stood back. "Make yourself decent. We've got work to do, woman."

Rory smiled and buttoned up her blouse then reached for her jacket.

"OK, time to go. Try it out on the way down the stairs." Lindsay said, desperately wanting to give Rory a benedictory kiss but knowing it would only be another source of pain.

Rory waggled her fingers in farewell and winked. "See you in Café Virginia when it's all over."

Lindsay watched her leave, then made some adjustments to the small receiver and tape recorder. Suddenly, Rory's voice emerged clearly from the speaker. "Your mission, should you choose to accept it, is to adopt celibacy as the only safe way to live..."

In spite of the seriousness of the moment, Lindsay couldn't help herself. She burst out laughing. "Oh, Rory," she said out loud. "Such bad timing."

Patrick sat in the passenger seat of Michael's hired car, staring at Bernie's house through a pair of binoculars. He let them drop and pulled out his phone. The number was answered on the second ring.

"Are you free and clear now?" he said without preamble.

"They've left," Bernie said.

"Good. Where are we meeting?"

"The Charles Rennie Mackintosh multi-storey car park at the bottom of Garnethill. Top floor. Eight o'clock." Bernie's voice was flat and depressed, the voice of a woman who has given up. It gladdened Patrick's heart to hear it.

"Fine. I'll be there. And no tricks, mind, or there'll be a couple more funerals in this city before too long." He stabbed a finger at the phone, ending the call. He allowed himself a satisfied smile and said, "Charles Rennie Mackintosh car park in Garnethill. Half an hour's time. You know what to do, boys. When she comes out the house with the boy, you follow her. If she goes anywhere except this car park, you stay on her tail and call me right away. If the boy comes out with anyone else, Kevin, you follow them. And Michael, you deal with the bitch. Is that all clear, now?"

"It's clear," Michael said.

"But she's not going to try anything on, is she?" Kevin asked. "Not after that wee warning."

"Of course she's not," Patrick said, confident and dismissive. "But I've always been a believer in contingency plans. That's probably why I'm still alive. I'll see youse later, boys." He opened the door and stepped out into the heavy drizzle, turning up his coat collar as he walked back to his car, parked further up the street. Although he had spent years battening down his emotions in favour of operational activity, Patrick couldn't suppress a surge of excitement that raised his pulse rate. Tonight, finally, he would take his son home. What better feeling could a man have?

Lindsay let herself out of Rory's flat and walked to her car. She put the receiver and tape recorder on the passenger seat, then lifted the narrow bench seat in the back of the MGB. When she'd first bought the car, she'd customised the seat with a set of hinges so the area beneath it could be used for extra storage space. She hadn't quite envisaged stowing one of her father's shotguns there, but it had turned out to be perfect for the job. She deliberately hadn't told Rory about the gun, aware that the knowledge would have made it impossible for Rory to carry out her end of the plan with anything approaching equanimity. But Lindsay didn't trust Patrick Coughlan and she had no intention of leaving Rory exposed and unprotected.

She leaned into the car and broke the gun open, slotting a pair of cartridges into the breech. It had been a long time since she'd handled a gun, years since she'd shot rabbits and pheasants with her father on the hills above Invercross, but she was pleased to find she hadn't lost the knack. Then she slammed it closed and put it on the floor behind the driver's seat, hiding it beneath a tatty tartan rug she'd borrowed from her father's workshop.

Lindsay leaned on the cloth roof of the car and tried to calm herself. It was still painful to breathe, never mind move around freely. But she had to be up to this. She had to forget her physical discomfort and focus on the plan. She reached into her pocket and took out a container of ibuprofen tablets. She swallowed 600mg and hoped for the best.

Lindsay climbed into the car and pulled a ski mask out of the pocket of her waxed jacket. She'd gone back home that afternoon in Sophie's absence and chosen her clothes with care. A black cotton polo neck, the jacket, black fleece trousers, black leather gloves and rubber soled black shoes. She rolled up the ski mask so that it resembled a watch cap and jammed it over her hair, then started the engine. She wanted some music to psych her up for what lay ahead and slotted Horse's *Both Sides* into the cassette player. "Never Not Going To" blasted out at her and she sang along with a sense of savage irony as she drove through the rainy streets in the gathering dusk to her rendezvous with Giles.

She pulled up outside the Victorian warehouse where Giles and Julia enjoyed a magnificent view of the river and the Finnieston crane from their converted loft apartment. A tall slim figure detached itself from the shadows of the doorway and crossed to the car. Giles was almost unrecognisable in camouflage trousers,

Doc Martens and a parka. "You look like Rambo on a night out," Lindsay observed as he piled into the car, shunting the electronic equipment on to his lap.

Giles raised an eyebrow. "And you don't?" he asked. "I have to wonder what I'm doing here."

"You can't resist playing cowboys and Indians."

"Hmm. Let me tell you, if Rory wasn't certifiably lucky, I wouldn't be here."

Lindsay drove off, cutting up from the quayside on the road that paralleled the motorway as far as Charing Cross, then followed the signs to the Charles Rennie Mackintosh car park.

"Why here?" Giles asked as they approached the entrance.

"Because of the system." Lindsay pointed to a sign that read, PAY AT MACHINE BEFORE RETURNING TO VEHICLE. She drove up to the entry barrier, lowered her window and took a ticket. The metal arm rose and she drove through. "There you go," she said, handing the ticket to Giles. They stared at each other for a long moment then he opened the door, unfolded his long legs and climbed out, leaning back into the car to give Lindsay the thumbs up sign.

"Good luck," he said.

"And you." Lindsay waited till she saw Giles walk over to the lifts and attach an OUT OF ORDER sticker to the doors. Then she drove on up, her damp tyres screaming on the cement as she climbed to the penultimate floor, the last covered level below the roof.

Lindsay parked near the "up" ramp and got out. She pocketed the electronic equipment, slipped the shotgun under her waxed jacket and walked cautiously up the ramp to the roof. Here, there were only a couple of other cars, and little scope for hiding. She checked out one of the parked cars, but the lines of sight were terrible. Adrenaline was making her jumpy and she began to panic at her inability to find somewhere to conceal herself. Then she spotted a large concrete bin used for storing grit near the door leading to the lifts. She hurried over there and stood by it, sighting along her arm like a child playing soldiers. This was better, she thought, dry-mouthed and sweating. She could see the ramps

247

clearly, as well as the whole area of the roof level. Lindsay freed the shotgun and squeezed down behind the bin, gasping as her ribs protested.

Meanwhile, nine floors below her, Patrick Coughlan slowed down as he approached the barrier. He looked sharply around him, but missed Giles, who had found a patch of shadow in the lee of the entrance. Patrick leaned out of the driver's window to snatch a ticket then edged forward, aiming for the ramp that would carry him to the meeting he'd dreamed of for years.

Michael hadn't taken his eyes off Bernie's front door since Patrick's departure. He knew his life would be worth nothing if he fucked up now and he was determined not to make a single mistake. Suddenly, he straightened up in his seat. "It's them!"

"The bitch and the boy?" Kevin exclaimed.

"The same." As Bernie ushered Jack towards her scarlet hatchback, Michael fastened his safety belt and dug Kevin in the ribs. "Start her up, Kevin."

Startled by the hard edge in his partner's voice, Kevin turned the key and floored the accelerator. The engine coughed and stalled. On the third try, it finally caught. "Sorry," he mumbled.

"Just don't fucking lose them." It wasn't a command to argue with.

Bernie strapped Jack into the child seat in the back of the car, then walked round to the driver's seat. The car nosed out of its parking place and made its way down Kinghorn Drive to the junction.

"But why won't you tell me where we're going?" Jack asked plaintively.

"Because it's an adventure," Bernie said, glancing in her rear view mirror, not in the least surprised to see a car pull out behind her.

"I don't want any more adventures. I want Tam." Jack sounded on the point of tears.

"I want Tam too," Bernie said, her voice trembling. "But we have to learn to manage on our own."

◆ ◆ ◆ ◆ ◆

Patrick's car edged on to the rooftop level of the car park. He cruised slowly from one end to the other, pausing at each parked car to check it was empty. Lindsay crouched behind the bin, the ski mask pulled over her face so nothing was visible in the gloom except the gleam of her eyes. She could feel sweat trickling down her neck and pooling in the small of her back. "Just park, you bastard," she said under her breath.

As if he heard her, Patrick drew to a halt and reversed neatly into a slot as far away from the other cars as he could get. *Perfect*, Lindsay thought.

As the sound of his engine died in the damp night air, nine floors down Rory was driving up to the car park barrier. She took a ticket and drove in, then stopped. Giles stepped out of the shadows and gave her the thumbs-up sign. Rory flashed a grin at him and drove upwards, heart thudding in her chest. She urgently wanted to pee, but realised it was purely psychological. Almost the last thing she'd done before she left had been to use the toilet. That knowledge didn't stop her feeling desperate, however.

Giles checked his watch. It showed five minutes to eight. He took a deep breath and crossed to the machine that issued the exit permits. He inserted the ticket Lindsay had given him, fed a handful of coins into the machine and took the exit ticket. He walked briskly across towards the barrier guarding the way out and leaned against the wall, trying to look as if he was waiting for someone.

Which of course he was. Bernie turned into the street and checked the dashboard clock. Two minutes to eight. She was right on time. She drove into the entrance, checking her tail was still in place a discreet distance behind her. She took a ticket from the machine, then, as the arm rose, drove hesitantly forward. While she hovered, apparently uncertain of the direction she should take, a Vauxhall Vectra drove into the entrance lane. The driver's arm appeared, taking a ticket, and the barrier rose again. The car drove through and edged towards Bernie.

The moment the entrance barrier returned to the horizontal, Bernie's car leapt forward in sudden acceleration. She pulled hard on the wheel, swinging round and heading fast for the exit. Giles jumped out of the shadows and inserted the exit ticket as she approached. The metal arm rose and Bernie speeded through, her tyres screeching as she hit the street at thirty miles an hour. Giles took off on foot, running through an alley towards their pre-arranged rendezvous.

Inside the Vectra, panic was raging. "The fucking bitch," Kevin screamed over and over again.

"She's set him up," Michael raged, throwing open the passenger door. "Get after the fucking cow. Don't fucking lose her." He dived out of the car just as Kevin accelerated and he rolled to the ground, twisting his ankle badly as he fell. He got to his feet, cursing and wincing as arrows of pain shot up his leg. As he stood, he realised he'd also done something to his left collarbone. He could hardly move his arm and every step he took provoked a painful grinding along his shoulder.

Kevin had the engine at screaming point, lifting his foot off the clutch and launching the car at the barrier. He hurtled forward straight into the metal pole, expecting it to snap under the impact. Not for the first time in his life, Kevin had misjudged the situation completely. The barrier, more solid than it looked, rocked and bent slightly. The car was more vulnerable. The wind-screen starred as the glass shattered and the car roof crumpled. "Jesus fuck!" Kevin wailed.

He threw the car into reverse then attacked the barrier again. This time, the pillar at the end of the windscreen bent under the impact, but the car's momentum carried it forward, only brought to a halt by the strength of the barrier. The car was comprehen-sively trapped. It could move neither forward nor back. Kevin struggled to open the driver's door, but it was stuck too. He couldn't squeeze over to the passenger door because the roof was crushed too low on that side. Nor could he stretch far enough to reach the mobile phone which had fallen into the footwell on the passenger side. As the magnitude of the disaster slowly began to penetrate, Kevin started to shake. "Ah, shit," he groaned.

Meanwhile, Michael had limped across to the lifts, only to dis-cover the "Out of Order" sign that Giles had stuck there. He didn't even bother to try the call button, settling instead for kicking the door with his uninjured foot. Breathing heavily, one arm hanging useless at his side, he turned towards the stairwell. His good arm reached inside his jacket and reappeared clutching a Glock automatic. "Fucking bitch," he swore as he began the long descent to the roof.

Rory had climbed the levels as fast as she safely could, swerving once to avoid a woman loading her boot with shopping. The red digital display read 7:59 as she turned on to the final ramp. It was still drizzling and visibility was poor on the roof level. But she could make out Patrick Coughlan standing in the shadows by his car. She parked about twenty feet away from him and got out, keeping her hands in sight and well away from her body. Her whole body was tense with apprehension, her blood pounding in her ears like a mad Burundi drummer. She took a few steps towards him.

Patrick remained motionless, his eyes watchful, his hands in his overcoat pockets. He said nothing until Rory was about six feet away from him. Then he spoke. "Who are you?" he said.

"I'm Lindsay Gordon's business partner."

Patrick's lip curled in a sneer. "Lindsay Gordon. The woman who can't take a telling."

Rory licked her dry lips, "Bernie asked me to come. You know she can't let you have the boy."

It felt like a long silence, but it was only a matter of seconds. "I wish you hadn't said that," Patrick said.

"Why? Because you'll have to deal with her the same way you dealt with Tam? And then me? And then Lindsay?" Rory's voice sounded far more defiant to her than she would have believed possible.

"You don't know me well enough to heed my warnings. Bernadette should know better, though."

"What Bernie knows is how her son would end up if she handed him over to you. A cold-blooded killer, fighting a pointless war, just like his daddy."

251

"A boy should know who his father is. I have a right to my son."

"And Tam? Didn't he have any rights?" Rory stood her ground, her eyes never leaving his face.

"He had no right to my son."

"He risked going to prison to get your son back to his mother," she pointed out.

"I've risked at least that much to put the boy where he belongs. In my house."

"Oh yeah, I forgot. Murder." It was, she knew, the key moment. She had to get the admission on tape, had to forge a weapon strong enough to keep this man at bay forever.

Patrick shook his head. "It wasn't murder. It was punishment. For taking what wasn't his."

"She won't let you have Jack. Not after what you did to Tam."

A cold smile, his teeth gleaming in the dim light. "Dead women don't have choices."

Rory started at the sound of a door smacking open against a concrete wall. She whirled round to see a figure silhouetted against the harsh fluorescence of the stairwell. An unfamiliar voice shouted, "Patrick! She's set you up! She's got away with the boy. We lost them!"

Rory's hand instinctively flew up to protect the microphone in an ambiguous gesture. Assuming she was going for a weapon, Michael's gun hand came up and he moved into the firing position. But before he could shoot, from behind the grit bin came the flash of gunfire and the backfire boom of a shotgun. Michael, blasted at point blank range, crumpled to the ground without a sound. Shocked at what she'd done, Lindsay stood looking down uncomprehendingly at the still form at her feet.

She was brought back to reality by the sound of shots. Suddenly alert, she took in the scene. Patrick was waving a handgun around, shooting wildly in her general direction, his panic the reaction of a man who hasn't seen active service for a very long time and is unaccustomed to taking responsibility for his own protection. Lindsay didn't think he could see her and had no conviction that he could hit her even if he could.

But as she stood motionless in the shadows, she saw Rory whirl back round to face Patrick. As if in slow motion, she saw Patrick's gun hand waver towards Rory. Lindsay roared, "No," and left the shadows at a sprint, the shotgun held at waist height, her finger on the trigger.

Patrick's hand jerked and Rory staggered before crashing to the ground. Lindsay felt her chest constrict as she charged across the roof, screaming unintelligibly. Patrick turned back towards her but before he could fire again, Lindsay's finger tightened implacably.

The blast caught him full in the chest and he collapsed, blood pouring from a hole the size of a football. Lindsay barely paused, knowing he was beyond help and not caring. She dropped the gun and fell to her knees beside Rory. Blood soaked her shirt and jacket, spreading from a wound high on the right side of her chest. Rory's face was parchment in the sodium lights, her eyes closed. Tears spilled from Lindsay's eyes as she checked for a pulse in Rory's neck. It was there, faint and thready, but it was there. She gently touched Rory's face with one hand, while putting pressure on the wound with the other. "Rory? Oh God, Rory, say something. Don't do this to me, don't die on me!" Her voice was agonised, mirroring the desperation she felt as Rory failed to move.

Lindsay pulled out her mobile phone and dialled the emergency services. "Which service do you require?" the anonymous voice asked kindly.

"Ambulance. My pal's been shot," Lindsay gabbled. "On the top floor of the Charles Rennie Mackintosh car park. You've got to hurry, she's bleeding badly. There's two other people hurt as well."

"That's the Mackintosh car park in Garnethill?"

"Yeah, yeah. Get somebody here, please."

"The police and ambulance will be with you shortly. Can you . . ." Lindsay cut off the call. She didn't have time for anything except Rory. She leaned over her to check she was still breathing. This time, her eyelids fluttered and opened. Rory looked dazed and bewildered.

"Rory?" Lindsay said, hardly able to believe her eyes.

"Lindsay?" It was a croak, but it was her name, unmistakably.

Lindsay suddenly remembered she was wearing the ski mask and yanked it off. "It's me, Rory. Listen, there's an ambulance coming, you're going to be OK. Just hang in there."

"Hurts...Did we get enough?" she groaned.

"It's sorted," Lindsay said.

"You look...You never said...a gun."

"You'd only have worried."

Rory coughed. "Cover your back...you need...cover your back."

"Never mind me." But nevertheless she took heed of Rory's concern. Lindsay slipped her hand inside Rory's bra, made even more fearful by the marble coldness of her skin. She pulled the mike clear and stuffed it into her pocket.

"Please," Rory whispered. "Gun. Get rid."

"OK." Lindsay didn't care about the consequences for herself, but being scared for her wasn't helping Rory. She grabbed the shotgun and stood up. "Fucking carnage. How do you explain fucking carnage?" She raced down a level to her own car and wrenched the door open. She lifted the bench seat and threw in the gun, the spare cartridges and all the electronic equipment. Then she pulled off her waxed jacket and tossed it on top.

Lindsay raced back up to the roof, the sound of distant sirens cutting through the constant hum of the city at night. She threw herself down beside Rory again, leaning over to press down on the wound. Her eyes were closed again and her skin looked even paler than before. "Oh fuck," Lindsay groaned. "Don't die on me, Rory."

Rory's eyelids parted in a narrow slit. "Lindsay..."

"Can you hear me?"

"Yeah..."

"This is really important. Try to remember. We came here in your car. Together. You were meeting Patrick Coughlan. Some IRA story. You were worried and I offered to come along for the ride. OK?"

"My car," Rory murmured.

"And then it all went off. We've got no idea what happened or who was involved. OK?"

Rory's mouth twitched. It was almost a smile. "Not a lie..."

Now the sirens were close, whooping in and out in a Doppler

effect as the emergency vehicles climbed through the car park. "You're going to be OK," Lindsay insisted.

"Coughlan...?" Rory said so softly it was almost lost in the background noise.

"He's dead. It's all over Rory. It's all right."

"Tell Bernie." Then her eyes flickered shut again, just as two police cars and a pair of ambulances screamed up the ramp. Lindsay got to her feet and waved her arms over her head. "Just don't find my fucking car, that's all," she muttered as the headlight beams pinned her like stage spotlights. There would be time enough for her to deal with what she'd done. For now, what mattered was saving Rory. And perhaps, in the process, saving herself.

Epilogue

It was, Lindsay thought, the most splendid bouquet of flowers she had ever spent money on. She didn't even know the names of most of the things in it. She only hoped the nurses could find a big enough vase. She walked through the hospital corridors towards the lift, still buzzy with lack of sleep and the satisfaction that comes from surviving a terrifying ordeal. She'd never been so scared in her life, nor so relieved at the outcome.

Lindsay emerged from the lift and took the short corridor that led to the private rooms. She nodded to a nurse who exclaimed at the flowers. Lindsay paused on the threshold and took a deep breath. Then she grabbed the handle and marched in.

Rory was sitting on a chair by the window, the animation on her face revealing she was in the middle of some anecdote. But Lindsay had no interest in her today. She turned to face the bed, where Sophie sat propped up, nursing Clare Julia Gordon Hartley, 36 hours old and the most beautiful creature Lindsay had ever clapped eyes on. A slow grin spread across her face and she leaned down to kiss Sophie and then their daughter, who remained oblivious to attention while there was milk to be downed.

Lindsay glanced up at Rory. "So, what do you think?" she said.

"She's gorgeous."

"That's the right answer," Sophie said. "You can come again."

Rory uncurled her legs from under her and stood up. "Try and

256

keep me away. How long are you going to be in for?"

"They usually keep mothers in for five days after a section, but I'm going to try to persuade them to let me out sooner than that. Hospitals are such unhealthy places," Sophie said. "Besides, Lindsay's getting off far too lightly just now."

"Well, I'll probably wait till you're both home." Rory reached for the flowers. "I'm going off now, I'll give these to one of the nurses and get her to stick them in a vase. Lindsay, what time are we kicking off tonight?"

"Eight o'clock, Café Virginia."

"Kicking off what?" Sophie asked, curious rather than suspicious. Doubt had disappeared some months before, for which Lindsay was profoundly grateful.

"Wetting the baby's head," Lindsay said. "Work contacts, mostly. All the gang from Radio NMC, plus people like Giles and Sandra."

"I'm so glad I'm missing that one," Sophie said dryly.

"See you soon," Rory said, stooping to kiss Clare's wispy black hair on her way out.

Sophie watched her leave, then reached for Lindsay's hand. "I'm glad you forced me to get to know Rory. She's great fun."

Lindsay shrugged, embarrassed. "I didn't see how I could avoid running into her, with us both so involved in the media scene. I just hoped the two of you would ignore me and get to know each other. Self-preservation, that's all it was."

"Well, it worked." Sophie shifted. "She's asleep. Do you want to hold your daughter?"

Lindsay picked up Clare as if she were a primed bomb and edged round to the chair by the window. "I can't believe how good she is. Did you get much sleep?"

Sophie grunted. "It wasn't too bad. She went three hours between feeds at one point, which was blissful. But it's not restful in here. We'll both do better once we get home."

The rest of the day passed in a drift of feeding, changing, bathing and conversation. Lindsay's parents turned up in the afternoon to drool over their grandchild, and Lindsay left her mother with Sophie for half an hour so she and her father could get some fresh air.

"It's all worked out for the best, then," Andy said as they walked along the banks of the Kelvin.

"Amazingly enough, yes," Lindsay said. "I couldn't believe it when they put Clare in my arms. It was like a hook going into my heart. Instant love."

"There's nothing like it," Andy agreed. "You forgive them anything, you know."

"Even stupidity," Lindsay said wryly.

"Even stupidity. Do you see much of Rory now you're doing the radio show?"

For the past five months, Lindsay had been the presenter of the midday news programme on Radio NMC. It was one of the few good things that had come out of her encounter with Tam and Bernie Gourlay. The station's boss had been a close friend of Tam's, and when his anchorman had left for BBC national radio, he'd called Lindsay to offer her the slot. She'd been at a loose end ever since she'd given up working with Rory as the price of reconciliation with Sophie, and it had turned out to be the perfect slot for her abrasive humour and incisive questioning. "I usually only see her when Sophie's around," she said. "It's safer that way."

Her father nodded. "Aye. Nice lassie, but trouble on legs."

Lindsay shook her head. "I'm the one that's trouble, Dad."

"Aye, well, that'll all change now. You've got responsibilities."

Lindsay grinned. "I know. Great, isn't it?"

She left the hospital in time to get to her counselling session at half past five. She'd gone into therapy while Rory had still been in hospital recovering from the gunshot wound that was bizarrely a mirror image of Lindsay's own. When she'd woken screaming in Rory's spare room for the third night running, she'd called Sophie for help. They'd had a cautious lunch together when Lindsay had revealed the truth about the events on the roof of the car park. Sophie had been horrified at Lindsay's risk-taking and adamant that she needed professional help.

"How can I talk to a therapist?" Lindsay had demanded. "As far as the cops are concerned, I'm just a bystander who got caught up in a Republican revenge shooting by chance. Thank God the only one of them left standing kept his mouth shut or I'd be on remand at Cornton Vale right now. I can't sit down with some New Age nambypamby and confess that I killed two men. They'd freak out."

"Leave it with me, I'll find someone," Sophie had promised. And she'd kept her word. Anne-Marie Melville was a medically qualified psychiatrist turned counsellor who regarded her duty of confidentiality as highly as a priest in the confessional. Lindsay reckoned Anne-Marie had probably saved her sanity.

That evening as she left Anne-Marie's consulting rooms, she was astonished to see Rory sitting on the bonnet of her car, soaking up the sunshine. "What are you doing here?" Lindsay asked.

"Nice to see you too," Rory said, sliding off the car and giving Lindsay a hug. "I just wanted to see you on your own before we got ripped into the drink. I knew this was your night for seeing Anne-Marie and I thought I'd grab you when you were vulnerable."

Lindsay grinned and hugged her back. "Living dangerously, huh?" She moved away and unlocked the car. "Come back to the house and have a drink, we'll go into town together."

They were silent on the short drive, each keeping her own counsel till they were sitting on the living room sofa, both clutching a cold beer. "Mmm, that's nice," Lindsay said, rolling the bottle against her forehead.

"Bernie called today. She's finally found a house she likes and the owners have accepted her offer."

"Where is it?"

"Cornwall. Near St Ives. Jack likes the sea. She was thrilled to hear about Clare."

"I suppose that's as near as we're going to get to a happy ending," Lindsay sighed.

"All things considered, we should probably be grateful we came out of it with nothing worse than matching scars," Rory said.

Lindsay reached for her hand. "I know it's not exactly what you hoped for. I'm sorry."

Rory shook her head. "Don't be. I'd only have broken your heart. And it taught me something important too."

"What? Don't mess with married women?" Lindsay said, only half teasing.

"There's that," Rory acknowledged ruefully. "But more importantly, I learned that I'm maybe not as much of a lost cause as I thought I was. I always reckoned me and love were as incompatible as a Mac and a PC. But what I felt for you . . . well, let's just say I'm not really scared any more."

"Oh, Rory," Lindsay said, putting down her beer and pulling Rory into her arms. "You deserve better than me."

Rory grinned up at her. "You think I don't know that?" She snuggled into Lindsay for a moment, then pulled away and said briskly. "Come on. It's time to go and paint the town lavender. You've got something to celebrate, Lindsay. The new life starts here."

V. L. McDermid

Val McDermid published her first Lindsay Gordon mystery, *Report for Murder*, in 1987. Since then she has written a further five books in the series featuring the Scottish lesbian journalist. The fifth, *Booked for Murder*, was nominated for a Lambda Literary Award. She has also written six novels featuring PI Kate Brannigan, four featuring psychologist Tony Hill and police officer Carol Jordan, and three standalones. An international best-seller, her books have been translated into almost 30 languages and the Hill & Jordan series has been adapted for the award-winning TV series, *Wire in the Blood*. Her many awards include the Gold Dagger (for *The Mermaids Singing*), the Los Angeles Times Book Prize, the Anthony, the Dilys, the Barry, the Macavity (for *A Place of Execution*), the Sherlock (for *The Distant Echo*) and the Grand Prix des Romans d'Aventure (for *Star Struck*).

Val grew up in a Scottish mining community and is a graduate of Oxford University. She worked as a journalist for 16 years, becoming National Bureau Chief of a major national Sunday tabloid. She quit journalism in 1991 to become a full-time writer. She is also a regular contributor to BBC radio. She has one son and divides her time between the city—Manchester—and the country—a seaside village in Northumberland.

Lindsay Gordon novels available from Bywater Books

Report for Murder
When a star musician is found garroted with her own cello string minutes before she is due on stage, Lindsay Gordon finds herself investigating a vicious murder.
ISBN 1-932859-06-3 $12.95

Common Murder
A protest group hits the headlines when unrest at a woman's peace camp explodes into murder. Already on the scene, journalist Lindsay Gordon finds that no one—ratepayer or reporter, policeman or peace woman—seems wholly above suspicion.
ISBN 1-932859-07-1 $12.95

Deadline for Murder
Lindsay Gordon is embroiled in an investigation involving blackmail, stolen government documents, and the vested interests of a group of people determined to keep her from finding the truth.
ISBN 1-932859-08-X $12.95

Conferences are Murder
When an unethical union leader is found dead, having catapulted out of Lindsay Gordon's tenth-floor hotel room, she uncovers a seething cauldron of blackmail, corruption, and abuse of power, all brought to the boil by her investigation.
ISBN 1-932859-09-8 $12.95

Booked for Murder
Lindsay Gordon delves beneath the glittering facade of the glamorous world of London publishing in search of a murderer. While hobnobbing with industry notables, she encounters a mix of soured relationships, desperate power plays, underhanded fraud, and seething rivalries.
ISBN 1-932859-10-1 $12.95

Order directly from Bywater Books by calling toll-free
866-390-7426 or at our website at www.bywaterbooks.com